DRUID'S FOLLY

A DRUIDVERSE URBAN FANTASY NOVEL

M.D. MASSEY

1

Fun fact: I'm pretty sure I can time travel.

Okay, so it's not exactly time traveling. It's more like probability searching, mentally flipping through possible alternative futures until you find the one you want. Then you follow that thread to see what happens. Welcome to chronomancy.

Here's the really trippy part. Because none of the events I'm seeing have happened yet, the timelines I witness don't really exist. But if I choose, I can step into a timeline. Or at least I think I can, theoretically. According to a certain quasi-god I know, by virtue of the fact that a chronomancer—or more accurately, a chronourge... chronourgist?—experiences that timeline, it becomes reality.

Weird? Yes. Scary? When you consider the implications, absolutely. And dangerous? I'm not sure I know the half of it, yet.

But I do know that chronomancy and chronourgy are what got Gwydion in hot water with the gods. That's why he's laying low in Maeve's demesne under an assumed name. As for why he started teaching me time magic, well—I guess it's just in his nature to do insane things.

Click—that's the quasi-god formerly known as Gwydion—is a trickster, through and through. Tricksters are seemingly morally obligated to sow chaos and sabotage the other gods' plans. So, when a trickster can't act directly to fulfill the functions of their assumed or given role, they seek out a proxy.

Whether by intention, circumstance, or chance, Click chose me as his surrogate. Now, I'm fully entangled in a trickster's schemes, and that's how I ended up here, standing in front of The Trickster's Council. Hungover and fighting a splitting headache, no less.

Click brought me here the night after my druid master's wake—against my will, of course. When I figured out what he'd done, I tried to leave, but it seemed the tricksters locked the place down when a meeting was in session. Now, I was laying on a very uncomfortable wooden bench, doing my best to hide my eyes from the light, while Click made a case for my probationary admission to the Trickster's Local #113.

I am not making that up.

And did I mention I asked for none of this?

"Dear members o' the committee, whilst I know this request is most irregular, I kin' personally vow fer' the lad's suitability ta' be appointed as one o' us. That is ta' say, a trickster. Apprentice level, o' course."

"Assembly the from him expel to move I," a raspy man's voice said from the middle of the stands.

The place looked like a Victorian-era courtroom when we first walked in, but it had morphed into a high school basketball arena in the last few moments. I only noticed this because the man's odd manner of speech compelled me to identify the speaker, risking a stabbing pain in my eye as I uncovered my face to scan the room.

My eyes settled on an older man in the first row, who had weathered bronze skin and long, salt and pepper hair that he wore in two identical braids. He was dressed in a buckskin shirt over worn jeans and flip-flops, and everything he had on was backward, opposite, or inside out. Despite his ridiculous appearance and strange way of speaking, he somehow managed to come across as distinguished—regal, even.

"I second the motion," I said, raising my hand from my supine position on the bench.

"Ya' can't expel him, Heyókȟa," Click replied with a hint of exasperation in his voice. "He's not yet been admitted ta' our ranks."

"Up screws he before, now out him kick to reason more the all," Heyókȟa replied.

"Sounds good to me," a perky female voice added from somewhere in the third or fourth row.

When I glanced over to give a thumb's up to the speaker, I noticed that the room had shifted into a college lecture hall. The woman in question wore a grey athletic t-shirt that said, *YOU'RE MY BOY, BLUE* in block letters, along with plaid pajama bottoms and fuzzy unicorn slippers, which I could see because she had her feet propped up on her desk. Her lustrous, dark hair hung in loose curls just past shoulder-length, framing a face that was rather attractive despite a strong jawline and largish Greek nose. On consideration, she reminded me a bit of Lisa Edelstein from *House*.

"Also, I heard him talking shit about Sun Wukong earlier," Unicorn Slippers continued. "I say we make him fight his way out of here."

"Exactly," I said before her words registered, then I almost barfed when I sat up too quickly. "Wait—say what?"

The Monkey King had been ignoring the proceedings, instead entertaining himself by playing *Angry Birds* on his phone. It was easy to tell what he was playing because he had the sound turned up and he kept chuckling to himself and commenting on "those crazy birds." He looked up from his seat at the center of the front row, eyeballing me with one brow cocked halfway up his forehead.

"What did the ginger say, Eris?" Sun Wukong asked.

"Oh, I don't know," she replied as she picked at her teeth while looking in a compact mirror. "Something about not believing you're as tough as they say."

"Now, wait a minute," I countered, standing up and

then sitting right back down again due to room spin. "I never said anything about The Monkey King."

A hush went over the room as Sun Wukong stood up, slamming his phone on the desk in front of him. "Who you calling a monkey, Stinky Breath?"

"Well, um," I stammered in a momentary fluster. "Aren't you The Monkey King?"

Sun Wukong vaulted the desk with one hand as he picked at his ear with the other. "Baboons are monkeys. Mandrills are monkeys. Macaques are monkeys." He made a fist, pointing at his chest with his thumb. "I'm an ape. Do I look like a monkey to you?"

"Look," I said, holding my hands up. "I'm no prima-tologist, so how in the heck should I know a monkey from an ape?"

A collective gasp rose from the other tricksters in the room.

"I think he just said you look like a monkey," Unicorn Slippers remarked.

Soon, the rest of the people in the stands—tricksters, every last one—were chanting, "Fight, fight, fight, fight!" Obnoxiously loud, I might add.

"No, no 'fight.' 'Leave,'" I said, wincing at how raising my voice made my headache worse. And the lights were so very bright. I dug around in my Craneskin Bag for some sunglasses, slapping them on before I tried to defuse the situation.

Suddenly, we weren't in a college lecture hall anymore. I now sat in a Roman-style stadium, more specifically a Roman *gladitorium*. Not to be confused with *herpes gladitorum*, which I understand can be quite painful. Like my headache.

"Ah, for cripes' sake," I said as I looked around the space. "I don't want to fight, I don't want to join your secret trickster cult, and I don't even want to be awake right now. Just send me back home, so I can go back to sleep and pretend this never happened."

"Nope, not gonna happen, Opie," Sun Wukong said as he bounced on his toes like a boxer. "You insulted me. Now, you pay the price."

"Aw, c'mon. I never said those things. You know that chick is lying. You can never trust a girl who wears animal slippers ironically—everyone knows that." I glanced around the stadium, finding my sometimes mentor and full-time instigator standing on a raised dais near the stands. "Click, help me out here. No, I take that back—get me out of here, now."

Click flashed a sheepish grin at me as he futzed with the zipper on his leather jacket. "About that—sorry, lad, but once the proceedin's commence, no one gets in or out. Rules, ya' see."

"Great," I muttered as I started stealth-shifting into my semi-Fomorian form. I really did not want to fight Sun Wukong, but if I had to do it, I wasn't going to kick his ass while dealing with a hangover. "You're going to owe me for this. You know that, right?"

"Does that mean ye'll consider our offer fer' membership?" he asked in an overly polite and mildly patronizing tone.

"One thing at a time, alright?" I shifted my gaze to address the monkey deity across the sand, who was spinning a metal staff in dizzying patterns around his body. "Oh, come on! Now we're doing weapons? Really?"

"He always fights with his staff," Eris said from the front row. "Well, not always, but definitely when he's pissed."

"You knowing nice. Kid, luck good," Heyoka added.

"Fuck her right in the—"

"Hey!" I yelled, cutting Loki off mid-heckle. "You cut that shit out, or no trip to Vegas for you. By the way, how the hell did you get out of jail?"

"Oh, you're no fun," he groused, slouching in his chair as he knocked back the last dregs of a bottle of Cristal. "And as for your question, have you really not figured that out yet? You were instrumental in my jail-break, after all."

"Ah, so that's what all that shit in Jotunheimr was about." I tapped a finger on my chin. "I bet you were the one who arranged Dian Cecht's trip, too. Guess I should've seen that coming. But you're still a prick—you and Click, both."

"Salty today, isn't he?" Loki said, addressing Click.

"He's hungover," Click responded apologetically.

"And about to get his ass kicked," Sun Wukong added. "Are we doing this, or what?"

"Fine," I said, working a few kinks out of my back and neck. Once I felt halfway human—or rather, halfway Fomorian—I drew an enchanted war club from my Bag. I didn't want to kill the little fella, after all. "C'mon, banana brains—let's do this."

"Your funeral," the monkey man said.

Without further ado, he swung his staff overhead. Before my eyes, the six-foot iron rod morphed, gaining a foot of girth and fifty feet in length while losing zero speed in the process. And it was coming right at the top of my skull.

Now, I've seen my share of Wuxia films, and I'm not saying I didn't expect the dude to have some moves. And yeah, I'm a fan of Donnie Yen, and I'm familiar with the legends—although I think *Journey to the West* was a much more entertaining film than any of the adaptations starring Yen. But what I didn't expect was for the hairy bastard to start swinging a flipping telephone pole at me.

Okay, so maybe I was sort of hoping he'd do some crazy shit, but I didn't really expect it to happen. I mean, the book was a fictional account, based on the real-life travels of a monk named Xuanzang in the seventh century. The author was said to have modeled Sun

Wukong on Hanuman, or possibly some previously existing monkey deity that was worshipped locally in Fuzhou.

So, I figured *this* Sun Wukong was just a minor deity who took on the persona to maintain worshippers or something. Far be it from me to tell someone they couldn't identify as a fictional monkey god-slash-demon. But no way did I expect said individual to actually exhibit powers that were approximate to the character in the novel.

Speaking of which, in the 16th century novel, the staff is a gift from the Dragon King. Sun Wukong is supposedly the only creature strong enough to use it, which is dumb, but okay. It's supposed to weigh something like nine tons, which would require the stupid monkey to have superhero-level strength—also silly, but again, whatevs.

I didn't care what the novel said, no fucking way the staff coming at me weighed that much. Then again, I wasn't stupid enough to stand still and find out. I dove sideways, rolling and coming up with the war club in a vertical guard. And a good thing I did, because Sun Wukong whipped the damned thing around at me, striking at chest level and bowling me over.

I knew better than to block force against force, especially not against something that could snap a mundane weapon in two. Sun Wukong's staff bled magic, and wherever he got it or whoever made it knew their way around an enchanter's workshop. Even though my war club was said to have been made by Goibniu and Luchta, no sense risking damage to it unnecessarily.

For that reason, I faded away from the strike when I blocked Sun Wukong's staff, defusing some of the blow's force but still taking a hard enough hit to toss me into the stadium wall. I hit a bas relief column, bouncing off and landing on one knee, leaning on the club while I tried to force air in my lungs.

Fuck, I think he broke some ribs.

"You had enough, shit for brains?" Sun Wukong asked. "Ready to apologize?"

Managing to get my bruised and battered diaphragm to function, I coughed up some blood and wiped red spittle from my lips. "Gotta hand it to you, that was a pretty solid hit. But that staff's not nearly heavy enough to be that big, and that tells me you're not as good at mass manipulation as you let on."

"Blah, blah, blah," he replied, using his hand to imitate my flapping jaw. "Less commentary, more apologizing."

I remained hunched over so no one would see as I prepared a rather tricky spell, something I'd not been capable of casting a few days ago. Recently I'd chanted the *teinm laida* to defeat the goddess Badb. The chant had been hidden in a magically sealed grimoire by my late druid master, Finnegas, and it represented the deepest knowledge of all druidkind. Chanting it was like looking into the mind of the universe, and when I spoke it, the secrets of the cosmos were revealed to me all at once.

The knowledge I attained during the chant showed me how to beat Badb. However, due to my semi-mortal limitations, I could only keep a small sliver of the vast knowledge the *teinm laida* had revealed. Part of what I chose to retain had to do with understanding the mechanics of time magic, and the other part was all the stuff I should've learned from Finnegas, my druid master, before his untimely passing.

Not specifics, mind you—that would be too much knowledge for my pea brain to handle all in one fell swoop. I didn't want to be the world's most knowledgeable vegetable, after all. But I did want to understand the advanced principles that made the difference between a journeyman and a master druid, and that's exactly what I retained.

Keeping my gaze lowered to feign a worse injury than I'd sustained, I continued. "Like I was saying, it's a neat trick, but you don't quite have the knack of it. Mass manipulation is tricky stuff. Most people think you do it by borrowing material and adding it to the object you're altering. But that's a very limiting technique, and it slows down the spell considerably."

"Get to the point," Sun Wukong sighed, leaning on his staff as he spun lazy circles in the air with his index finger. "We have things to do."

I flashed a Cheshire grin as I looked up. "The right way to do it is not to borrow mass, but gravity. Like this."

Much of druidry was simply understanding how the laws and forces of nature worked, and all druid magic consisted of working in harmony with those energies to get the desired result. Specific spells were really just the application of that core skill. Knowing what I did, it wasn't hard to create a powerful magnetic field in the earth under Sun Wukong's iron staff. And if I led him to believe I could manipulate gravity, well—they did want me to be a trickster, right?

I spoke a single word in Celtic as I made an arcane gesture in the air. Instantly, the staff in Sun Wukong's hands tipped over, crashing to the ground and yanking him with it faster than he could let go. As it slammed to the packed sand, the staff sunk several inches deep, trapping his fingers under the shaft. The monkey deity let out an "eep," and then he was screaming bloody murder about his smashed fingers.

"That son of a bitch broke my hand," he cursed as he desperately struggled to pull his injured digits free.

While he bitched and moaned, I strolled across the sand, triggering my full transformation while taking my time getting to him. I didn't really need to transform, as I had already won the fight, but my ribs weren't healing fast enough, and I still had a lingering headache. So, fuck it—I decided to showboat.

As I walked, my bones elongated, splitting my skin in multiple places as my soft tissues fought to catch up. Muscles tore and healed as they grew longer, reattaching themselves in new and interesting locations, while my skin mended itself, growing thicker and much more keratinous as the transformation neared completion. Finally, it was over, leaving me in the form of a ten-foot-tall monster who looked like the love child of Quasimodo and the Jolly Green Giant... albeit, without the green skin.

"Now, tell me, ape," I rumbled, glaring down at him as I slipped my war club back in my Bag, replacing it with my Fomorian-sized greatsword, Orna. "Do you still insist that I apologize, or can we call it even and get on with whatever cockamamie scheme Click has cooked up?"

The monkey man—or demon, or whatever the hell he was—looked up at me with sheer, unadulterated anger writ across his features. His eyes narrowed dangerously, and when he spoke, his voice was a low, menacing hiss.

"Never," he said as he yanked hard, ripping his fingers from his hand.

Aw, shit—here we go.

2

'm gonna come at you like a spider monkey.

He didn't actually say it, but Sun Wukong may as well have, because that's what he did. Rather than using martial arts, he basically went, well, *apeshit* on me. Unsurprisingly, the fucker was strong—and crazy.

When he first attacked, he jumped up as I tried to grab him, vaulting around my arm like I was a jungle gym. Then, he landed on my shoulders, at which point he proceeded to beat me with that bloody stump of a hand while hanging on to me with the other.

I reached up to grab him with my free hand, and he skittered over to the other shoulder, hitting me all the while. When I tried to grab him again, he did the same thing, switching to the other side. Meanwhile he was turning my face into mush, and I couldn't tell if all the blood that was flying around was his or mine.

Orna was no good at this range—to be effective,

zweihanders needed space and distance. So, I stabbed the sword in the dirt and went mano a mano with the monkey man. Once I had two hands to grab with, he couldn't evade me while still staying up there, so he leapt off to avoid a direct grapple. Then, he loped around me on all fours, knuckle-running like a gorilla as he looked for an opening.

"You messed with the wrong ape, ugly," Sun Wukong said.

"Gonna have a hard time winning with only one functional hand, you maniac."

"Hah! I could beat you with one hand tied behind my back," he replied. The monkey god came at me in a sprint, using all fours to cover the ground between us in an instant. I thought he would jump at my face, but instead he sort of bowled into me at knee level, knocking me on my ass. As I fell, he wasted no time in climbing atop me and pummeling me in the balls, stomach, face—anywhere he could get a shot in.

Shit, it was like fighting a whole damned troop of monkeys the way he fought. And hell if I couldn't get a grip on him. Every time I swiped at him, my hands closed on thin air.

Bottom line—this prick was beating my ass like a redheaded stepchild. Not that I couldn't take it, but it was sort of embarrassing, considering the audience.

"Kick his ass!" someone shouted from the stands.

"Kill him!"

"Bite his nose off!"

Okay, that's just a little too specific.

It was like being at a pro wrestling match in a small town in the deep south, late at night when everyone in the audience was three deep in their second twelve pack. Damn, but these fools were rowdy.

Somehow, I managed to roll to my knees. When the monkey man tried to jump on my back from behind, I got a lucky back kick in that sent him flying. Which was fortunate, because I was a mess. While my injuries would heal shortly, blood poured off my face in streams, pooling beneath me and staining the ground red.

I looked up, and instead of the monkey, I was greeted by Click's smiling face. Except he wasn't smiling. "Lad, yer embarassin' me. Get the lead out an' start winnin' already."

"I'm going to kill you for bringing me here—you know that, right?"

"That's the spirit! Get angry, and then focus all that rage on winnin' this fight. Now, go," he said, patting me on the shoulder. "The monkey god awaits."

"Arrrrgggggh!" was all I heard next. I looked behind me and saw Sun Wukong charging like a damned rabid bull, arms flailing as he beat his chest like a drum.

Oh, fuck this already.

I doubted I could hit him with a directed spell, like a lightning bolt, or a fireball, or an ice spike—he was just too damned fast. And anyway, I didn't want to kill him, 'cause it would probably make me more than a few enemies here. Instead, I said a trigger word, unleashing a spell I'd been working on since before my fight with Badb.

"*Cuaifeach iomghaoth.*"

The spell came on quickly, unleashing a whirlwind of air that circulated at hundreds of miles an hour in a circumference ranging thirty feet from my person. Since the arena floor was covered in packed sand, this had the effect of turning the ring into a sandblaster... and Sun Wukong was caught right in the middle of it.

As I looked on, the crazy fucker struggled to reach me, digging his fingers and toes into the sand as he pulled himself closer, step by step. All the while the supernatural sandstorm peeled his fur and skin away, a layer at a time.

"Give it up," I yelled. "You'll be dead before you reach me."

He either didn't hear me, or he ignored me. I decided it was the latter, because this guy seemed to be as stubborn as he was nuts.

Fuck this.

I pushed myself upright so I could better direct the storm, gesticulating like a symphony conductor as I directed the wind to lift the monkey man off the ground. Then, I funneled the air up, shooting Sun Wukong a good thirty feet overhead. I released the sand when I did so, because the guy was already bloody and battered, and he was missing skin and fur in bare and abraded patches all over his body.

However, I kept him in the maelstrom, tightening its

radius until he was suspended in the air and spinning in place at several revolutions a second.

"Oh, I don't feel so good," he said, right before he barfed.

Whatever he'd had for breakfast spewed out in sort of splattering rain, all over the other tricksters in the stands. Some of them, like Loki, had seen what was coming and prepared. At some point he'd donned a long yellow rain slicker and hid behind a clear plastic umbrella so he could see the fight. Others ducked behind their seats or beneath tarps and plastic sheeting, like audience members at a Gallagher show.

But some of them weren't as prescient, Eris chief among them. She was struck in the face with a glob of something green and sticky that likely smelled as bad as it looked.

"Oh, yuck," she cried as she slung it to the ground. "Okay, I'm going to the lounge. Tell me how this ends." Then, the goddess disappeared, without so much as opening a portal to facilitate her exit.

"Impressive," I said before turning my attention to the monkey deity spinning in the air over my head. "Hey, Sun Wukong—you ready to chill?"

"Yes! Let me down, you—*urp*—pink baboon—" he cursed, just before he barfed all over the crowd again.

I don't know why, but that tickled my funny bone. I started laughing, then it became a full-on giggle fit. Soon, I was barely able to guide the monkey deity down safely before I ended up rolling on the ground.

Sun Wukong landed on his bottom, at which point he sort of fell over like a drunk. That made me laugh even harder. He pushed himself up, groggily at first then gradually steadier, scowling at me and the mess he'd made all over the arena.

But the more I laughed, the more he relaxed, until finally he started laughing too. We went on like that for a couple of minutes, until the laughter subsided.

"I'm sorry I called you a monkey," I said.

"I apologize for calling you a pink baboon," he replied.

"Ah, it was worth it for the lulz," I wheezed, wiping my eyes. "Hey, where'd everyone go?"

The stadium was empty, except for us two. The crazy thing was, I hadn't even noticed anyone leave. Deific magic was weird like that.

"To the bar, most likely. Or the showers, for those who lack the powers of disintegration and transformation." He pushed off the ground to stand, brushing himself off and checking his bare spots. In most places, his skin had already grown back, and his hair was starting to come back in as well.

"Should we join them?" I asked.

"Why not?" he said. "But you're buying the first round, rookie."

A few minutes later, I was sitting across from Sun Wukong and Click, sipping a pint of dark, aromatic draft in what looked like a SOHO pub. The place was complete with dim yet comfortable lighting, dark wood trim, and a bartender who had the look of a retired professional boxer, crooked nose and all.

"So, I gotta ask," I said, cradling my mug in both hands.

"Yes?" Sun Wukong replied archly.

"Naw, nevermind. I've said enough."

Click took a sip of ale and wiped his mouth on the back of his hand. "He's really Sun Wukong, if that's what yer' wonderin'. Belief forms reality where deities are concerned."

"Seems like I've heard that somewhere before," I said, snapping my fingers. "Ah, right—it was Maman Brigitte who once told me something to that effect."

"Hubba, hubba," the monkey deity said. "She's one Tuath Dé I would not kick out of my treehouse."

"Too rich for my blood," I said. "Besides, she wants to fix me up with her granddaughter. We even went on a date once. It was fun, but sort of a disaster."

"As is always the case when dealin' with gods n' demigods, lad." Click set his mug on the table. "Speakin' o' such, the Council voted whilst ya' were still tangling with Sun Wukong here. Good news—yer' in."

I kept my eyes on the beer in my hands, lips pursed as I responded. "Did I ever say I wanted to be in?"

"Well, no... but it's a huge honor, lad—huge."

"Pfah, if the pink baboon doesn't want in, it's his business. Why push it, bard?"

"Because he wants something," I said. "Somehow, my being admitted to the Council—"

"Not the Council," Click interjected. "Trickster Local #113. And as an apprentice, o' course."

"Er, right. Anyway, he's getting something out of this. I don't know what it is, but that's a fact."

"Of course he wants something," Sun Wukong said. "Tricksters always have a con running. It's what we do."

"Yeah, but what I don't understand is *why* you're tricksters. Okay, so I get why deities like Eris are what they are—she represents an elemental force of nature in her pantheon. But why the whole—" I gestured at our surroundings as I swept my gaze around the pub "—old boys' club thing?"

"And girls," Eris shouted from across the room.

"Right, goes without saying," I said. "But why?"

"You can answer this one," the monkey deity said to Click. "I need to take a leak."

Sun Wukong pushed away from the table and stood, then he strutted off through the pub, making jokes and small talk with gods and goddesses at every table along the way.

"Man, that guy is cocky," I remarked. I looked at Click over my mug as I took a slug of beer. "Anyway, you were saying?"

Click swirled his ale around in the tulip-shaped glass in his hands, watching the amber liquid as he spoke. "While some'd consider us nothin' more n' a mythological punchline, we're actually more important than that. A lot more important."

"How so?"

He tsked and set his glass down. "Hmm. Well, the universe has a way o' balancing things out. Kinda' like how some humans evolved to become more n' their brethren, so as they could protect the mortals from the others races an' creatures."

"You're referring to heroes."

"Precisely. A power differential existed, and nature stepped in ta' correct it." He pointed his thumbs at his chest. "We're nature's answer ta' power hungry, despotic gods."

"By official designation, or by choice?"

Click thrust his lower lip out and shrugged. "Both, I s'pose? We sow chaos and throw the odd wrench inta' the plans o' the gods. Is it nurture or nature what guides our hands? Destiny er will? Who kin' say? All I know is that fer' about as long as the gods have been bein' right pricks, we tricksters have been there to put 'em in their place."

"You are aware that, in most myths and legends, you all are painted as the bad guys, right?"

"There's not a shred o' truth ta' those accusations," Click replied as he drew himself up indignantly.

"Oh, really?" I squinted as I pinched my thumb and forefinger together. "Perhaps a wee bit? Just a smidgen, wouldn't you say?"

"Aye, mayhaps there's a grain o' truth ta' some o' those tales. But fer' the most part, we're on the side o' the angels."

"You, er, don't believe in angels."

"Just an expression, lad. Don't be so literal."

I exhaled heavily as I considered what he was asking. Then, I realized I didn't precisely know what he was asking. "Um, so what's it mean to join a local and become a trickster?"

"Apprentice. But that's a fair question. It simply means ye'll act on the side o' chaos when'e'er possible, sowing discord and confusion ta' thwart the other gods' plans. An' ya' agree ta' help the other members, should they get inta' a tight spot during the course o' trickster work."

"So basically the shit I do on a daily basis."

He slowly nodded. "'Bout sums it up."

"And what do I get out of this?"

Click's brow furrowed. "Well, the favor an' assistance o' the rest o' the members, o' course. An' ye'll be off limits to the others' when it comes ta' their tricks n' schemes. Honestly, ya' can't beat it fer' sheer convenience, 'specially if it keeps ya' off Loki's shit list."

"Assistance, you say?"

"Within reason." Click looked at his glass as he glanced at me beneath hooded eyes. "So, are ya' in?"

I had to admit, having a bunch of sneaky-ass gods on my side sounded pretty good. Especially considering that there were other gods out there plotting my death, even as I sat in a pocket dimension sipping beer with Click. But these were tricksters I was dealing with, and hell if I wasn't going to make some demands. I wanted an escape clause, just in case.

"On two conditions," I replied.

"Name 'em."

"One, I can withdraw my membership if it isn't working out, at any time—past, present, or future."

"Done," Click said.

"And two, you have to show me how to walk the Twisted Paths."

Click frowned. "Phew. That's a tall order, lad. I know ya' somehow shat yerself outta' trouble with Badb and inta' druid mastery. But are ya' certain ya' kin handle it?"

"Believe me, I'm game."

He rubbed his chin, eyes on the ceiling as he considered my terms. After a time, he relaxed, meeting my gaze and extending his hand. "Okay, it's a deal."

I hesitated before I shook his hand, wondering if this was the smartest decision. But I needed allies, and I really needed to get back to the Hellpocalypse. Not only did I want to rescue Anna, Mickey, and the boys, but I also suspected I'd find answers there regarding who or what was pitting itself against me, in the grand scheme of things.

Eh, there's nothing for it. May as well deal myself in.

"Alright, I'll do it," I said, shaking his hand.

"Hey, everybody," Click exclaimed to the crowd in the bar. "The kid is in!"

A shout went up all around, and the other tricksters started cheering my name. "Col-in, Col-in, Col-in, Col-in!" I had to admit, it felt pretty cool. But somewhere deep in the pit of my gut, I had a suspicion not everyone here was feeling that chant.

3

Being the conscientious boyfriend I am, I returned to the junkyard with coffee and kolaches in hand. Werewolves generally didn't get hangovers, but Fallyn was always more pleasant after waking up to caffeinated beverages and lots of fat and carbs. When I walked in my old room in the warehouse, she was lying in bed, scrolling on her phone and looking like a million bucks, despite the bedhead and no makeup.

"Hey, did I wake you?"

"Nah, the early shift beat you to it. How the hell they managed to come in after Finnegas' wake last night is beyond me." She raised her chin, sniffing in my general direction. "Are those kolaches I smell?"

"Yep, and coffee from the roadside trailer down the street. It's not Luther's, but they roast a mean bean."

She made the universal gesture for 'come here.' "Gimme."

"Yes, ma'am." I kicked my shoes off and hopped up on the bed, handing her the bag and her coffee while somehow managing to avoid spilling my own.

"Mmm, that's heaven," she said around a mouthful of strawberry cheese kolache. "How do they get the pastry to be so soft and chewy?"

"They don't use pastry dough. It's more like bread, really."

"I don't care what it is. The German immigrant who invented it should be entombed at Arlington."

"They're Czech, and I think you have to have served to be buried there."

"The inventor served our nation. Trust me on this."

I smiled and leaned over to kiss her on the cheek. "It's good to have you back."

Fallyn stole a kiss, smearing my lips with sugar and strawberry filling. She wiped her mouth after she gunked up mine.

"Iz good uh be bawk," she said, smiling like a three-year-old on cake day.

"You slimed me, twerp," I groused as I grabbed a napkin from the bag.

"You love it."

"Ahem—do I need to leave, or is this going to stay platonic?" a nasally voice said from the corner of the room.

"Larry!" we yelled simultaneously.

"What?" he asked as he coalesced into view. "I figured the she-wolf smelled me for sure."

"That would be a negative," Fallyn said as she pulled the blankets over her legs. She was wearing a pair of my boxers and one of my old t-shirts, but from the right angle you could see all the way to France.

"Since when did you get all modest?" I asked.

"Since Larry likes to stare. Speaking of which, how long have you been in here?"

The chupacabra tilted his head. "Not long. I followed the druid in." He paused, licking his chops as he stared at the white paper bag in Fallyn's hands. "Got any without dairy in there?"

Fallyn hugged the bag to her chest. "Not for creepers, I don't."

"Oh, give him a kolache. You know he'll stick around until you feed him."

"Fine."

She pulled a plain cherry kolache out of the bag, tossing it in a high arc with a terminus that approximated the location of the dog's snout. Larry snatched it out of the air, swallowing it in one gulp.

"That's almost a crime. Larry, you're supposed to take time to taste the damned things."

He looked at me with his overly large tongue lolling out the side of his mouth. "C'mon, druid. Not like it's vegan sausage or something."

I stood and made a shooing motion with my hands. "Alright, you've been fed. Time to go."

"What? I just got here."

"Nope," I said as I opened the door. "I only recently

got my girlfriend back, and I want to spend some time with her. Alone."

Larry stared at me for several seconds, blank-eyed. "Oh—you want to have sex."

Fallyn threw the crumpled-up bag at him, nailing him in one of his googly eyes. "None of your damned business, mange-mouth. Now, go, before I have to go all alpha on you."

"She's serious, Larry. She's the Austin Pack's Alpha now."

"Yeah, yeah, I know when I'm not wanted." He gave us a literal hang-dog look, leaving the room with his tail between his legs.

After I shut the door behind him, I locked it. Then, I spun to face Fallyn with a mischievous grin on my face.

"To the Grove?"

"Damn well better. Now that I'm fed, I'm feeling a little hot. Might want to cool off with a naked dip in that spring-fed pool."

"I can hear you out here," Larry yelled through the door.

"We don't care," we replied in one voice.

I stalked to the bed and pounced on Fallyn, pinning her wrists until she muscled out and reversed position on me. Once that was settled, I transported us to the Grove. Frankly, there wasn't much conversation to be had after that.

"You're doing what?"

Fallyn and I were roughly halfway through the second day of our staycation in the Druid Grove. Time moved differently in my own personal pocket dimension, so it was hard to tell precisely how long we'd been here. The Grove tried its best to keep its light cycles synched with Earth, but the entity's plant-like thought processes had a hard time getting it right.

Sentient plants, mind you. Rather, my Druid Oak was a sentient plant. The Grove was a sentient, I dunno —pocket dimension, I guess. The Oak had grown from a magic acorn The Dagda had gifted me, and when it matured a pocket dimension—The Grove—had been created inside it. Well, not really inside, but that's the easiest way to describe it. The two entities were both separate yet connected to each other on an existential level, almost like fraternal twins.

Since planting the Oak and bonding with the two, I'd become attached to them and kind of saw them as my children. Which was weird, all things considered. Besides that, it was nice having someplace I could go to get away, work on druidry, and steal time. Due to the time differential, I could portal in here and take all the time I needed for recovering, sleeping, and developing new spells. When I exited Earthside the equivalent of several days later, only a few minutes would have passed in the primary time stream.

But that wasn't even the best thing about the Oak and Grove, not by a long shot. This Oak was the first of its kind to be birthed in two millennia, and the Dagda had wanted to ensure its survival. So, he gave it the ability to portal itself away from danger. A side effect of the Oak's ability to teleport was that it could teleport me as well, anywhere on Earth and even to some places beyond.

Additionally, the two entities were made from pure druid magic. As a mortal, my ability to use magic was limited by my own innate magical reserves, which were insignificant compared to the nearly unlimited supply of magic that high fae and gods could access. The fae drew on Underhill, which the Celtic gods had created from their own intrinsic magic. That's why humans were at such a disadvantage when it came to fighting the fae and the gods—we were always outgunned.

The Dagda saw this and pitied the humans. To even the odds he taught mortals druidry, and then he gave us the groves. By tapping into a grove's power, a master druid could hold their own against a high fae wizard or sorceress... and, in rare cases, even with a god.

The groves were the druids' secret weapon, back in the day. And it was probably why certain Celtic gods conspired with the Romans to burn down all the groves. That's what Badb had tried to do to my Grove, and that was also why she was floating around in the Void in a vegetative state due to the frontal lobotomy I gave her.

Mess with my kids? I don't think so.

Eventually, other gods would try to do the same. But right now, I was more concerned with my pissed-off alpha werewolf girlfriend. I'd kind of dropped the whole "I'm going back to the Hellpocalypse" thing in her lap in the course of casual conversation. And, surprise—she'd fucking flipped.

"It's not that big a deal, Fallyn. I know how to time travel now. I'll just step out of this time stream and into that one, take care of some business, and be right back an instant later. It'll be like I wasn't even gone."

"Not even gone? Are you out of your mind? Do you recall what happened the last time you were there, when Click stranded you? You still have nightmares about it. I know, because every night you fight vampires and ghouls in your sleep. Sheesh, I can't count the number of times you've cast that sunlight spell in the room, and then woken up shaking, sweating, and screaming."

I hung my head because I knew she was right. "Maybe that's why I have to go back—to face those demons."

She pursed her lips as she shook her finger at me. "Oh no, mister, you are *not* trying that bullshit with me. You're not going back to face your demons. You're going back to try to save an entire, fucked-up post-apocalyptic world. And don't tell me you're not, because I know you and your freaking messiah complex all too well."

"I like to think it's part of my boyish charm." Oops, that was the wrong thing to say, apparently. Fallyn's eyes were turning from hazel to yellow, her pupils were changing, and she was starting to sprout fur. *Yikes.*

"Are you seriously joking about this? Really? Colin, we just got back together after a year-and-a-half apart. What if you get stuck there, and I'm left here, wondering what happened to you? Or what if you pull a Rip Van Winkle and come back an old man? Or come back when I'm an old lady?"

"You're a werewolf, Fallyn. Werewolves have long lives. I'd have to mess up by a mile for that to happen. Besides, Click is going to be right beside me, helping me out."

She threw her hands up in the air—hands that had noticeably longer fingernails than they had just seconds ago. "Oh, that makes me feel so much better, that you'll have a trickster god with you in the zombie apocalypse."

"He's the expert at this stuff, Fallyn. Only a few gods can work time magic, and he's the only one who's done it on a regular basis for thousands of years."

"And doesn't that tell you something about how dangerous it is? Meaning, there are time gods out there who apparently don't fuck with chrono-magic the way Click does. Have you ever considered that he's batshit crazy?"

I knew Click was batshit crazy, so I didn't answer that question. Instead, I lowered my voice, attempting to defuse the situation.

"Fallyn, that timeline exists because Click plopped me into it to prove a point. I'm responsible for all those people who are suffering there. That's why I have to go back. I couldn't live with myself if I didn't."

She grabbed a big handful of her auburn hair as if to pull it out. "Ugh! See, that's what I'm talking about. Do you even understand the physics of how this time travel stuff works? If they didn't exist before you showed up there, how do you know they still exist when you're not there?"

I rubbed a hand across my two-day stubble before answering. "I know, because I can see them. Remember when I told you that after I chanted the *teinm laida*, I could only keep a small portion of the knowledge it revealed?"

She seemed to deflate a little, probably because she knew the other shoe was about to drop. Fallyn nodded her head slowly as she answered.

"Right, and you chose to retain knowledge related to mastering druidry."

"And I kept a little knowledge about how time magic works. I understand it all, Fallyn. The chant revealed it because it's the other half of what I chose to remember."

She plopped down on a nearby bench. "Holy hell, Colin. What made you—? Never mind, I know why you did it." Fallyn covered her face with her hands. "Arrgh, why do you have to be so noble all the time? Can't you be just a little selfish every now and again?"

I sat down on the bench next to her, slowly so I didn't irritate her wolf side. "I'll just pop over there and come right back. I promise."

She shook her head, and when she looked at me there were tears in her eyes. "No, you won't. You'll stay there until you fix everything that's in your power to repair. And it'll change you, Colin. I can feel it. My wolf is telling me not to let my mate go, because it fears this is going to spell disaster for you."

I tried cupping her face in my hand, but she pushed it away. "No, uh-uh. I can't even right now. Ugh, I can't even look at you. Just take me back to the clubhouse."

"Fallyn—"

She grabbed my wrists, hard, and held them in her lap with her werewolf strength. Then, she looked me in the eyes, and what I saw there wasn't just Fallyn. It was also her wolf, staring right into my soul.

"Listen to me, Colin. I won't stop you if this is what you want to do. But you need to understand what you're doing. I'm a 'thrope, and we mate for life. So help me, if you leave me here, I will find a time deity to send me where you are, just so I can kick your ass all the way back to this timeline. You hear me?"

"Yes, ma'am."

"There you go again, cracking jokes." She gave me the hand, backing away as she stood from the bench. Then, she craned her neck and yelled up at the sky. "Tree! I wanna go home, now."

The way things were going was breaking my heart. But I had no choice—I had to see it through.

"I swear—"

"Don't," she said, looking away from me with her arms crossed. "Just tell your fucking tree to send me home."

Do it, I thought as I sent the Oak a mental picture of the Pack's back-up clubhouse, where they were still gathered. A split-second later, Fallyn was gone.

"Eh, she'll be okay after she calms down. Right?"

The Grove sent me an image of a she-wolf baring her teeth.

"Okay, maybe I'll give her a couple of days to cool off. Anyway, I need time to get ready. The Hellpocalypse is no place to visit unprepared."

I spent some time inside the Grove, arranging the contents of my Craneskin Bag and making a list of items I should pick up before leaving. Medicine, MREs, ammunition—lots and lots of ammunition—and tools, the kind that would be useful for getting the odd vehicle running.

The Craneskin Bag was my birthright as the last descendent of Fionn MacCumhaill—that and the enmity of the countless *aes sídhe* he'd pissed off over the course of his life. The Bag followed me everywhere I went, and even if it was taken from me or lost, it would eventually show up of its own accord. Handy, but also a pain in the ass—partially because it was butt-ugly, but mostly because it immediately marked my identity to those who knew who I was.

I could carry a near-infinite amount of stuff in the Bag, but what I carried was limited to things that fit through the opening. Anything else I needed, like a welding machine, generators, solar panels, and the like, I'd have to scavenge, scrounge, or steal once I got to the Hellpocalypse. Heavy weapons and explosives as well. It wasn't like I could just go down to the local HEB and buy frag grenades, after all.

Once my Bag and list were in order, I headed Earthside to waste some time while I let Fallyn cool off. First, I headed to the junkyard to check in with Maureen, the half-kelpie who'd been my druid master's Girl Friday and confidante for centuries. Maureen and the old man had practically raised me after my Fomorian mother had given up on the task, and frankly she was more of a mother to me than my own mom.

I had the Oak drop me off behind the building, then I popped my head in the door and found her behind the counter, typing away at the keyboard.

"Hey, Maureen, need anything?"

"I see ya' recovered from the wake," she said without looking up from the screen.

I chewed my lip as I gauged the temperature of the room. "I did. How are you doing today? You know, after the funeral and all."

"As well as kin' be expected."

Her face was an inscrutable mask as she tossed me a stack of stapled pages. Obviously, she didn't want to talk about it. "A few auction vehicles were delivered. Ya' might see what ya' can do about gettin' 'em runnin'. The lads are good with pullin' parts, but they lack yer' skill with diagnosing and such."

"Fair enough. Anything else you need?"

She crossed her arms and gave me a glum expression. "Someone needs ta' go rifle through the remains o' Éire Imports, see what might be salvaged. I can't bring myself ta' do it. Mind headin' up there today?"

"Can do," I said with a smile, even though I dreaded the task. "I'll be in the yard if anyone needs me."

"As if," she countered. "The place runs like a top. No owner interference needed, lad."

"Okay, okay. And, as always, your presence is appreciated."

"Dangerously close ta' a thanks, boyo. But noted."

Ducking out the door with a chuckle, I checked out the auction vehicles on the list Maureen had given me. One was an older Datsun that looked like a parts vehicle, but I knew an enthusiast would pay top dollar for a rust-free specimen like that. Another was a Mini Cooper with eighty kilometers on the odie—parts, for sure— and a third was a Honda minivan that, with some TLC, would serve some family well for several more years.

I spent half an hour getting the Datsun to run, stealing a set of points, plugs, and wires from an engine we had sitting in the shop. Then, I gave the Honda a once-over, noting it needed better rubber and a front-end wheel alignment before we passed it on.

Otherwise, it was in good condition, so I marked it as such before leaving the work order on the dash. Then, I cast a chameleon spell on myself and headed to Éire Imports.

When I portalled in, a couple of school-aged kids were picking through the rubble. They looked to be about twelve years old, and why they weren't in school was anyone's guess. I was about to start chewing ass, but then I realized that could've been Jesse and me, ten years ago or so.

Geez, I feel old.

"Hey, there's a sword here," one kid said, pulling a warped trainer from under a pile of bricks. "Aw, man, it's bent."

His female companion looked at it and shrugged. "Danny found a dagger last night. A real one—it was sharp and everything. Keep looking."

"Ahem," I said, clearing my throat loudly. I'd snuck right up on them, and they hadn't even noticed. The boy jumped at the sound of my voice, while the girl ran immediately.

Smart kid. Kind of crappy to leave her wing man, though.

The boy dropped the sword, and it clattered loudly as it hit the bricks at his feet. "We wasn't stealing anything, mister. Honest."

"And people don't call me ginger."

"That's a girl's name."

"So it is. And what would your name be?"

"Jeff. But everyone calls me J.J., because my last name starts with J."

"Nice to meet you, J.J. I'm Colin," I said with a nod.

"I thought you said your name was Ginger," he replied, wiping his nose on his sleeve.

I had to stifle a laugh—the kid was a riot. "You know this place belongs to someone, right?"

J.J. looked down at his feet. "Yeah. But the other kids have been digging here, and we just thought—that is, Clary and me—that it was okay."

"Well, it's not," I said, crossing my arms and giving him my best imperious look. The kid seemed kind of scared, so I let the tension out of my stance as I continued. "Anyway, I used to work here, and I'm supposed to be looking through the rubble for anything we can salvage. Fact is, I could use some help."

"Really?" he said with excitement in his voice. Suddenly, his face fell. "That sounds like a lot of work, though."

"Yes, but I'll let you keep anything interesting you find that I don't want. Deal?"

"Yessir!"

4

The kid and I spent the better part of the morning rifling through the rubble, with me keeping a close eye on him so he didn't get hurt. When the work was done, we'd recovered a pile of weapons that I planned to toss in my Bag after the kid left. We'd also found a few pictures and personal items, mementos that wouldn't mean anything to anyone but Maureen, Jesse, and me. As soon as I got the chance, I'd deliver a share of that collection to each of them.

J.J. was sitting on what used to be the back dock, and I was organizing our finds, when I sensed a powerful magical emanation close by—fae magic.

Portal spell, has to be.

"Kid, you'd better run along," I said as I scanned the area in the magical spectrum.

"Can I keep this thing?" he said as he struggled to lift a mace with a huge, spiked head.

"No," I replied, keeping my eye on the spatial disturbance I'd spotted twenty yards across the parking lot. I pulled out my money clip, peeling off a bill. "Here's twenty bucks. Now, go home, and don't spend it all in one place."

The kid snagged the twenty out of my hand, sprinting off to do who knew what mischief. I watched him leave out of the corner of my eye, saving my attention for the danger that lurked close by. Soon, a female figure coalesced. She wore a long, dark cloak, dark leather pants and gloves, and leather high-heeled boots.

Fuamnach.

Without a moment's hesitation, I called on my magic, readying several druid battle spells and setting them on a hair trigger. One gesture, and I'd hit the Tuath Dé sorceress with half the spells in my arsenal. It wasn't in my nature to attack first, and that's all that stopped me from unloading on her before she spoke.

"Wait, I'm not here to do battle," she said in the elitist, Mid-Atlantic accent she affected. "Not that I don't intend to put you in your place, someday. However, I have more pressing matters to attend presently."

Magic crackled in the air around me as she spoke, invisible to anyone not versed in the mystic arts. Rather than lower my guard, I let the spells hover in the air as a warning to the goddess who stood before me.

"You tread on sacred ground, witch, so you'd better talk fast."

"When they told me you'd survived your confrontation with Badb, I didn't believe it. Something about you is different, druid—I can see it." She cradled her chin in her hand. "The Seer fooled us all, didn't he? If only we'd seen his plan sooner. Now, you'll be that much more difficult to dispose of—when the time comes, that is."

"The clock is ticking," I replied icily.

"Yes, of course. As you know, my son and I are at odds."

"He's not your son."

She rolled her eyes. "If you say so. Regardless, I need to find him."

"Lemme get this straight—you want me to rat out Crowley? Seriously?"

"I never jest. And by way of recompense, I would be willing to call a truce between us for—oh, say, a century?" I stared at her, tightlipped. "Oh, very well—make it two, then. Do we have a deal?"

Silence hung in the air for several heartbeats. Then, I laughed. "You fucking Tuath Dé just don't get it, do you? I'm not like you, you bougie-ass, neutral-color-wearing, back-stabbing, psychopathic harridan. I don't sell out my friends, and I can't be bought or bribed."

"Pfah," she replied with a backhanded wave. "Anyone can be bought. This is an urgent matter, and I don't have time to dicker. Name your price, druid. Power? Influence? Knowledge? I could tell you how to leverage the land you've claimed in Mag Mell, you know. Do you realize how powerful you'd be, if you were only able to utilize that magic to its fullest? You could be a god."

"Holy shit, but you deities are stupid. What in the great green froggity fuck makes you think I want to be a god?"

"All humans crave immortality. Your kind longs for it. It's for that reason that mortals flock to the *neamh-mairbh*, giving themselves up to be fed upon like cattle. Surely you wouldn't pass on such an opportunity. I will not offer twice."

"Then listen closely, you imperious, hatchet-faced, gonnorheic harpy. I will never—I repeat, never—betray my friends for the sake of whatever table scraps you trumped-up, self-important, short-sighted *little gods* deign to proffer. So, take your offer, shove it up your ass, and fuck off back to whatever hidey-hole in Underhill that Peg Powler chased you to."

"Hmm, yes. I'd forgotten how charming you could be when you set your mind to it. Very well, have it your way." A portal opened up behind her, a seven-foot-tall oval of nothingness, beyond which I could see only mist and shadow. She half-turned toward the hole in the fabric of space, only to pause and address me one last time over her shoulder. "But, druid, do remember that 'never' is a very long time. Take it from someone who knows."

I shot her the bird with both barrels, my eyes locked on hers until she exited the scene wearing a knowing smirk that said I hadn't impressed her in the least.

Whether due to paranoia or cautionary common sense, I stared at the space the portal had occupied, long after it winked out behind her. When I was certain she'd gone, I was left with nothing more than regret over not attempting to kill her, and concern over the fact that she'd personally come looking for Crowley.

Considering that she'd leveled her adoptive son's farm all on her lonesome, I might've been relieved that we didn't tangle. However, I had spells in reserve that she'd never seen me use, and I was fairly confident she was still underestimating me. The only reason I hadn't tried to kill her was because Crowley would never forgive me for denying him the opportunity.

I've no clue if I could take Fuamnach, but could Crowley?

It was a question for the ages, and maybe one that would be answered in the near future. I might have warned the guy, but he wasn't answering his phone, and I had no idea where he'd gone. So, I settled for leaving a message for him on Belladonna's voicemail, on the odd chance she'd see him and forward the intel. Later, I'd track him down and make sure he received it, but right now, I needed to find Fallyn and patch things up before I headed to the Hellpocalypse.

When I popped into the front yard of the Austin Pack's clubhouse—the one they used for training new 'thropes and hunting game—a half-dozen Pack members were in the yard. Normally they'd be hanging out, working on their bikes, and other meaningless shit. But today, they were drilling hand-to-hand combat techniques, the sort of superhero-ish stuff that only a 'thrope, vamp, or fae could pull off.

None of them could see me—I'd cast a chameleon spell on myself, force of habit—but one of the females held up a hand, signaling to the others that something was off. She began sniffing around, as did the rest of them, until an imperious female voice called from the front porch of the clubhouse.

"It's merely the druid. Return to your training." I dropped the spell, shimmering into view as Lita addressed me. "I suppose you're looking for Fallyn. She's not here."

"Okay. I guess we'll get to that in a minute," I said as I strolled up to the porch, avoiding the 'thropes who were sparring along the way. "But what I'd like to know is, what are you still doing here?"

She fixed me with her almost-yellow hazel eyes, staring down that Romanesque nose at me like I was a bug she was about to squash. "That, druid, is none of your business."

"Ah, right—you and Samson have that on again, off again thing going. Still on, I take it?"

She sneered, showing enough of her pearly whites to display an overly-long canine. "You tread on dangerous ground. You are not needed here. Speak your business and be off."

"My, but we *are* prickly today." She stared at me, her eyes drilling a hole in my forehead, so I continued. "Fine. Where. Is. Fallyn?"

"Gone, as I said," she answered, pulling her long, flowing black hair into a ponytail and tying it with a short length of cord in the back. She turned her gaze to the combatants in the yard. "No, no, no. Tera, how many times do I have to tell you, never cross your feet when moving laterally. Either leap, spring, or shuffle."

The female who'd first sensed my arrival lowered her head. She had short dark hair cut in a punky style, and she looked more like a hairdresser than a warrior. But she moved well, and her larger male sparring partner was having a hard time dealing with her speed and agility.

"Yes, mistress," the girl said. "But who's going to be quick enough to take advantage of such a small mistake?"

Lita glared at her, then she swept her gaze across the lot of them. "Oh? You think you won't face someone who can exploit the weaknesses in your strategies and tactics? What about the vampires, or the fae? Or even the druid here—did he not recently dismantle your former alpha, and in front of the entire pack?"

The group answered with nods all around, but Tera was still unconvinced. "But Mistress Lita, I'm just an aesthetician. I'm not an enforcer, and I'm damned sure not a frontline fighter. Why the hell should I have to know this stuff?"

Lita scowled, causing the lot of them to lower their gaze at her displeasure. "Samson has been too easy on you, letting you choose to be less than you are. A pack is only as strong as its weakest link. Every pack member must be ready to step in at a moment's notice to protect the Pack. You cannot simply rely on your supernatural gifts to save you, not considering what may threaten a pack like yours. Now, do as I say, or you'll be sparring me instead of Thomas."

"Yes, ma'am," Tera replied.

"Expecting trouble?" I asked.

Lita kept her eyes on the group of trainees. "A pack alpha should always expect trouble and prepare for it. Samson relied too much on the peace he brokered with the vampires and the fae, and now this pack is weak and vulnerable. If my daughter is to lead it, then I will see to it they become a finely tuned fighting force."

"Makes sense. Speaking of, where is your daughter?"

The titan smirked. "She showed up here in a fuss, railing on about what an idiot you were, and how you were going to get yourself killed. I did not disabuse her of the notion."

"And?"

"And she asked to be sent on assignment. I am still running an international mercenary operation, despite being preoccupied with cleaning up Samson's messes. I pulled a dossier and gave it to her, then she left without a word."

I rubbed my forehead and groaned, not liking the sound of this at all. "When will she be back?"

Lita frowned as she hollered at one of the 'thropes. "Faster, Lucas, faster! You'll never survive a skirmish with another pack like that." She flicked her gaze to me, then back to her trainees. "Who can say? Often, the contracts we take are complex affairs, requiring a great deal of reconnaissance and planning before execution. She could be gone for days, or months. Such is the nature of our work."

"Fuck."

"Not likely, until she returns. Will there be anything else?"

I rubbed my chin as I exhaled heavily. "No, Cruella —not today." I'd leave a message on Fallyn's voicemail, since she definitely wouldn't be picking up while she was on a job. Fallyn hadn't told me much about the work she did for her mother, only that it was dangerous and that she and her team went dark when on assignment. I was about to leave when a thought crossed my mind. "You know, Lita, you can't break us up."

"I'm aware of that," she replied. "But I'm reasonably confident you'll get yourself killed sometime in the near future. I am a patient titan. I can wait."

"Nice to know you care, Mom."

In an instant, she had me by my lapels, pinning me to a nearby porch column. "I told you never to call me that."

"Oops, must've forgot," I said, flashing her a shit-eating grin. "Man, I can't wait to spend the holidays in the Alps with you. Ooh, we could come for Thanksgiving, Christmas, Easter—how are the summers there? Is there enough powder to ski?"

The titan's eyes narrowed, then she dropped me to the ground. "Play your games, druid. One day, you'll jest with the wrong immortal, and that day will be your last."

I straightened my clothing, dusting myself off unnecessarily. "Right. Nice chat. Tell Samson I said hi."

She snarled, which I took as my cue to leave. It was time to find Click and head to the Hellpocalypse.

When I officially joined the Trickster Local #113, Click was assigned as my mentor. The choice didn't surprise me in the least, as he was the one trying to get me to join the damned club in the first place. But I felt a bit like Groucho Marx at the moment, wondering why I would ever want to belong to a club that would have me as a member.

I was no deity, that was for certain. Neither was I completely mortal, being the son of a Fomorian mother and a father who was a natural born hero, a human born with exceptional physical talents who protected the human race.

But I was no god. I had no desire to become one, either. Yet Click had convinced me it wasn't necessary to be a god to be a trickster. In the annals of myth and legend, there was a long and storied history of demigods and heroes becoming tricksters. Odysseus, Cú Chulainn, Wakdjunga, and Olifat, to name a few. Humans often had to outsmart the gods to survive their schemes and designs, which almost always ran contrary to the best interests of humankind. It wasn't much of a leap for me to do the same. Hell, it was what I'd been doing all along.

One of the "benefits" of apprenticing to a trickster god was instant communication. Click was now somehow in tune with me, and from what I'd gathered, all I needed to do was speak his name to summon him. I didn't necessarily consider that an advantage, considering that I frequently wished I'd never met the quasi-god. Still, it was better than roaming the city calling his name out at random.

"Click, you there?" I said, feeling like a fool for talking to myself. I'd come to the junkyard after leaving the Pack's clubhouse. It was after hours, and no one was around to hear, but I still felt like a moron.

Hmm... no answer. Maybe I have to raise my—

"Aye, lad. What kin I do for ya'?"

I jumped at the sound of his voice, which came from behind me. "Shit, why do you and Larry always do that? Just because you can turn invisible and sneak up on people, it doesn't mean you should."

Click thumbed his chest. "Trickster. Ya' were sayin'?"

"Fair enough. I suppose I should expect nothing

less." An odd thought occurred to me, one that I expressed before I fully considered the implications. "Why haven't you invited Larry to join? He seems like he fits the bill."

A sour expression crossed Click's face. "If yer' insinuatin' that me and the mange-ridden freak o' scientific experimentation have somethin' in common—"

"No, not at all," I said, raising my hands apologetically. "It's just that he seems the type. I mean, Coyote is a member of your group, right? And Raven—Raven has to be a member."

"True, but they're shifters. They kin take on human form. We have ta' have some standards, after all, else we'd have every talkin' animal in the cosmos tryin' ta' join our ranks."

"Okay, but Larry can shift too. At least, he claims to be able to do so."

"Aye, an' backwards at that. Most shifters remain human except when they turn involuntarily once a month. That mutated pile o' excrement does it in reverse, only becoming human once a month."

"Seems like Heyoka would be all for that."

"Don'cha go puttin' ideas in his head," Click said, shaking a finger in my face. "Now, why'd ya' call me here?"

"It's time. I want to go to the Hellpocalypse."

Click's expression soured even further. "Are ya' certain, lad? In truth, I only meant ta' leave ya' there fer a moment. 'Twas havin' a spell, else I'd not have left ya' there fer' so long."

"A spell?"

He circled his index finger around his ear. "Comes and goes, a side effect o' gainin' immortality the hard way."

"Which is?"

He sat on the hood of a rusted-out seventies station wagon. "I shouldna' be tellin' ya' this, but ya' kin become immortal, if ya' have the magic an' ya' choose ta' give up yer' mortality. But it's a hefty bill ta' pay, and not everyone comes through the process unscathed."

"I see. What you're saying is, I could become immortal?"

He shook his head in the negative, then up and down, and finally around in circles. "Yes? No? Maybe? What I do know is that, if I have another spell whilst yer' in that other timeline, I won't be of sound mind ta' come round ta' save ya'."

"That—huh. Yeah, that is a little ominous. But I understand time magic now."

"Oh? How?"

I held a finger up as if to say eureka. "I learned it when I chanted the *teinm laida*—that, and the principles of druid mastery."

"Crafty lad, ya' are, which is why I chose ya' as my apprentice. But knowin' and doin' are two different things."

I flashed him a crooked frown as I scratched behind

my ear. "I had a feeling you'd say that. How long do you think it'll take me to be able to do it on my own?"

He threw his hands up in the air. "One time? Ten? A hundred? I have no clue. Everyone who takes up the practices o' chronomancy an' chronourgy are different, an' they progress at varying paces." He tapped a finger on his chin. "But then again, ya' have shown promise."

"You don't sound too sure," I said with skepticism in my voice.

"I'm not. Time magic is as wild and imprecise as the mystic arts kin get. All I kin do is teach you, an' hope ya' don't get lost between timelines or open a black hole that swallows the entire galaxy."

"That doesn't sound ominous at all."

He gave an offhanded wave. "A cautious person never causes an avalanche."

"Don't you mean, 'a cautious person never changes the world,' or something?"

"That too." He glanced around, as if searching for a thought that escaped him. "Now, what was I goin' ta' say? Ah, yes. If ya' get o'er there an' ya' can't find yer way back, stop. Jest sit tight an' stay where ya' are, else I may never trace yer' steps when I eventually come lookin' fer ya."

"Eventually," I said, framing the word in air quotes.

"Sure! Ya' kin count on me, lad," he said, rubbing his hands together like a mischievous child. "Now, where are we goin'a again?"

5

A fter reminding Click where exactly I wanted to go —repeatedly, in fact—he began instructing me in the ways of Walking the Twisted Paths.

"Time magic is forbidden magic, lad—always remember that. Ne'er let a soul see ya' walk the Paths. Always do it in secret and kill anyone who witnesses such an act."

"Say what? You want me to murder someone in cold blood, just because they saw me using time magic?"

"Aye. What if they tell someone, who tells someone else, who tells a god like The Dagda, or Odin, or Amun-Ra, that yer' feckin' 'round with chronomancy and chronourgy? Or worse, what if they're a feckin' mage o' no small skill, and they try ta' emulate yer' spell without knowin' what they're doin'?" He opened his hands and spread his fingers wide in the universal sign for *kaboom*. "Ya' want yer' own timeline ta' just *poof*, disappear?"

I thought about it before giving a short nod. "You have a point. But what if I just mind-wiped them?"

"If ya' can't listen ta' me 'bout this, how are ya' goin' ta' learn ta' walk the Paths?"

"To be fair, you never told me this before," I replied as I crossed my arms over my chest. "If I'd have known there was killing involved, I might have refused your offer."

"An' ya'd be deader than a doornail."

"I'm not killing anyone. I'll just make sure no one sees me working time magic. Simple."

He sighed. "Fine, have it yer' way. Now, when yer' walkin' the Paths—"

"Wait a minute—aren't you skipping ahead? We haven't even discussed how to get on the Paths."

"Huh? I thought that was obvious. Ya' picture 'em in yer' mind, an' when ya' see the one ya' want, ya' step inta' the feckin' thing."

I arched an eyebrow at him because that sounded really sketchy to me. "That's it? If I can see the thread, I can walk it?"

"Certainly. But it's holdin' it when yer' walkin' it that's the trick. It takes concentration, willpower, an' lots o' magical energy."

"So, it's like wielding magic—I think it, will it, and it happens." I cocked my head at an angle. "Are there any trigger words or gestures to do? Do I need to memorize a chant or anything?"

He scowled. "Nah. That sort o' thing is fer' amateurs."

"Can runes be invested with time magic?"

His eyes grew big as saucers as he wagged a finger side to side. "Don't even think about it, lad. The wrong person could find your enchanted item, and then we'd all be screwed." Click grabbed a twig from the ground, then he knelt and started drawing in the dirt. "As I was sayin', the hard part is holdin' on ta' the damned thread while ya' walk it."

"How so?"

"Look here," he said, pointing to the squiggly lines he'd drawn.

"Looks like a lightning bolt. And not a very good one."

"Smart alecky upstart, that's supposed ta' be a time-line branch, o' which there are infinite offshoots. Anything that could happen, has happened in the interminable branches o' the Twisted Paths."

"Then, how can we follow them? Or find the one we want?"

"Ah, ya' *are* yer' own startin' point. Surely ya've figured this out, flippin' through the time streams like ya' have been."

I gave a grudging nod. "I figured as much, but I didn't want to be presumptuous. What's so hard about holding onto one of these streams?"

"Well, ya' don't always catch one at the exact point ya'

want. Meanin' ya' have to ride it until ya' get to yer' intended destination. S'like ridin' a tiger, lad—damned feckin' hard. Ya' never want ta' do it when yer' not at yer' best, that's fer sure. Else ye'll get tossed off an' land who knows where. I lost ma' grip once, got tossed inta' the late Pleistocene." He closed his eyes and shivered. "The women there were uglier than the ass-end o' Sgoidamur's mule, lemme tell ya'."

Click stared off into space for several seconds, until I snapped my fingers in front of his face. "Click. Click!"

"Wha'? Oh, yeah. So, don't let go o' that thread, no matter what ya' do. 'Tis yer' lifeline, and if ya' lose it, ya' might not make it back ta' yer own timeline. Got it?"

"Yep. Now, how are we going to do this? Are you going to take me there like you did last time? Or am I doing this myself while you watch?"

"While I watch? Oh, o' course—ya' meant time travelin'. That sounds 'bout right. Walk, an' I'll observe."

"'About right'? You mean you aren't sure?"

He shrugged. "Been fore'er an' a day since I learned time magic. Can't blame me fer' bein' sketchy on the details." He rubbed his hands together impishly. "So, are ya' ready?"

I looked skyward, saying a silent prayer. "I guess now is as good a time as any." I stabbed a finger at Click as I fixed him with a stern look. "But if I fuck up, you pull me out right away, okay?"

"Sure, sure. Now quit feckin' about. I'm supposed ta' meet Loki fer' brunch at the gentlemen's club at ten."

"They serve food at those places?"

"Good food, in fact. Only reason why I go, the way those girls always pester me fer' money. Ya'd think they'd kick those dodgy panhandlers out o' such establishments."

I nodded slowly. "Uh-huh." Click appeared to be having a moment, and I wondered if this was the best time to be walking the Paths for the first time.

Ah, fuck it.

I closed my eyes and slowed my breathing, then I began flipping through the time streams in my mind.

Here goes nothing.

It took me a while to find the time stream I was looking for, even though I'd spied on it several times since I'd chanted the *teinm laida*. Click had once said that time-line came up repeatedly in his own searches, but I had to follow several until I located it.

Time magic allowed for that, as you basically sat in your own stasis field while you looked through hundreds or even thousands of branches. The branches were infinite, but probability allowed me to narrow them down to "stronger" branches—those Paths that burned brighter in the theater of my mind.

There.

I saw the same scene that I'd witnessed through Click's portal when he'd yanked me back from the Hellpocalypse, albeit from a bird's eye view. Anna, running to warn everyone of an incursion, and a horde of zombies hot on her heels. If I wanted, I could sort of zoom out and see things that were happening in other places. But my intention was to find this place and these people, so the magic led me here.

Holy hell, there's a lot of them.

Before, my view was limited by Click's portal opening. But, now, I saw what I couldn't before—a small swarm of hundreds of deaders slogging through the swamp toward our camp.

The ones Anna had seen were just the tip of the spear—a few dozen faster, newer zombies who led the vanguard. The real danger was behind them in the main body of the herd. There'd be no fighting all those walking corpses, no matter how much stronger, faster, and tougher I was now.

No, I'd have to use magic. And that meant getting Anna and the kids out of camp so I could work. They all knew what to do, but the canoe and flatboat I'd hidden at the tip of the peninsula couldn't hold them all. It'd take at least two trips across the lake, which meant I needed to work fast.

I just need a little privacy, is all. Nothing to it.

I was still in my own timeline, however, and I really didn't know for certain how to get from "here" to "there."

"Click, are you with me?"

"Aye, lad."

His voice in my ear almost made me lose my concentration, and my handle on the time stream as well. "Shit, is it really necessary to be that close?"

"I didn't know how far yer' mind had gone inta' the Paths. Sorry."

"Whatever. I can see where I want to go. Now, what do I do?"

"Can ya' see yerself?"

I shook my head, keeping my eyes closed so I could hold the image in my mind. "No, this must've been right after you yanked me back to this timeline."

"Phew, that's a relief. Okay, then all ya' have ta' do is jump."

"Jump? As in, jump up and down?"

"Naw, don't be daft. Ya' hafta' jump yerself inta' the timeline, mentally as it were. Imagine pullin' yerself inta' that timestream, an' it'll happen."

"That's it?"

"'That's it?' he asks, as if it's so easy. Mark my words, it'll be a struggle, fer' sure. But don't let go—jest push through, no matter what ya' think is happenin' to ya'."

I gave a thumbs up gesture, still keeping my eyes shut tight. "Okay, here goes—"

In my mind, I saw myself stepping into that timeline, as if stepping through a portal in time and space. At first, I felt nothing as I imagined my foot moving forward into that reality. Then, that "nothing" became a gradually increasing pressure that built exponentially, the further I willed my foot to go.

The sensation was sort of like popping a balloon by

sitting on it, when the balloon doesn't seem like it wants to give. Except this took a tremendous effort of will, causing the kind of mental strain I hadn't felt since I tried to cast my first spell. Suddenly, I felt like a beginner learning magic for the first time, struggling to form the power inside and around me into a cogent spell-form that would achieve the desired result.

Why didn't it feel like this when Click did it?

It occurred to me that maybe it had to him, but since I was just a passenger I hadn't noticed. And, man, was it hard—like pushing a ten-ton boulder up a mountain with my mind. It felt different than druid magic, too, as if the universe itself resisted my efforts to fuck with its rules and bypass the safeguards placed on the streams of time.

That weight felt like it was crushing me, so much so that I'd tensed every muscle in my body. Sweat had broken out on my brow, and I was literally shaking under the strain.

"Almost there, lad—don't give up," Click admonished from somewhere nearby but very far way. I was right there on the edge, just like he said—I could feel it. With a loud groan and a monumental effort of will, I gave one final mental push.

"C'mon, c'mon—fuuuuuuuccccck!" I screamed.

I felt a *pop*, and I was through. The air was different, everything smelled different, and even the ground beneath my feet had changed. I opened my eyes to look around, and sure enough I'd made it. But instead of hearing a zombie horde and Anna's shouted warnings, I heard Click's voice in my head.

"That's fantastic, lad. Now, don't ferget ta' anchor the—"

Skrtich. It sounded almost like reaching the edge of a radio station's broadcast territory, as Click's voice drifted off into static.

"Click. Click! What am I supposed to anchor?"

Nothing.

I had little time to concern myself with Click's unfinished message, however. Now I *could* hear the dead—hundreds of them, in fact, moaning in the distance, while the vanguard of the horde groaned even louder nearby.

Spotted. Gotta' get the group out of here. Then, it's time to fight.

I'd armed myself with the same hand-and-a-half sword I'd used the last time I was here—or, at least, a close facsimile of it. In fact, I was wearing the same outfit I'd worn in my final moments here, down to the last detail. I'd known all along that I was coming back someday, so I kept the clothes in my Bag; that way, I wouldn't raise suspicions by looking too fresh and clean cut. I'd let my hair and beard grow in the Grove, too. Couldn't imitate the smell, but I did skip a few baths to make up for it.

The dead were coming up from the south, but they

were slow, so we had time to act. I ran out of the tree line, yelling instructions to Anna, both to coordinate and to get the attention of the dead.

"Head to the boats—I'll hold them off as long as I can."

Anna's cold blue eyes met mine, and with a shared nod, she was off. Now, it was time to deal with the dead.

The leading edge of the horde had fixated on me, which was conveniently disconcerting. I had no doubt in my ability to handle a few dozen zombies, even with the odd ghoul mixed in, but I could still be infected. My skin was still human in my stealth-shifted form— vulnerable to cuts, scrapes, and, of course, bites. Thinking back to the time I'd had to fight off the mysteriously potent vyrus that existed in this timeline gave me the chills, and I decided then and there I wouldn't risk it happening a second time.

Magic it is.

A quick backward glance told me Anna, Mickey, and the kids were long gone, having already disappeared into the trees on the northern boundary of camp. That left me free to do what I do best—chew bubble gum and kick ass with druidry. And I was all out of bubble gum.

With a thought and a trigger word, I turned the ground to quicksand-like mud, all the way across the peninsula, effectively turning a twenty-foot swathe of land into a moat. It took way more out of me than normal, but I chalked that up to the fact that I'd cast the spell so quickly. Shaking off the fatigue, I stood my ground, waiting for the dead to converge on my location.

It didn't take long—the smelly bastards were stupid as fuck. Soon the first few had stumbled into my trap, sinking up to their waists in gooey, sticky mud. Instead of taking that as a sign to steer clear, the rest of the vanguard followed their basic zombie instincts, which meant going after the nearest moving thing that had brains to eat and warm blood in its veins—me.

Within minutes, two-dozen zombies were stuck in my mud moat, groaning and moaning up a storm. However, more were coming behind them—a lot more —and if I didn't do something, they would fill the gap with bodies and cross the treacherous ground by using their buddies as an inhuman bridge.

No bueno.

I was just about to turn the whole fucking field into one huge mudpit, when I saw him.

Holy shit, that's Brian.

Brian was Anna's little brother. The kid was in a tree on the other side of my moat, about seven feet off the ground, kicking at a beanpole thin male zombie in mechanic's coveralls that was trying to pull him down. The tree he'd climbed was little more than a sapling, and it was clear he couldn't climb much higher. I had to go get him, before he ended up becoming deader cheddar.

Fuck, I can't let him see me doing magic. Time to improvise.

I was pretty sure the kid hadn't noticed me yet, so intent was he on not getting eaten. So, I cast a chameleon spell on myself, then I sunk the zombs the rest of the way into the ground, hardening the surface after. Again, the spells took a lot more out of me than usual, but I ignored the sensation. Once I had solid ground between me and the kid, I ran full tilt using my Fomorian speed, dropping the chameleon spell about twenty feet away and slowing to human speed.

I sprinted the final ten feet, lopping the zombie off at the knees before it noticed I was there. A quick downward thrust to the face, and the former mechanic was out of action. I looked up at Brian, beckoning for him to jump out of the tree.

"C'mon, more are coming. We gotta boogie, kid."

"Where'd you come from, Mr. Colin?" he asked as he clambered down from the tree. "I thought I got left behind, and then you appeared out of nowhere."

"Yeah, we'll talk about that later. Right now, you gotta haul ass to the boats."

"Dude, you said a bad word. Better not let my sis' hear you talk like that."

Only an innocent kid like Brian would worry about getting into trouble at a time like this.

"I won't say anything if you don't," I said, chuckling despite the situation. "Now, go—scram before the rest of them show up."

"Yessir," he said, running off across the clearing like a scared rabbit.

I watched him go, then I turned my attention to the mass of undead that were starting to appear amidst the trees to the south.

Fuck it.

I gathered my will, directing it into the ground between the trees and the lake water that surrounded the isthmus. The ground was already fairly sodden here, and it didn't take much to turn the whole damned stretch of land into a swamp. Hell, it was halfway there already, and all it took was a bit of magic to finish the job. When it was done, I felt dizzy and a little nauseous, and I found myself wondering why magic use was tiring me out now that I was back in the Hellpocalypse.

That should hold the dead for now. Time to see how Anna and Mickey are doing.

6

A fter sticking around to make certain the dead wouldn't get through my trap any time soon, I took a moment to get my bearings. There were things I needed to do, and one particular item was first on my list. However, the group's welfare was priority one, so I'd deal with my personal matters once they were safely across the lake.

Here I am—back in the never-ending nightmare of constant worry and stress.

It felt odd being back here, and despite the upgrades I'd had since my last visit, I felt increasing levels of anxiety taking hold as I remembered how fucking difficult those six months had been. Taking care of a group of two adults and two dozen or so school-aged boys was no walk in the park. My days were filled with finding increasingly scarce resources like food, water, and medicine, and my nights were spent making sure we didn't lose anyone to roaming groups of zombies, or the many revenants and vampires that inhabited this version of my home state.

Nothing for it but to push through. One step at a time, Colin.

As I headed for the boats, I continued reassuring myself with positive self-talk, focusing on my breathing just as Finnegas taught me. By the time I reached the northernmost tip of the peninsula, I'd calmed down and Anna was loading up the second group of kids. Since I didn't see him, I assumed Mickey was probably with the first group on the northeast side of the lake, at our rally point in the state park. It wasn't the safest place—no place was, really—but it was fairly remote, and there were areas of dense forest nearby in case the group needed to hide.

"How we doing?" I asked as I strolled out of the trees.

"Halfway there," Anna replied as she flashed me a forced smile.

She'd been a rock since I stumbled upon the group, shortly after Click dumped me here the first time. Pale and willowy, with long, wavy brown hair she kept pulled back in a ponytail, Anna might've looked frail, but there was steel behind those Anne Hathaway looks and upper-middle-class manners. Her baby blue eyes conveyed the urgency and worry she felt, so I held my hands up in a calming gesture.

"Relax, it's under control. The dead are having a hard time dealing with the swampy conditions in the narrow part of the isthmus, and I dealt with the ones that made it through. We have time."

Her shoulders relaxed, but she continued to encourage the boys to board the boat and canoe as quickly as possible. "C'mon, let's go. That's it—Matthew, help Thomas with his backpack. Danny, move some of that load to the front of the canoe—it's back heavy and it'll be harder to steer."

Anna was good with the boys, calm and patient. Me, not so much. They looked up to me, that was for certain, but I lacked her composure when it came to dealing with a couple dozen rowdy, whiny, and sometimes sick children. For that reason, I left the direction and coaching to her while I stood watch, just in case any of the dead had made it through the swamp I'd created.

And a good thing I did. The last child was clambering into the flatboat when a ghoul came stumbling out of the tree line.

"Miss Anna, look," one of the boys whispered.

"Don't worry, I got this," I said. More were coming— I could hear them bounding toward us. "Get them across the lake, and don't come back for me. I'll come around the long way and meet you at the rally point."

"Colin, no—there are too many," Anna urged softly.

The ghoul had finally spotted us, and her keening wail would soon bring others of her kind. Ghouls were stronger, smarter, and faster versions of your average zombie. Zombies with upgrades, due to a physiological affinity for the vyrus. They were a step up from zombies, and a step down from vampire-like revenants. One ghoul was no problem, but a dozen could be an issue. I hoped only a few had made it through the muck after this one.

"Just do it. I promise I won't be long," I said as I pushed the canoe and then the flatboat out into the lake. Anna jumped in the boat, sloshing through knee-deep water as I strolled up the bank to cut off the ghoul before it could reach the boats.

The boys already had oars in the water by the time the ghoul had reached me. The creature was an older Anglo woman, maybe early fifties at the time of her death, but she'd been in shape when she was alive. She wore jogging tights, one running shoe, and a Nike pullover, and what remained of her light brown hair had been pulled back in a ragged ponytail. The outfit was marred by gore and bloodstains—not to mention the fact that half her face was missing as well.

She was quick, coming at me at a near sprint with her arms extended and her fingers curled into claws, all the better to seize me and chow down on my neck and face. It seemed they really did prefer brains, as I'd seen zombies and ghouls alike smashing a recently killed human's head open like a melon to get at the warm, gray stuff inside. However, they'd gladly chow down on any warm flesh they could get their hands on, and I had no doubt this one would sink her blackened teeth into any bit of exposed skin she found.

Not today, Jillian Michaels. Time to put you out of your misery.

As usual, the ghoul went high as she lunged at me, so I went low, swinging the hand-and-a-half sword in a broad, horizontal arc that cut her off at the knees. I spun counterclockwise on the follow-through, bringing the blade overhead in a smooth spin that allowed me to behead the poor lady before her torso hit the ground.

By this time, the boats were far enough out in the lake to be safe from the half-dozen ghouls that approached from the south. I watched the kids and Anna from shore, then I headed back up the slope to deal with the rest of the dead so they wouldn't follow me to the rally point.

The ghouls weren't much trouble, and it only took a minute or so to chop them down and put them to rest. That was always a priority when I fought the undead, to release them from whatever hell they were experiencing. Nobody knew how much they remembered from their previous lives, but based on their proclivities for revisiting their old haunts, I suspected they retained something of their pre-infection memories.

That was enough reason to make sure the dead stayed that way after I tangled with them. I couldn't imagine wandering the earth as a zombie or ghoul, existing in a sort of half-living fugue until you wore your limbs down to nubs. And even then, you'd still be held captive to the way the vyrus animated your decaying, decrepit body.

Fuck that.

Anna, Mickey, and I had made a pact not long after we banded together, that if one of us were infected, the others would do the deed to end our suffering. Same with the kids, although we hadn't told them that. That didn't stop Brian from bringing it up once, though. He was the smartest of them, if not the oldest, and the natural leader of the group. Freaking kids were full of surprises, not the least of which was a hyper-aware prescience regarding the shit adults worried about.

It was a hell of a way to be forced to grow up, and I was determined to give them the most normal child-hood I could. That meant getting the group someplace that was easily defended and relatively safe from the dead and other supernatural predators that roamed the rapidly deteriorating cities and towns across the state.

I was roughly a mile from the rally point when a distant groan tore me from my reverie, forcing me back to the present and the tasks at hand. From where I stood in the trees along the shore, I could see Mickey keeping watch over the boys across a large inlet of the lake. Things were quiet, which meant they were safe, for now, so I could attend to some personal business.

I headed north, crossing the park trailway and traversing the woods until I came to a six-foot cedar fence that guarded the backyard of a two-story McMansion. The saved maps images on my fully charged phone revealed an entire neighborhood of homes north of the park—some upscale, others, not so much. I had highway maps of the state in my Bag, and most major cities as well. However, satellite images offered plenty more detail, so I'd spent considerable time saving images of our intended route on my phone before I left.

Most GPS satellites were still working, although eventually their orbits would decay, and they'd all go kaboom. However, most cell towers had failed by now, along with any remaining internet servers that hadn't been taken out by EMPs when the bombs fell. Anything that wasn't on paper or saved digitally on semi-permanent media was toast in this timeline.

Damned shame.

As for the neighborhood, that many homes meant food and other resources, but it also meant lots of wandering dead. All I needed was some privacy to run some magical diagnostics, and then I'd move on before I attracted their attention. I observed the house and yard from the safety of cover and a chameleon spell for ten minutes, then I checked out the streets in front. A few undead roamed further down the block, but this house was clear.

I leapt the fence, landing in the tall grass on the other side with cat-like grace, a benefit of being in my stealth-shifted form. Then, I leapt to the second-story roof, where a cracked window offered the easiest point of entry to the home.

Upon entering an upstairs bedroom, I nearly stumbled on a scattered array of clothing and personal items, the detritus of a family's hasty flight from their home. It looked to have been a teenage girl's room, based on the boy band posters on the wall and the mod, 90s-style decor. The family was long gone, so I wasted little time wondering about their fate as I lifted a dresser, setting it down with all due care to maintain relative quiet as I barred the door.

Time to see what's what, I thought as I sat on the fake zebra stripe carpet, adopting a lotus position as I cleared my head. Altering my breathing pattern, I dropped deep into a trance as I reached out with my druid sense, scanning the area miles around for threats.

The fact that it took more effort to use my druid senses was yet another indication that I'd likely be disappointed by the next to-do item on my list. Despite the effort it took, I was able to scan the area around the park, borrowing the eyes and ears of a red-tailed hawk to locate a large horde ten miles north, and a smaller group of a few hundred at the northernmost edge of this neighborhood. I made note of their positions and direction of travel, then I scanned for areas that prey animals like deer and hogs were avoiding. Soon, I located the lairs of two nos-types that had holed up in buildings along our route.

Of course you did, you bastards.

Nosferatu were feral vamps, but they weren't stupid, and they knew humans tended to travel along established routes. For that reason, they liked to hide out along major roads and highways, like hunters setting up tree blinds along game trails. We could avoid them by traveling during the day, but if I had time, I'd take them out in advance of our departure.

Now for the important stuff.

Clearing my mind of those concerns, I opened myself to a familiar telepathic channel through which only three creatures in existence communicated—the one I shared with my Oak and Grove. All I got on this plane was dead silence, meaning that the Oak had been destroyed, or it had vamoosed to the Void. I had no idea whether the Colin who'd inhabited this reality had bonded with his Oak. If not, I suspected that if I could locate the Oak that existed here, I might be able to complete the bond in his stead.

There'd be more time to look for it later, if it still lived. On a whim, I tried reaching through the Paths to reach the Oak in my own timeline, but that was a bust as well.

Looks like I'm on my own. Shit.

While these revelations weren't a surprise, they did pose some interesting challenges. For one, I had come to rely on my Oak and Grove for an excess of magical energy on which I could draw. Having that pool of magical power put me on par with most fae mages, if not in experience, then in sheer power. That I didn't have that reservoir at hand meant I'd be casting spells using my own reserves, which, while not inconsiderable, were limited.

If I ran into any serious baddies, that could put me at a severe disadvantage. Thus, one of my priorities after getting the group settled would be to track down the Oak that existed in this timeline. Failing that, I'd need to plant a new one here. And that meant traveling to Underhill to visit the Dagda.

One thing at a time.

With my immediate to-do list complete, I eased out of my trance. Then, I searched the house for fresh water and food—no sense in depleting what I had in my Bag, after all. After scrounging up some bottled water and a few cans of beans and soup, I headed for the rally point a mile or so distant, wondering how I was going to get nearly thirty people from here to Austin.

When I walked into the makeshift camp that Anna and Mickey had set up at the rally point, tensions were high. Mickey was busy getting the younger kids ready for bed, while a few of the older boys kept watch with Anna. Everyone knew this area wasn't secure, but a person could only go so long without water, food, and sleep. Addressing human needs meant that taking risks was part and parcel of surviving in the Hellpocalypse.

I signaled with a bird call before entering camp, then

I dropped my chameleon spell and exited the trees, carefully dropping the trash bag full of bottled water and canned food I'd slung over my shoulder. The boys descended on it immediately, divvying it up between them while saving a share for Anna, Mickey, and the kids on watch. You ate, shat, and slept when you could in the apocalypse, and that was a fact they knew empirically.

While the boys filled their bellies, I called Anna off to the side so we could speak privately. "Killed one of the ugly ones on the way here. It was holed up in a house asleep, and I happened to stumble on it and stake it by sheer luck."

"You killed a vampire?" she asked, crossing her arms as she gave me a skeptical look.

"Like I said, I was lucky. But you know how the rest of them avoid that scent. I didn't bring the body into camp because I didn't want to freak the kids out. But I intend to drag it around camp before I leave. Hopefully the scent will keep the zombs away."

It was a lie, obviously. What I actually planned to do was ward the shit out of the perimeter. Anna wasn't ready to know the full extent of my story, not yet. For now, I'd have to lie to her and Mickey. I didn't like it, but it was what it was.

She hung her head for a moment as she considered the news. "Was it close to us? How many more could there be? You know we can't fight those things at night."

The urgency in her voice betrayed her worry over

my "find," and I berated myself for not thinking about how disturbing the story might be to her.

"It's okay," I said, placing a hand on her shoulder. "Those things are territorial, right? That means there won't be another one for miles. And we'll be long gone before any others figure out that this one's hunting grounds are uncontested. We're good, for now."

She looked at me with narrowed eyes. "Something's different about you. You look—I don't know, refreshed. Sound like it, too. You didn't raid a pharmacy or something on your way here, did you?"

"Um, no. Must be the adrenaline, I guess."

She shrugged my hand off her shoulder, but not unkindly. Anna wasn't much for physical contact, at least not with men. "Makes sense, considering how many of those things you killed today. You must be bone tired." She took a moment to scan the area, making sure the kids were safe. "But if you do find some Adderall, or even some No-Doz, let me know. I could use a pick-me-up right about now."

"You taking first watch?" I asked.

"Yeah, as soon as the kids go out for the night. This place is really exposed, Colin. I don't like it."

I glanced around the area, and frankly I had to agree with her. We were in the middle of a makeshift fortress that had been made by circling several RVs, wagon train style. Rocks and debris had been used to fill in the gaps beneath the vehicles, and the tires had been flattened to reduce the gaps underneath. Whoever had done it was long gone, but it would do for a few nights, especially after I set up a ward cordon.

"I know, but it's all we have right now. Look, I have a plan to get us out of here, but I'm going to need to leave you guys alone while I put it in motion."

Anna's eyes widened, the whites of her eyes showing in the fading daylight. "You're going out there—at night?"

I shrugged. "Can't be helped. We can't stay here, so I have to find someplace more secure for us. The sooner I get on that, the better."

"Going out at night is risky as hell. If we lose you—"

"Stop. You know we don't talk like that. We do what's necessary, and we survive. I'll be back by morning, and then I'll let you know what I'm planning, okay? Trust me, it's all going to work out."

"Famous last words," she muttered, crossing her arms and pulling her threadbare pleated coat tighter around her.

Flashing her my best devil-may-care smile, I ended the conversation by attending to Brian, who'd been waiting patiently off to the side to speak.

"Hey, buddy, what's up?"

He scratched the tangled mess of hair on his head and looked at his shoes. "I gotta' do number two, but I'm afraid to go inside the RV by myself."

Stifling a grin, I patted him on the shoulder. "The dark scares me sometimes, too. C'mon, I'll go with you, and we can be brave together."

A glance over my shoulder allowed me to catch the tail end of an approving look from Anna. Then, she was off to help the kids clean up after their meal so they could settle down for the night.

After Brian took care of business, I walked him back to where the others were bedding down, then I headed out into the night. I had a lot of work to do warding the campsite, and a lot of ground to cover before morning.

Time to enact phase one of my grand plan—finding transportation. Now, I wonder where I might find an armored personnel carrier out here in the middle of BFE?

7

I had spent a great deal of time in the Grove planning what I'd need to do when I came back to the Hellpocalypse. One of the biggest challenges I expected to face was finding a secure location to set up a permanent home for the group. Thankfully, I knew Austin like the back of my hand, and it only took a few hours of searching online maps and satellite images to come up with something that could work.

For starters, I needed someplace that could be easily defended, that was relatively remote and that was large enough to house over two dozen people. Second, the location had to be close enough to resources like food, water, and technology so I could easily scavenge for those items. And lastly, it needed to be located in an area where there would be an ample amount of game to hunt, in case local stores of supplies ran out at some point.

I knew from past experience in the Hellpocalypse that the biggest threat to our group wouldn't come from the dead. Instead, it would come from other humans who would want to take away our resources in order to facilitate their own survival. I could keep the dead away with my skills and talents, but keeping away roving bands of marauding raiders was another matter.

The solution I devised was simple and elegant, if a bit sketchy at first glance. And that was to set up a safe zone near an area of Austin that was still hot with radiation from nuclear fallout. Austin had been hit with a tactical nuclear strike the day the dead attacked, and due to prevailing winds and weather patterns, that small nuclear strike left a great deal of irradiated dust and other fallout to the south and east of the city.

Unlike the movies, you weren't likely to find a Geiger counter just laying around at a military checkpoint or installation. For that reason, I felt that fear of radiation poisoning would be enough to keep most people away from Austin, except for the very stupid and those ignorant of the effects of nuclear radiation. But for a druid who could "see" radiation, nuclear fallout only presented a minor impediment to travel and settlement in the area.

I'd mapped out the radiated areas of the city using technology from my own timeline, approximating weather conditions and wind patterns on the day of the blast. After that, it was simply a matter of entering all that info into a nuclear attack simulator to determine places in the city that would be less radiated, as well as a relatively safe path to access those areas.

I finally narrowed it down to a location in the southwest corner of Austin, in the hills where the very wealthy had lived. There were plenty of estates in the area that would work well for our purposes, but I had my sights set on one in particular that ticked all the boxes on my list. The only question was how much radiation had actually hit the area, and whether or not I could create a radiation-free safe zone in the middle of a hotspot that was hot enough to keep most humans away.

Was it crazy? Yeah, but it just might work. All I had to do was find a way to transport the group a hundred miles across a zombie-infested wasteland full of desperate survivors and bloodthirsty vampires.

Piece of cake.

After I set up wards around the camp, I took off on foot toward the nearest large city, which was Bryan-College Station to the northwest. The cities bordered each other and had been home to a pre-apocalypse population of about two-hundred-thousand people, as well as a large, publicly funded university. Therefore, I figured it was my best bet for acquiring transportation. I'd settle for a school bus, but I had my hopes set on finding something more suitable for the journey.

Before the shit hit the fan, the drive to Austin would've only taken a couple of hours, tops. However, the highways were clogged with abandoned and wrecked cars and all manner of debris, including crashed airplanes, overturned tractor trailers, and road-blocks that had been set up by enterprising civilians who'd decided to become highwaymen—and women—after things went to shit.

There were plenty of backroads we could travel to avoid most of that, but I needed a vehicle or vehicles that could carry lots of people while safely maneuvering off-road for short distances as well. That meant I needed to find off-road modified vans or armored personnel carriers. Due to the security factor, I was leaning toward the latter of the two options.

It was a good bet that a city as large as Bryan-College Station had a SWAT team that owned at least one APC. Hell, the military had practically been giving the damned things away to local LEO agencies after the wars in the Middle East. The problem was, there was a strong likelihood that those vehicles had been deployed when things went sideways. Knowing my luck, I was going to have a bitch of a time finding one, but at least I knew where to start looking—right in the heart of downtown College Station, which was going to be zombie central.

A thirty-five-mile jaunt at Fomorian speed took me a bit less than an hour, what with the time I spent avoiding zombie hordes and killing the odd ghoul that got in my way. As I ran, I relied on speed instead of magic to stay out of trouble, as I couldn't maintain a chameleon spell for that long without depleting my magic reserves. My instincts told me I'd need to conserve whatever juice I had for staying hidden once I hit city limits, and I was right.

To put it bluntly, College Station was a city of the dead.

Everywhere I looked, the undead roamed in groups of three or more, following the routes of their former lives in automaton fashion. Further into the city, the concentration of zombs increased until they were packed shoulder to shoulder in a tight mass near the downtown area.

Right where I need to go. Great.

The good news was that wherever you found a zombie horde, you could be certain that the area was vamp-free. Zeds didn't like the smell of vampires, and they avoided their territory like the plague.

Plague. Heh.

That was some dark fucking humor. I needed to get us somewhere secure, and fast, before I went to the same dark place I'd fallen into before Click pulled me out of here.

One thing at a time. Transportation, then the road trip from hell. Then shelter, fortifications, and infrastructure.

Shit, that's a lot to think about.

I took a deep breath, exhaling slowly to center

myself. Then I cast a decent chameleon spell and silence spell on myself and leapt to the next building.

The silence spell would keep the dead from detecting my presence, but it wouldn't keep me from falling through a roof into a room full of stasis-locked zombies. That's why I chose to remain in my stealth-shifted form. My full Fomorian form might've been a deterrent to revenants and ghouls, but it didn't do shit to keep the zombs from bum-rushing me. And I was damned heavy in that form. Sure, I could leap farther and run just as fast, and I was impervious to almost anything the dead could throw at me, but I was more likely to crash through a rooftop in that form.

No, thank you.

As I leapt from roof to roof, building to building, the dead maintained their usual cacophony of moans and groans. That was a good sign because it meant they hadn't sensed me. As long as that low, monotonous background noise stayed at a level volume, I was in the clear. It was when they changed their tune that I had to worry.

Lucky for me, this part of town was nothing but apartments built to house college kids and the businesses that once serviced that population. It wasn't hard to stick to the rooftops, and I only had to make the occasional foray at ground level to cross major roadways. By the time I reached Texas Avenue and Harvey Mitchell, the crowd had gotten so thick I had to wait and time my landing before crossing the intersection.

My ultimate destination was only about a half-mile north of that location. While there weren't many buildings between me and the station, there was a sort of greenbelt that led right to the station's backdoor. Once I located a vehicle and got it running, I planned to take Highway 6 south out of town, then loop back around to leave the vehicle with Anna and Mickey.

And then, I'll have to do it all over again.

I pushed those concerns to the back of my mind as I leapt from the roof of a thrift store to the top of an auto parts store. I was about to leap down and cross the highway when I realized I might need some things from inside. After tiptoeing to the edge of the roof, I glanced over the side to check out the storefront. It was mostly intact, having been boarded up by some enterprising manager or owner when the shit hit the fan.

I scanned the parking lot, noting that most of the dead in the area had congregated in front of the Wally World across the street. At first, I thought their behavior was simply due to latent memories, then I saw movement on top of the building.

Who in their right fucking mind would stay in the city after all this shit went down?

The answer was simple, of course. Much like the dead, people were creatures of habit who sought comfort and convenience. And some stupid fucker thought it would be a smart idea to hole up on top of a department store and grocery, to have easy access to food and supplies. According to the bed sheets hanging from the sides of the building, they were now trapped by the horde.

STRANDED, said one such banner. *HELP,* said another. I'd seen this before, way too many times. While my first instinct was to assist them, experience had taught me that it was all I could do to help my own group. Shaking my head at my own stupidity in even considering the attempt, I broke the lock on the roof hatch to the auto parts store. Then, I opened it and dropped into the darkness below.

My Fomorian-enhanced eyesight was more than a match for the gloom inside the store. It was crazy how dark the world got at night without the light pollution from millions of headlights, streetlights, and outdoor fixtures shining into the night sky. I hadn't known darkness until I came to the Hellpocalypse, that was for sure.

Inside the store, it was darker than the inside of a gravedigger's front pocket, and it smelled just as bad. Something had died in here. Chances were good that if it smelled that bad after all this time, it was still moving around. The only light coming in the place was from the hatch above me, and it would draw the dead like moths to a flame. I stayed absolutely still, knowing that a change in light and shadow would draw the dead to my location.

I didn't have to wait long. Soon, a dark shadowy

figure skittered along the wall to my left, nearly hidden behind the tall shelves where the majority of the parts were kept. The way it moved, there was only two things it could be. With this many dead around, I was banking that it was a revenant.

I hate revs.

Revenants were like vamps, just dumber and a lot more feral. Some of them maintained a rudimentary intelligence from when they were alive, but their thought processes were mostly limited to an instinctive predatory cunning. They moved almost as fast as vampires, they were nearly as strong, and when they came at you, it was usually from behind. But the worst thing about them was that they screamed when they were injured—and screaming attracted more dead.

I had my silver-plated Bowie on my belt, so I silently released the retention strap and wrapped my hand around the hilt. Then, I waited for the thing to position itself for the inevitable surprise attack.

Seconds later, the thing had positioned itself on a shelf behind me. It made a hell of a lot of noise, which told me it was either newly made or hungry as hell. Why it hadn't crossed the street to pick off the people at the hypermarket was beyond me. Or, maybe it had, but they'd managed to scare it off.

Revs were tough, but they also liked easy prey. I did my best to appear as hapless as possible as I waited for it to pounce. Moving slower now that it was close, it crept to the edge of the shelf, tensing itself for an attack.

Here we go.

The rev leapt off the shelves, spread eagle with its hands extended like talons, the better to grab me and sink its teeth in my neck. While it was in midair, I drew the Bowie knife, dropping beneath the arc of its trajectory as I spun and slashed overhead.

I was strong and fast in this form, and more than a match for the rev, but I didn't want to get infected again. Caution made me a little too conservative with my attack, so the blade missed the thing's neck, instead catching it across the lower torso.

Moving as I cut to avoid the splatter, I spun to see the results of my attack. Although I'd cut it in two above its pelvis, the damage had done nothing to hinder its ability to make noise. Just as I was about to silence it, the thing let out a high, keening wail that echoed off the cinderblock walls and metal roof above.

"Ah, shit," I said as I leapt forward.

I flipped the knife into a reverse grip and drove it hilt-deep in the rev's skull. The thing's howling cry stopped, and it fell limp, the echoes reverberating in the silence like the moment after you hit the snooze button on an alarm clock. Instinctively, I stood stock still, listening in the desperate hope that the sound hadn't carried outside the building.

No dice. The ambient moans and groans that had remained at a constant level in the background were now rising to a fever pitch outside. Seconds later, the first zombie began to bang against the weathered plywood boards covering the front windows of the store.

"Ah, crap."

I pulled the knife out of the rev's head, placing my booted foot on its lower set of teeth for leverage. As brute force overcame suction, the blade came out with a sickening *pop*. After cleaning it on the rev's AC/DC concert t-shirt, I stuck it back in the sheath as I examined the corpse.

Just a kid, no more than fifteen or sixteen. Shit.

I wondered if he'd been part of the group that was living at the super store across the street. The thought had little bearing on my group's survival, so I dismissed it immediately. Reminding myself that introspection was a luxury in the Hellpocalypse, I turned my attention to gathering the stuff I'd need to get an APC running.

Let's see... a portable jump starter, a fresh battery... no, make that two. Ah hell, I have a flipping bag of holding, I'll just take all of them. Fuel stabilizer for both diesel and gas engines, enzyme fuel treatment, a five-gallon gas can, metric and SAE wrenches and sockets, and a basic portable tool kit. Yep, that should do it.

By the time I'd tossed all that crap in the Bag, the zombies out front were almost through the doors. Glass shattered and crashed in tiny pieces all over the tile floor, and the plywood creaked and groaned under the strain of the pressing horde. That I could hear the sound the barrier made over the roar of the dead was telling, a clear sign I needed to GTFO.

On a whim, I stopped at the counter and grabbed a handful of candy and gum, as well as a bunch of flashlights and batteries. *Hell with it, the kids need something to cheer them up,* I thought, just as the front doors gave. With an involuntary yelp, I skidded around the corner of the front counter and into the warehouse area until I reached the roof hatch where I'd entered the store.

Just as I was about to leap through the square opening above, a shadow peeked over the edge of the hatch.

Well, damn. This night just keeps getting better and better.

8

"Well, you just going to stand there and get eaten, or you coming up?"

It was a voice I recognized, but the last one I expected to hear. "Sledge, is that you?" I asked after dropping my silence spell.

"Jump now, talk later, kid. There's about a thousand of those fuckers at the front door."

Shit.

"Right," I said as I jumped through the hole while trying to remember how much this version of Sledge would know about my abilities. He obviously knew a lot, because instead of giving me a hand, he stepped back and let me pass through the opening.

After I landed in a crouch next to him, he leaned in to yell in my ear, a necessity now that I was outside where the roar of the horde was overwhelmingly loud.

"Good thing I recognized your scent, else we'd have left you for the dead. Trina's gonna provide a distraction," he said with a glance at his digital wristwatch. "In three... two... one."

A car alarm began sounding in the distance, about a block to the north and west of us.

Sledge gave a sly wink, nodding in the opposite direction. "Time to go, druid."

He leapt off the side of the building, landing atop a lone deader about fifty feet away. His engineer's boots crushed the zombie's head into mush as he rode the thing down to the pavement. Then he was off at a run, heading north across the multi-lane road and behind the muffler shop and bank across the street.

I backed up almost to the opposite side of the store, sprinting and leaping off the roof at a dead run. I sailed about ten yards past the zombie Sledge had crushed on impact, landing silently in the tall grass near the shoulder of the road. Then, I ran.

Small groups of zombies and loners were heading across the road toward the noise of the blaring car alarm, but none saw me as I dodged and swerved around them. Sledge waited for me behind the bank, acknowledging me by sniffing the air as I arrived. He led and I followed as we snuck around the far side of the super store. There only the least mobile dead remained, crawling and dragging themselves along the pavement toward the noise across the street.

We each took time to crush the heads of those stragglers, knowing that once they saw us, they'd raise an alarm that would draw the rest of the horde. I noted the fortifications that had been made around the building, consisting of overturned cars and metal shipping containers that were lined up around the store, cutting off door access and shoring up the walls against the press of a large mob of dead. I'd seen large groups like the one we'd just escaped breach brick walls with the sheer weight of their combined mass, so it made sense that the 'thropes would take the time and risk to set up these precautions.

Sledge leapt atop a shipping container, using it as a steppingstone to reach the roof, bounding over the concertina wire that lined the periphery in a continuous spiral loop. I followed him in like manner, noting that human and 'thrope sentries were posted inside makeshift sniper towers at every corner of the building. The towers were hunting blinds, of the type sold by department and sporting goods stores around deer season. It was wise to use the blinds, as they allowed the sentries to remain hidden while they manned their posts.

I noted the sentries were armed with crossbows instead of silenced rifles. *Smart.* This group had done a good job of setting up in a bad place. I thought it was a risky location, but I could see why they'd done it. So long as they dealt with the zombies, they wouldn't have to worry about other humans competing for the resources inside the store.

Sledge waited for me to take it all in, then he motioned for me to follow him. I trailed close on his tail, counting heads as I went. A handful of 'thropes, no more than a half-dozen, and twice that many humans.

They'll be running low on supplies in a couple of months. I wonder what they plan to do then?

We entered a large camping tent that had been set up on the roof, its corners anchored to the roofing membrane and sheathing with screws and large washers. Inside, a roof hatch led down to the store below. We descended on a rope ladder into what must've once been the store's warehouse. A few humans slept on cots here and there, and a roving guard patrolled the area carrying a machete and a pistol crossbow.

Lycanthrope. They're splitting up guard duty according to who can see in the dark.

"If you're wondering what we plan to do when shit runs out, we have a plan for that," Sledge said when we'd passed through the sleeping area into a break room that now served as the group's galley. He pulled out two styrofoam cups from a package on the counter and poured each half-full of water from an Igloo cooler.

"Thanks, man."

"I'd offer you more, but we can only purify so much every day." He shrugged. "Have a seat."

Sledge plopped down at a cafeteria-style table, and I joined him, sipping my water as I took it all in. After a minute or so of silence, I asked the burning question. "Where are the rest of the Pack?"

"Dunno. I know Samson's alive, but he's off somewhere up north investigating what caused all this shit." He smirked. "Bet your worried about Fallyn. Far as I know, she was high in the Alps at that fancy school when it went down. She's fine."

Internally, I gave a sigh of relief. "How in the hell did you guys end up out here?"

Sledge chuckled humorlessly. "Trina, Guerra, and I were out at the back-up clubhouse when the bombs fell. After the zombies started showing up, we realized that was a shit place to make a stand. The camp was great for privacy, not so much for defense. Hell, we didn't even have a security fence around the property."

"And the mine was basically a death trap," I said. "One way in, one way out."

"Yep. Some of us had family around town and in other areas of the state. Trina's girl—well, she died in the blast, and Guerra's last close relative passed on decades ago. My niece was attending school out here, so when the Pack split up to find survivors, they came with."

"And then?"

"Then? We found my niece leading an oddball group of humans in the top floor of one of the dorms on campus. It was a clusterfuck, I tell you. If we hadn't seen their flags..." His voice trailed off. Sledge had the sort of haunted look I'd seen so many times before, so I let it lie.

"Speaking of signs, what's with yours? Looks like you guys are doing okay here."

The big, burly 'thrope ran his tongue inside his front lip as he considered my question. "The humans in the group insisted on it. Some of 'em still think the government is going to show up and bail us out. Stupid, but I can't blame them for holding out hope."

"Yeah, that's not going to happen," I said. "What's your plan for when supplies start to get thin?"

He sniffed twice, wiping his nose with his sleeve. "Those who want, we'll see if the wolf accepts them. The ones who survive being turned can come with. Folks who refuse'll be dead weight when we move, so we'll leave them behind. Simple as that."

"Harsh. But I get it." I thought of the kids, wondering what would've happened to them if I hadn't been there.

"And you? How did you end up here? I mean, we thought you were dead. In fact, you're the first magic-user I've seen since this shit started."

I exhaled heavily, leaning an elbow on the table as I rubbed my face with my hand. "That's a long story. If you care to hear it, I could really use some help."

"That's—wow, that's a crazy story."

I hadn't told him about the time travel, just the parts

of my story that involved saving the LARPers. "Yeah. That's why I need someone to lend a hand. If I could get both vehicles to my group at once—"

"It'd mean being able to hit the road before any zombies you draw have a chance to attack your camp." He grimaced. "Damn it, but we're shorthanded here. Trina's out on a supply run, looking for parts we need."

"Bike or car?"

"For our hogs. Much easier to get around on a bike than it is in a car. So long as you stay ahead of the horde, that is."

"And Guerra?"

"Scouting. That rev you killed? It'd been coming around, trying to pick us off, but it was more a nuisance than anything. But word is, there's a vamp hanging around the outskirts of town."

"If it moves in, you'll likely see the dead disperse. They don't like being around vampires, unless a vamp is controlling them."

"They can do that?"

I nodded slowly. "The old ones can. If you see a mob hanging out around a vamp's aerie, steer clear."

"Noted," he said, shaking his head. "How d'you know all this shit?"

"Been hunting them, trying to figure out what happened. And as soon as I get my group to a safe, defensible location, I'm going to start tracking down the fuckers who caused all this mess."

Sledge crossed his arms as he leaned back in his

chair, causing it to creak under his weight. "Gotta be the Vampyri Council."

Truer than you know, brother.

I couldn't tell him about what had happened in my timeline, how we all banded together to narrowly avert this disaster. But he was on the right track, for sure.

"Is that what Samson thinks?" I asked.

"It's what we all think. Shit, the world goes to hell in a hand basket, the fae dis-a-fucking-pear overnight, and the damned vamps multiply like rabbits—not to mention the other undead. Smells like the bloodsuckers fucked us all, don't it?"

"Yeah, it does." I arched an eyebrow as I looked at the ceiling. "But right now, you and I both have more pressing matters. So, what do you say? Can you lend me a hand and help me get those vehicles to my group?"

He stroked his long, scraggly red beard. "Tell you what. You go find Guerra and see if there's a vamp out there. If there is, help him get rid of it. Then I'll send him with you to get those vehicles."

Well, fuck.

I'd expected some sort of barter, but I hadn't expected Sledge to be so mercenary about it. Shouldn't have been a surprise, though. This *was* a zombie apocalypse, after all.

"Deal," I said, extending my hand. When he took it, I pulled him in so we were leaning across the table from each other. "But it goes without saying that if you guys fuck me, I'm not going to take it well."

He narrowed his eyes, and I saw just a flash of yellow in his pupils. Then, he relaxed. I released his hand, and Sledge sat back in his chair with a huge grin on his face.

"Pack is Pack for life, so you don't gotta worry about that. Anyway, hell if I'm going to fuck with the only magic-user left in Texas. Not only would Fallyn cut my nuts off if I screwed you over, but we might have to call on you someday. Magic's hard to come by in this new, screwed up world."

"Good to know. Now, where the hell did you send Guerra again?"

Sledge indicated a spot on the northwest side of Bryan on a battered map that was pinned to the break room wall. I didn't want to let him know I had a working cell phone on me, so I waited until I left the superstore before I pulled up my own map to gauge the distance and get a better handle on the local terrain. It was a seven-mile jaunt, which I could do in under ten minutes on city streets, with enough motivation.

Motivation? Yeah, I have plenty of that.

I took off at a run up Texas Avenue, not even bothering to use conventional means of stealth. My spells would hold for this short sprint, then I'd reassess once I found Guerra. This vamp was supposed to be hiding out in a church. Obviously, it had a sense of humor—or irony, take your pick. Neither would save it from a more permanent death once I got hold of it, though.

The street was packed with dead for blocks-long stretches, so I was forced to sidetrack along parallel routes, dodging the horde and taking on difficult terrain to avoid the swarm that had taken over the former college town. Once I reached the outskirts of the city, the dead thinned out, and I got back on the main road. That led me to my destination: the Brazos Family Worship Center, which happened to be next to a cemetery.

Fucking brilliant.

Vamps couldn't raise the dead, thankfully—they could only turn the living into undead by infecting and then killing their prey. Undeath was usually an unintended consequence of feeding, and not done purposely by vampires except to create another vamp. Zombies drew unnecessary attention to their makers, and even rogue vamps usually killed the lesser undead they created, making zombies a rarity in the pre-apocalypse world.

Humans only occasionally rose as zombies or ghouls after death by exsanguination, because normally, the vyrus just wasn't that good at creating undead. The speed at which the vyrus spread in this timeline indicated that the Vampyri had unleashed a much more virulent version on the population. In my own timeline, I had come across just such a strain, but thankfully I'd managed to kill those responsible and contain the infection.

As I neared the church, I set aside such thoughts so I could focus on more immediate concerns. Namely, that the area reeked of vampires. The church itself was a large, squat limestone building with a metal roof and few windows—the ideal vampire hideout. No doubt, that's where it had holed up.

I found the vampire—so where's Guerra?

My gaze followed the roofline of the building, all the way to the water tower behind it. If I had been sent here to scout the place, that's where I would have set up. I steered clear of the church, circling around the south until I reached the base of the tower. A few dead wandered around outside the perimeter fence, so I vaulted it opposite of where they'd gathered.

The door at the base was unlocked, which told me whoever had entered wasn't worried about zombies. I headed into the pump-house, keeping an eye out for trouble as I climbed the access tunnel stairs, which led above the lower tank. From there, I took another narrow corridor to the roof access ladder. The hatch was open above, but I had no idea who might be up there, so I readied a spell as I scrambled to the top.

When I peeked out the hatch, I saw Guerra on his stomach near the edge of the tower on the southeast side. I dropped my concealment spells and climbed out, crouching first, then low-crawling to come up beside him so I could emulate his position.

"Caught your scent when you came up the ladder. Sledge send you?"

"Yeah. Heard you got a vamp to kill?"

He frowned, which was pretty much his resting expression. The guy was a dead ringer for Danny Trejo, so much so that I'd often wanted to ask him if he really *was* the actor.

"A whole mess of them, actually," Guerra said. "An older one—the leader—and a bunch of newbies. *Pendejos.*" He spat, never taking his eyes off the church. "They've been using the church as a base to terrorize the survivors in the surrounding countryside. Pretty much nothing but farms and woodland from here north to Dallas. Lots of people out there, trying to get by."

"And?"

"Here's the weird thing. They aren't killing all of them. Instead, they're rounding them up and keeping them alive inside the church."

"No shit?"

He exhaled sharply. "No shit."

Bryan-College Station was just a hop, skip, and a jump from Dallas, at least as far as distance in Texas was measured. I wondered if this coven was gathering cattle for their own use, or if they were rounding them up for their leaders in Dallas. No better time than the present to find out.

"Huh. How many are there?"

Guerra held his hand out, rocking it back and forth. "A half-dozen, plus the leader, *más o menos.*"

"If they're feeding on those people, the ones they've captured won't last for long." I flashed him an evil grin.

"What say we go down there after sunrise and fuck up some vamps?"

If I thought my grin was evil, Guerra's was downright diabolical. "You read my mind, *amigo*. You read my fucking mind."

9

W e took the long way down from the tower. No sense risking injury before a fight. Sure, we could both heal up pretty quickly, but who knew if we were being watched?

When I reached the bottom, I stepped aside to give the 'thrope room to drop down. He took the last twenty feet in a slide, landing with supernatural grace on the concrete floor of the pump room. I cleared my throat, not sure how I should broach the subject of entering the vamp lair.

"You got something to say, druid, say it."

"I know this was your assignment, but I've taken out a lot of nests, and I kind of have a method."

Guerra thrust out his lower lip as he stroked his goatee. "I'm listenin'."

"Vamps can't resist fucking with the typical hapless victim who stumbles in their path. So, I use that to my advantage. I pretend like I'm scavenging for food and supplies, using my apparent helplessness to draw them in."

"And then?"

"Then, I drop the hammer. If you're good with this approach, I'll go in and do my thing. You stay outside to clean up any of the fuckers that try to escape. Sun should take care of the young ones, but if there's more than one mature vamp, a suntan might not kill them. I've seen—"

He held up a calloused, scarred hand. "Got it. Not my first rodeo. So, what's the signal?"

I grinned. "You'll know. When you hear the screaming, keep your eyes peeled. Make sure you come in hot, because I might need help with the leader."

"Oh yeah? I've seen you at work, *mago*. One injured vamp shouldn't be a problem for you."

I coughed into my hand. "I, uh—well, I need him alive."

The 'thrope gave a shake of his head as he sighed with displeasure. "You gotta be kidding me."

"Best way to get intel is from the source. I have a feeling this group is collecting cattle for the vamps in Dallas."

He grimaced. "Heard rumors. Didn't think it was a thing, though."

I *knew* it was a thing. In this timeline, I'd tortured and questioned a female vampire named Clara just yesterday. It seemed like ages ago now, because it was to me, but I remembered everything that conversation had revealed about their operations in Dallas.

"I interrogated a vamp—um, not too long ago. She told me they have downtown Dallas hooked up with power, water, fuel, the whole bit. Apparently, it's like living in the fifties. Not exactly the return of modern society, but close enough. I'm headed up there to see it for myself, as soon as I get my group settled. The more I know before I make that trip, the better."

"Okay, we do it your way." He rubbed his beard before continuing. "But I think you're crazy for sticking your nose in Vampyri business. Likely to get it cut off, you know what I'm saying?"

"Yeah, but I have my reasons." I swung my gaze to the east. "Sun's coming up. You ready?"

"Born ready. It's your show."

I gave him a nod, then I ran out the door of the tower, turning right and leaping the fence to the north, away from the gathered dead. I circled around to the east, sticking to the thick undergrowth to stay hidden as I approached the front of the church.

Guerra would be in place, or he wouldn't. He was a pro, and probably one of the oldest 'thropes in the Austin Pack. Or what was left of it. I wasn't about to insult him by micromanaging or waiting for him to get in position, so I turned my attention to playing the help-less scavenger as I entered the church.

The front doors were glass, and strangely intact. Despite the growing daylight, I couldn't see past the

entry hall on the other side of the doors. I pulled my
Bowie knife from the sheath, tapping the butt on the
door glass several times for effect. It was a good ruse—
anyone who survived for any length of time out here
would check for dead before entering a darkened
building.

May as well play it up.

Sheathing the knife, I unzipped my pants and
whipped my Jimmy out. Then, I pissed on the hinges,
grunting as I pointed the stream so it reached the top
hinge. Urine made a decent field expedient lubricant for
noisy doors, and it was a trick I'd used more than once
for real. Plus, the urine turned the vamps on—sick
fuckers were all about making their prey piss
themselves.

Once I zipped back up, I slowly opened the door,
wedging it with my foot as I peered inside. After a sufficient waiting period, I stepped past the threshold, my
gaze darting around nervously as I artificially increased
my heart rate and rate of breathing. It wasn't long before
my enhanced ears caught the sound of movement in the
nave ahead.

No human moves like that. Gotta be a vamp.

Once you had the knack, it was easy to tell vamp
sounds from human sounds. For one, the stupid fuckers
didn't breathe, and their hearts beat so slowly they
almost didn't have a pulse. Plus, they moved like cock-
roaches after flipping the lights on in a darkened room,

with creepy-fast, furtive movements no mundane human could duplicate.

I only hear one. Weird.

I had means of scouting the area ahead, but the first method—a sort of magical sonar—might tip the vamp off that I was a magic-user. The second involved borrowing the eyes of any animals that might be hiding within the building. That approach would leave me momentarily vulnerable because I'd have to drop into a druid trance to use it, and no way was I risking that in a vamp nest.

Guess I'm going in blind. Fuck it, I'm in the mood for killing vamps.

I queued up my favorite vampire slaying spell, a casting of my own design that released stored sunlight in a brilliant, extended flash. Devastating to bloodsuckers, not so much for me.

Time to dance.

I nudged one of the closed double doors to the nave open with one hand, holding my knife at the ready in the other. Then, I pulled a penlight out of my pocket, firing it up and flashing the thin, weak beam around the room. It was empty, except for the lone vamp that I heard skitter along the wall. Within seconds, it was poised above the entrance to the nave like a trapdoor spider, waiting to pounce.

Fuck.

I didn't want to waste the spell on one vamp, because it'd take me all day to recharge the damned thing. So, it was time to improvise. My intuition told me this vamp was hungry, which meant it'd probably pounce right when I walked through the doors.

I could kill it. But what if it's the leader?

That would fuck my plan up royal. I needed to subdue the vamp without arousing the rest of its nest mates, wherever they were at the moment. I searched the nave and entry hall again, this time without the penlight. Seconds later, I found what I was looking for, sitting on either side of the front doors.

Bingo, motherfucker. Your ass is mine.

After giving each a cursory glance, I picked one of the two potted plants by the front door, opting for the one that appeared to have the most life left in it. Thankfully, whoever had been in charge of the decor in this place had opted for live, drought-resistant plants for the front entry, and someone had been sneaking water to this snake plant to keep it at least borderline alive.

First, I used a bit of druidry to draw moisture from the air, infusing the soil with ample amounts so I could accelerate the plant's recovery. Once I'd performed a rapid rehab on the poor, mostly neglected houseplant, I dragged the thing to the nave's doorway, using it to lodge one side open as if I wanted the extra light.

Then, holding a good bit of druid magic at the ready, I stepped into the nave. Immediately, the vampire dropped from its perch near the ceiling of the room, with the obvious intention of landing atop an easy meal. I foiled the vamp's plan by sidestepping, just as I released all that pent up druid magic in a rush, channeling it into the plant and causing it to grow ten times its normal height in an instant.

Little-known fact, snake plant fibers are so strong they're used by indigenous peoples to make bowstrings. Before the vamp hit the floor, the plant's long, slender leaves had wrapped around it many times, tying its legs together and binding its arms to its sides. As the coup de grace, I wrapped a leaf around its face, cutting off its ability to cry out to its fellow vamps.

As the vampire fell to the ground with a thud, I listened carefully for any sign that other vamps had heard the noise. When no one came to investigate, I waited to make sure the vampire couldn't escape the bonds I'd created. It was struggling up a storm, but it appeared to be young and not very strong at all—or, at least, not strong enough to break through several layers of thickened, fibrous leaves.

Luck of the Irish strikes again. Let's see if it holds.

I dropped to one knee next to the vamp, drawing my Bowie knife in the same motion. The vamp's gaze darted around, first at me, then at the room around us. I waited for it to realize it was alone and pretty much fucked. Once its eyes focused solely on me, I gave it a good long look.

It had been a teenager when it was turned, maybe

sixteen or seventeen. This one was male and Caucasian, with dark, shaggy hair, pockmarked skin, and a thin, sallow look about it that wasn't just due to the vyrus. It stared at me with cold, grey eyes that were filled with hate and fear.

"Ah, that's the thing about gaining all that power," I whispered, so low that none could hear but us. "You start to think you're invincible. Then, something else comes along that's a hell of a lot stronger, and you find out you're not so tough after all."

The vamp began to struggle again, grunting and cursing in muffled syllables beneath the makeshift gag I'd created. I waited for its efforts to reach a crescendo, then I dragged the tip of the silver-plated Bowie across its forehead, leaving a thin trail of sizzling, burned flesh behind. The smoke and steam rising from the wound smelled like hot iron and burning corpses, turning my stomach.

It had been a while since I had to deal with this sort of thing, and I'd lost my taste for it during the time I'd spent away from the Hellpocalypse. To counter my discomfort, I let a bit of my Hyde-side come to the fore, allowing it to take over so I could do what needed to be done. The Fomorian in me was always eager to hurt my enemies, and that side of my personality had no compunctions about torturing vampires.

"Now," I began, in a voice that was much deeper than it had been moments before. "I want you to tell me where the rest of your coven mates are, and where you're keeping the humans. If you refuse, or if you cry out, I'm going to start cutting pieces off you. Understand?"

The vamp's gaze darted to the knife and back to me. Then, it nodded and grunted something that sounded like acquiescence.

"Good. I'm going to loosen the gag. If you squeal, I'm cutting your nose off your face."

With a gesture and a thought, the leaves covering the vampire's mouth parted, leaving just enough of a gap for it to speak. It gulped air greedily, even though the thing didn't need it—a sure sign of a new vamp if ever there was one.

"Don't hurt me, alright? I didn't ask for this, and I'm just doing what Clarence says."

"Clarence? He's your master—the one who made you?" The vamp nodded. I'd figured as much. Clarence was an old-fashioned name, and if the coven leader was making vamps, he was no spring chicken. "Where is Clarence right now?"

"Downstairs, resting with the others. They left me up here to make sure none of the humans tried to escape."

"And you left the door unlocked, hoping some fool would stroll in here and give you an easy meal." He averted his eyes, which was all the answer I needed. "Tell me, what's the layout downstairs?"

"There's a big room with a bunch of tables, like a cafeteria, right when you come down the stairs. It runs the length of the building until you get to the kitchen. All the classrooms are along the far wall, then there's some bathrooms in the back."

"Where does Clarence sleep?"

"In the pantry. He's paranoid like that. The rest crash out in the classrooms."

I tapped the knife's tip on the kid's chest. "And where are the humans?"

"They stay in the cafeteria."

"How many are alive?"

"M-most of them. Clarence won't let us feed on them, not much anyway. We're supposed to take them back to Dallas when we have enough."

His explanation sounded about right, considering that few humans survived being frequently fed on by vampires. That was likely why the vamps had been sticking around. They needed enough humans to feed on, with some left over to take to Clarence's masters.

I didn't even bother saying anything else. I just stabbed the kid through the eye, punching his ticket before he even knew what was happening.

"You're a cold motherfucker, druid."

I snapped my head around, spotting Guerra in the front hallway. I hadn't heard him enter, which said a lot for his ability to move stealthily.

"It was a mercy."

"Maybe. Makes me wonder what you'd do to a feral 'thrope."

Wiping my blade clean on the kid's shirt, I released

my druidic magic, allowing the plant to wither away to dried, brown foliage. Accelerating plant growth like that meant you also accelerated the plant's lifespan. Everything in magic had a cost.

"Same thing I would've done before the bombs fell. Put the 'thrope down before they could do any more harm."

He frowned and nodded. "Least I know where you stand. We headed downstairs, or what?"

I stood, sheathing the knife. "Yep. Going to have to go in fast. Wait for the flash, then come in after me ready to fight."

Once we found the staircase, I didn't even bother with stealth, because I wanted to make a scene. I came down the stairs two at a time, hollering at the top of my lungs with my hand-and-a-half sword in my left hand and concentrated magic in my right.

"Wakey, wakey, eggs and bakey, motherfuckers!"

When I hit the bottom of the stairs, the humans were cowering in the center of the room. The huddled, bloodstained captives sat in tattered clothing inside a makeshift pen that had been made by stacking tables end on end. The whole thing could've been knocked down by a child, but it wasn't the rickety walls that kept them there.

No, it was the seven vamps that burst out of the

rooms on the far wall to converge on me. They were young, but still fast, and it only took a second or two for them to get in range. My right fist was already raised overhead, and when I said the trigger word to my spell, the lot of them were arranged in a neat semicircle in front of me.

"*Solas*," I said, opening my hand so the magically stored sunlight could pour forth and fill the room.

When the light hit the vampires, they immediately began to burn and crisp, even as they continued their intended line of travel to where I stood. Fresh young vamps seemed to be more resistant to instant immolation, but they also had less overall resistance to UV rays, or whatever the hell it was in sunlight that killed them. Five collapsed in shriveled heaps halfway across the large room, while the other two remained mostly intact.

The two smoldering corpses moved at speed, screaming in agony that locked their brains up, keeping them from changing their course. I sidestepped the one on the right, using Fomorian speed to avoid colliding with it as I lopped off its head with a horizontal forehand cut at neck level. Using the momentum of the blade, I pivoted on my front foot while swinging the sword in a tight, overhead arc. Carrying that motion through until I'd pivoted 180 degrees, I stepped forward in time to catch the last vamp as it bounced off the wall, cutting it in half with a powerful overhead swipe that split it from the base of its neck to its left hip.

Guerra waited on the stairs, scanning the room with

eyes that were much better at seeing in the dark than mine. I kicked the smoking corpse in front of me, ignoring the cries of the humans behind me as I examined the remains of the vamp I'd just cut down.

"Huh, must not have been as old as I—"

"Look out!" Guerra cried, pointing over my shoulder.

There was no way he could've intervened, because I was directly between him and the vamp that struck me from behind. Something struck me between the shoulder blades with jackhammer force, then I flew through the air toward the wall next to the stairwell. My sword flew out of my hands, and I crashed into the concrete wall with a sickening crunch.

10

Years of martial arts training saved me from a crushed skull. I managed to perform a half-ass front break fall, even as my body hit the wall at an oblique angle. My left shoulder took the brunt of the impact, crumpling against the solid foot-thick wall backed up by tons of earth behind it. Even my Fomorian bone structure couldn't take that much abuse, and I knew by the sound and the pain that my shoulder socket and collar bone were both pulverized.

Well, shit—that's going to take some time to heal.

When I turned around to face the thing that had blindsided me, I found that Guerra had beaten me to the task. The 'thrope and the vampire engaged each other in a series of rapid-fire strikes, kicks, blocks, and defensive maneuvers that would've been a blur if not for my Fomorian eyes. The humans remained huddled in the center of the room, and I only spared them a glance to ensure they wouldn't become unintended casualties of the supernatural battle.

I might've been in a hell of a lot of pain, but I had still retained enough of my sense of irony to know that the scene in front of me was all kinds of hilarious. The guy Guerra fought—who I assumed was Clarence—looked like the prototypical Dunder-Mifflin employee, khakis, short-sleeved button down, beer gut and all. I mean, this guy could've been a dead ringer for Kevin, easy, and he was giving the 'thrope hell on a fist-for-fist basis.

"Yo, druid—you gonna' help me, or what?" the werewolf yelled as he dodged a vicious spinning hook kick aimed at his head. Seeing the fat dude breaking out moves like Jackie Chan was just the icing on the cake, and before I knew it, I was giggling like a kid who'd just answered his teacher's question with a fart.

"Looks to me like you got this," I wheezed between giggles.

The chubby vamp hissed at me, taking his eyes off Guerra while still managing to side kick him halfway across the room. Guerra recovered in a crouching fighting stance, but with his left lower rib cage caved in. To give him some time, I drew my suppressed Glock 17 out of my Bag, and I shot the vampire in the knee with a silver-tipped round. Meanwhile, the 'thrope shoved his fingers under his broken ribs, popping them back into place with a sickening crunch.

"Gee, thanks," the 'thrope commented. "But you're

going to have to do better than that if you want to take
him alive. It's all I can do to keep from killing him before
he does any serious damage."

The vampire screeched as he clutched his shattered
knee, then he leapt back to the corner of the room,
clinging to the walls near the ceiling like a human
spider.

"Doesn't talk much, does he?" I asked.

"No, but he sure can throw *chingasos*. Shoot him
again—I need a breather."

"Age getting to you, old man?"

As Guerra flipped me off, I took a bead on the thing,
firing three more rounds as it skittered along the wall in
an attempt to dodge the gunfire. Good thing I was
almost as quick as Clarence. The first two shots missed,
but the third took him in the left elbow, which must've
really cramped his style. Despite his injuries, he still
managed to scamper under the metal roll-up door that
closed off the serving window from the cafeteria,
making a temporary escape into the kitchen.

"After all that work, you'd better not let him get
away," Guerra complained as he leaned forward with his
hands on his knees.

"He's not going far," I said as I passed Guerra at a
sprint with my left arm dangling uselessly at my side.
"Relax, I've got him."

Guerra waved me on while giving me an 'I'm too old
for this shit' look. I kicked the door to the kitchen open
without slowing, bursting into the room just in time to

see the vamp shove a large, stainless steel refrigerator six feet along the wall. The fridge crashed into a commercial range, while Clarence ducked into a man-sized hole that had been dug into the concrete and earth beyond.

"Shit on a stick," I muttered as I fired off two more rounds on the fly.

Shooting and running did not go together, no matter what actors did in Hollywood action flicks. Still, I managed to wing the fucker as he slipped into the tunnel. Soon I was right behind him, but instead of following him into that death trap, I holstered my pistol and made an arcane gesture at the ceiling of the tunnel.

"*Titim*," I said, closing my fist and pulling downward. Thirty yards ahead, the tunnel collapsed on top of the vamp, burying him in many tons of earth and stone. It wasn't a difficult spell, but the scope took the wind out of me. Not having access to my Oak and Grove sucked.

"Think that'll hold him?" Guerra asked, startling me as he peered over my shoulder.

"Gah! Stop doing that. And the answer is no, not for long." I pointed at my injury, which was looking a little lumpy. "Do me a favor and set my shoulder. It's starting to heal wrong, and I don't want to have to go full Fomorian in front of these people."

"Why do you think I didn't shift?" he said as he grabbed my upper arm, probing my shoulder while he moved it around. He narrowed his eyes, then he yanked, pushed, and twisted, eliciting a blood-curdling yell from yours truly. "Don't move it 'til it heals."

"Right. Not my first rodeo, either."

"¡*Híjole!* Who pissed in your cornflakes?" he said, holding his hands up front of him. He frowned as he looked past me down the tunnel. "Uh-oh, I think our boy is digging himself out."

I glanced over my shoulder at the cave-in, and sure enough, four chubby fingers were emerging from the dirt and debris. "He's a persistent little shit. Dumbass should've dug out the other way, though. Give me a sec and I'll make sure he doesn't go anywhere."

I closed my eyes, slowing my breathing and centering myself, which took additional effort due to the popping and cracking noises my shoulder made as it healed. Soon, I'd dropped into a decent druid trance, one that allowed me to 'feel' the earth and stone around me, including the pile the vampire was currently struggling to escape.

With a thought, I directed druid magic into the earth around the vamp, compressing it and hardening it into stone, even as I cleared the rest of it away. When I opened my eyes, a large earth-colored boulder sat in the middle of the tunnel, with the vampire's head, chubby fingers, and feet sticking out the sides and ends. Propping myself up against the tunnel wall with my uninjured hand, I admired my handiwork as I recovered from the effort.

"Neat trick," Guerra observed. "Hope he doesn't have to take a piss."

After we'd finished convincing Clarence's captives that we weren't vampires and had no intention of hurting them, Guerra took them up to the chapel. Once they were settled with whatever food and water we could scrounge, he rejoined me in the basement to discuss our next moves.

"I know what you're going to do with the vamp, but what about the humans?"

I scratched my head, noting that I'd picked up a case of lice over the last couple of days. *Joy.* "They look like new recruits to me. I say you explain the facts of 'thropehood to them and give them a choice. They can join your group and risk getting turned, or they can head back to their homes and brave the zombie apocalypse as-is."

He sniffed and cleared his throat. "Harsh, but better than cutting them loose. Can I count on you to help me ferry any recruits back to the store?"

"Shit, man, why take the risk? Have them set up an outpost in the water tower. There's bound to be some fresh water left in the tanks, and it's a lot more secure than anyplace else I've seen around here. Keep the fence and ground-level door locked, set up a couple of zip lines to nearby rooftops for an emergency escape plan, and you're set."

"Yeah, but who's gonna babysit them until they get turned?"

I patted him on the shoulder as I walked to the kitchen. "Looks like someone just volunteered."

"Fuck. You'd better tell them to send someone else, soon as you get back to camp."

"Will do." I snapped my fingers, remembering what Sledge had said. "Ah, shit. I'm going to need you for another errand. Work in trade for helping you with this nest, is what Sledge said. Once I finish with Clarence, I'll head back to fetch your replacement. Deal?"

He looked at the ceiling with a growl. "Do I have a choice?"

Chuckling to myself, I entered the kitchen, where I'd left Clarence inside his stone prison. I didn't give a shit about his comfort level, but I was worried about a tunnel cave-in and didn't want to accidentally lose him to daylight before I had a chance to interrogate him.

When I walked in, I rolled him over so he was facing me, albeit at a perpendicular angle, and then I pulled up a stool. I sat a few feet in front of him, cleaning my nails with my Bowie knife as I waited for him to speak.

"Silver doesn't scare me," he said, his beady eyes fixed on my blade. "I've felt it plenty of times."

"Huh. Based on your name and how you move, I'd have said you were made in the late 1800s. But your speech pattern says mid-1950s. Got turned by a real master, eh?"

He squinted those beady eyes, as if he were unsure whether to answer my question. "Most humans don't know the difference between a mature vampire, a master, and an elder—what you call primaries."

"Oh, I've been around the block. Plus, before all this shit happened, I was kind of tight with the Austin coven leader. Speaking of, you wouldn't know where I could find him, would you?"

Clarence chuckled as he affected a bemused expression. "Luther always did have a soft spot for humans. Yeah, I know where to find him. He's with my master in Dallas being slowly starved to death, the traitor."

Interesting.

"So, when you stupid fuckers set your plan in motion, you didn't exactly have the entirety of the Vampire Nations on board. Which meant you'd have a civil war on your hands after the bombs dropped, unless you got a primary to bring the rogue covens to heel."

Clarence scowled. "You do know a lot for a human."

"Oh, I'm more than human. But you've already figured that out. So, getting back to my story—I figure they pulled a primary through before the bombs dropped, putting that vamp in a new host body while they let it get nice and fat on primo human blood. Then, they had it go to the covens that might be trouble, putting down the ones who resisted and recruiting the rest to the cause. Am I getting warm?"

"Yeah, but you're completely wrong about something. There wasn't just one primary. There were three."

Shit.

"Wild-ass guess here," I said as I trimmed my nails with my Bowie. "The primary who confronted the Austin coven was Luther's maker. That's why he wasn't killed."

"Not as dumb as you look," Clarence said.

"That makes two of us, chubby." I rolled my chair closer, leaning in to get eye to eye with the vamp as I tapped the blade on the stone that held him. "But what I really want to know is, what the hell is going on in Dallas?"

"The new world order, for lack of a better term. We picked Dallas because of the climate and its central location. We also have capital cities in Miami and Los Angeles. Fuck the colder states. Those other things can have them."

"Other things?"

"You'd be surprised what comes through when you open a gate to the opposite side of the Veil. If you ever travel north of Saint Louis, you'll see what I mean."

"Ah," I said as I flipped the knife between my fingers. "Go on."

"Every major nation in the world was divvied up between clans, with a primary at the top and their brood running the show beneath them. We pulled the wool over your fucking eyes, and none of you dumb shits saw it coming."

"Huh. So, why so chatty, Clarence? You have to know I'm going to head to Dallas and fuck some shit up. I mean, you assholes went to an ass-load of trouble to get rid of all the mage circles, so obviously you're afraid of what they might've done. Why tell me where to find your leaders?"

"Because, druid," he said in a much deeper, older-sounding voice. "What he sees, I see."

"Ah, so now I'm talking to the primary—or elder, I guess you would say."

"I am an elder of my kind, and one of the first, yes. I made the one you see before you, and dozens more. You humans thought there weren't any primaries left on Earth, but you were wrong. We've been here for decades, planning the remaking of Earth. And look at you now—the best you can field is a lone druid, who thinks he can change the world. Pathetic."

I rolled my eyes and cracked my neck. After you'd defeated a god or two, these "big bad" monologues got old, quick. Of course, I'd defeated those gods with the help of my druid oak, and an assist from beyond by my late druid master, Finnegas. But this guy didn't need to know that.

"Alright, I've heard enough. I'm going to end Clarence's miserable existence, then I'm coming for you."

Clarence's eyes shone red as the elder vampire gave a short, dismissive laugh. "What can a single druid do against one like me? Come, then, if you care so little for your own life."

I stabbed my knife through Clarence's temple, twisting the blade to make sure it did the trick. Once he stopped twitching, I burned him with druid fire, until nothing remained but bone scraps and ash.

"Oh, I can do a lot. Just you wait, motherfucker. Just you wait."

———————

A few hours later, I returned with Trina in tow. She'd agreed to babysit those captives who decided to stick around, at least until they were able to fend for themselves. Which was probably a good thing—she was likely to eat one of the newbies if she had to deal with them for more than a day or two.

As for why they hadn't turned any humans yet, Trina said they were looking for a safe place to do it. Problem was, not everyone survived the process. You pretty much had to get savaged by a 'thrope to be infected, and then it was a matter of whether the 'thrope vyrus took hold before you died. Turning humans into 'thropes was a noisy, bloody affair, and the group was worried the process would attract every zombie in a ten-mile radius to their door.

"Underground," I suggested as we reached the front doors to the church. "I can help you set something up if you like. All you need to do is find some sewer tunnels, clear them, and let me do the rest. I can secure them pretty easily."

"Then, shit, why not set up a permanent camp like that?" she asked as her expression turned sour. "I mean, fuck—Sledge has had us on top of that store for months. It'd be nice to get somewhere underground that was soundproof and not in constant need of multiple armed guards to protect it. You don't know what I'd do for just one good night's sleep."

I scratched my nose, scanning the environment for undead that might've decided to follow us to the church. I'd cast a chameleon spell on us, but I couldn't spare the magic to make it thorough, or to hide our every scent and sound.

Clear, for now.

"Tell you what, you find the place, and I'll make it happen. Visit me in Austin when the time comes."

"Austin. You serious? That place glows in the dark, last I heard."

I chewed my lip as I decided how much I could tell her without tipping my hand on the whole time travel thing. "Parts of it got a lot of radiation. But based on what I've heard, the blast radius was only a couple of miles wide. From what I remember, we had a northern blowing in the day the bombs dropped, which meant strong winds to the south-southeast. I figure most of the fallout dropped on southeast Austin north of Buda, then southeast to Lockhart and Luling. If we skirt those zones, we should be safe."

"Mmm... Lockhart and Luling," she said, licking her lips. "What I wouldn't do for some barbecue right now."

"What, canned Vienna sausages aren't cutting it?"

"Pfft. We hunt, but it's just never enough. Damned zombs eat everything in their path." She scanned around, just as I had, and pointed out a small group that had taken an interest in us. "Speaking of which, that's a lot of driving, and plenty of road to cover. Fucking people are savages these days. And the slavers—don't get me started on them."

I pulled a pistol crossbow from my Bag, cocking and loading it. Then, I set it aside as I snagged a couple of throwing knives as well. Trina just picked up a chunk of concrete from the ground.

"Yeah, I'm aware. I have a plan for that."

The zombs had reached the entrance to the church parking lot, so I tossed both knives, then I grabbed my crossbow without even looking to see if I hit my target. The sound of metal sinking into putrefied flesh was all the verification I needed, and I followed it up with the crossbow, just as Trina took the last zombie's head off with that chunk of rock.

She did a pitcher's victory dance, punching the air with her fist at waist level. "Damn, I miss baseball. I played in a fastball league before all this shit happened, did you know that?"

"I didn't," I said, making a note to get to know more about the Trina in my timeline when I got home. Hellpocalypse living could make you sentimental like that. After you weren't living it, at least. "I gotta fetch Guerra and boogie. Got people waiting on me."

Who I hope are still okay.

The wards would hold for several days, but you never knew when some random animal would come along and fuck up your work by overturning a marker stone or some stupid shit. I needed to get back to them, pronto.

"Yeah, I get it. So, you fucking this girl you saved, or what?"

"Huh?"

"C'mon, druid. Sledge told me all about it when I got back this morning. Said you're protecting a bunch of kids, some college girl, and an older guy." Her brow furrowed. "Wait a minute—you're not fucking the older guy, are you?"

"What? No! Sheesh, Trina. And what's with the twenty questions, anyway? I don't remember you being this nosy—" *Oops, almost slipped.* "—er, before."

"What do you expect? I'm bored, dude. Fucking apocalypse is nothing but boredom. Same shit, every day. Guard duty. Patrol. Supply runs. Empty shit buckets. Cut the heads off people whose luck ran out doing any and all of the above. You're the most excitement we've had for weeks. I'm just trying to milk it for all its worth."

I rubbed my forehead with my palm as I scanned for more dead. "Okay, I get that. If it helps, I don't think Anna's into guys."

"Ooh, now we're talking."

Trina said it, but something in her eyes told me her heart wasn't in it. Turns out getting over losing someone isn't as easy in the apocalypse as those shows on TV led you to believe.

I smiled sympathetically. "You don't have to put on an act for me."

"That easy to tell, huh? Must be, if a dipshit like you noticed."

"Eh, I just know the look."

"It comes and goes, but these last few days—our anniversary is coming up, and I can't stop thinking about her. Suze might've been a pain in the ass, but she was my pain in the ass, you know?" She hung her head and stared at her shoes. "Just don't tell anyone else, okay? I need Sledge and Guerra to know they can rely on me. Pack for life, right?"

"Pack for life," I said, holding my fist up.

She gave me a bump, then she pasted on a shit-eating grin as she headed for the front door of the church. "Better go get your shit—I see more coming. Have fun cleaning them up, 'cause I'm going inside and taking a nap."

"Gee thanks," I replied as I spotted the dead approaching in the distance. I might've heard a chuckle from inside the building, or it could've been my imagination. With a sigh, I cast a couple of concealment spells before retrieving my weapons.

11

It was late afternoon before Guerra and I headed for the police station, and by then, I was getting antsy. My group had been alone too long, and I desperately needed to check in on them. It really made me wish that I had my Oak here with me, but I'd just have to deal with the inconvenience until I could find a workaround.

"You say you need two of these things?" Guerra said at an almost inaudible volume as we landed on the roof of a fast-food joint.

"Yeah, either that or an armored bus. There are too many of us to fit in one APC."

"Then there's someplace we need to stop along the way. As far as capacity goes, the biggest APC you'll find is a Stryker, and you're going to be hard-pressed to get two of those things all the way to Austin without breaking down. But I think I have a better alternative."

"Lead the way," I said, wondering what the 'thrope had up his sleeve.

Guerra led me southeast, past the main camp all the way to the southern outskirts of College Station. About a half-mile outside of town, we cut off the road, taking a parallel route through the tall grass and sparse woods that bordered the highway. The low drone of the dead told me a large group was milling about somewhere close by, and it grew louder the further south we went. When the noise became overwhelming, we headed back toward the road, but at a much slower, more cautious pace.

Guerra dropped to his stomach to low-crawl up a berm, and I did the same. When he got to the top, I shimmied up beside him to look at what we'd come all the way out here to see. Below us, an army of undead stood in a holding pattern in and around a National Guard roadblock that had likely been set up to prevent the dead from spreading north out of Houston. The authorities may as well have been pissing in the wind, for all the good such measures did.

I had to admit, they'd done a good job of blocking off the road. Metal shipping containers had been arranged two levels high, all the way across the road from berm to berm. And on either side, the berms had been built up around the ends to prevent anything from getting by easily. Add to that a lot of concertina wire and a chain-link gate, and you ended up with a fairly defensible position.

That was, if you were fighting living beings. The highway was the main artery north, so for anyone traveling in a conventional vehicle, this spot was a natural choke point. Unfortunately, the dead lacked all but the most basic, instinctive thought processes, so they didn't act like living humans. They were no respecters of routes, or barriers, or choke points. When they swarmed, they just rolled over whatever was in their way. Failing that, they went around and kept on going.

The spent casings around the two gun nests atop the shipping container wall told part of the story, and the trampled corpses up and down the highway south told the rest. A swarm had come up from Houston, following the path of least resistance, and when the leading edge got close, the Guard opened fire. The resulting noise had turned the swarm into a stampede, the roadblock had been overrun, and the horde went through Bryan-College Station like a plague of locusts, killing everything in their path.

As always, some of the dead stayed behind. Sometimes it was because they were following patterns they remembered from their previous life, but usually it was because they had fixated on their prey or stopped for a meal. Once the main body of the horde had passed, they were left to wander aimlessly in the area where they had last found food.

The thousand or so dead below us were what was left of the horde that came through here, and hell if I wasn't glad I missed that party. After I finished analyzing the scene, I turned my attention to finding what Guerra had wanted to show me, and it didn't take long to spot the prize. Smack dab in the middle of the herd sat an M939 heavy truck that had been modified with armored sides and a crew-served weapon on top.

The crew was long gone, and if they weren't down there milling about, they were sitting in some zomb's stomach for sure. As for the truck, those things ran on diesel, of which there was always plenty at gas stations up and down the road. Most cars ran on gasoline, so when the shit hit the fan, that's what ran out first. Diesel was more stable, too, and the 8.3-liter Cummins engine they put in those heavy military trucks was damn near bullet-proof.

It'd be a tight fit, but we'd manage. I'd have to remove the Browning .50 cal from the back to make room for the kids, but the thing was practically useless in a running battle anyway. All it'd do is bring in more dead, and it was probably rust-locked to boot. If we needed that much firepower, magic would have to do.

I nudged Guerra, nodding in the direction from which we came. When we'd retreated a reasonable distance from the checkpoint, I nodded and scratched my chin.

"Well, it does suit our purposes, but getting to it is going to be a bitch. And starting could take a while, too. What's your plan?"

"Wouldn't bring you out here if I didn't have a plan,

ese," he said with an evil gleam in his eye. "Trust me, I got it all figured out."

A minute or so of explanation later, I remained unconvinced. "Seriously? That's your plan?"

"You got a better idea? Not like we brought a bunch of explosives with us or something. Anyway, if we did set up an explosion down the road, it might bring in another herd we haven't seen yet. The last thing I need is to draw more of those things down on their heads back at camp. Trust me, this will work."

"If you say so," I replied. "Just make sure you don't swing back around until you hear that engine roaring."

"Yes, Mom," Guerra replied with a scowl as he scanned the horde below from our perch atop the highway berm.

I'd cast chameleon and sound containment spells on us, so we were mostly hidden. But the dead below must've caught our scent, because they were getting restless. It was weird how the damned things could hear and smell even when they didn't have noses or ears, like the vyrus created secondary organs for that purpose or something.

"We'd better get moving. You ready?"

The 'thrope smirked. "I already told you, I was born ready." He picked up a tire iron and hubcap that sat on the ground next to him, then he headed down the backside of the berm.

"Just remember, once I drop that chameleon spell, I won't be able to cast it on you again from a distance. So, make sure you haul ass once they see you."

"Relax, druid. You worry too much." Guerra flashed a devil may care grin, then he sprinted southeast in order to swing around the other side of the checkpoint barrier.

"Somebody has to," I muttered as I slid a few feet down the other side toward the mob.

The werewolf was quick, I'd give him that, because less than a minute later I heard him banging on that hubcap like a kid with a new drum set. The dead started going nuts almost immediately, but they weren't sure where to go since they couldn't see the source of the noise. I dropped Guerra's chameleon spell, and he shimmered into view right in front of the mangled chain-link gates.

"Here I am—come get me, motherfuckers!" he yelled as he beat on the hubcap like a dinner bell.

As soon as the dead closest to the gate saw the 'thrope, the tone and volume of their moans hit a higher pitch. That was their signal to the rest of the herd that they'd spotted a warm meal. Very warm, in fact, as a werewolf's body heat tended to run a few degrees higher than a human's. I wondered if the dead could see heat like certain other supernatural species could, then I dismissed the idea since they'd have noticed us, despite the chameleon spell.

Anyway, Guerra had already started jogging down the highway, singing some song in Spanish at the top of his lungs about a dude who was begging to come back to his ex. It was pretty funny, actually, and I had to stifle a laugh as I watched him zigzagging down the road, beating on the hubcap and singing his lungs out.

"*Y volver, volver, volver-r-r-r,*" he crooned, hanging on to that last syllable for dear life as he stayed about twenty feet ahead of the front of the horde.

"Not bad," I chuckled as I slid down the berm. "Too bad there's no Hellpocalypse Idol."

As Guerra's wailing and banging receded into the distance, I picked my way through the remaining dead, the ones who had shattered spines and missing legs who couldn't easily keep up with the herd. Rather than killing them, I avoided them. I had no idea what condition the truck was in, and it might take me five minutes or an hour to get it running. Moreover, a glance up the highway towards College Station revealed several smaller groups headed this way.

"Must've heard the ruckus. Shit."

That was going to put a serious cramp in my style. No way was I going to be able to get this damned thing started while fighting off a couple dozen zombs and ghouls. It was time to improvise.

I reached into my Bag, rummaging around until I found what I was looking for—a couple of Sharpies with a thick stroke. Moving as quickly as I could without getting bitten, I ran to the northwest side of the checkpoint, where several police cars and Humvees sat scattered across the road. Some had been turned over and others were burned out husks, but I didn't need them to run. I picked out a few that sat in strategic positions across the road, then began to mark them with glyphs and runes until I had a cordon of wards ready to go.

Slapping my hand on the last one, I infused it with a bit of druid magic, watching as it flared to life. Silver light sparked across the ward lines like a lit fuse, filling each ward rune before jumping to the next, then the next one after that. Soon, all the wards glowed with a silvery light, powering a ward barrier that would prevent all dead from entering the area until the wards became damaged.

Repeating the process at the gate, I made sure the wards were marked high enough on the wall so the zombs wouldn't smudge them if they came back. No zombie would willingly go near a ward rune that was attuned to repel the undead, but if they had a thousand or so of their cohort pressing in behind them, it wouldn't matter. Best to do it right the first time, just in case.

I stepped back to admire my handiwork, just as one of the creepy-crawlies inside the checkpoint reached the gate entrance. As soon as it neared the smashed gate, a spark of magic arced off the nearest metal shipping container, landing on the thing's head and zapping it with a *sizzle-pop*. The thing moaned and turned around, obviously not wanting anything to do with druidic magic.

"Now for the truck."

I didn't even bother changing the battery yet, as there wasn't time. Instead, I hooked up the portable jumper I'd gotten from the auto parts store, using some druid magic to give the system a little extra juice so I could start warming up the glow plugs. Then, I removed the fuel cap and probed the tank with my druid senses for water condensation. I used a little more magic to draw as much water as I could from the tank, then I poured in a bottle of water remover and a bottle of cetane booster. Since the fuel cap had a good seal, the fuel was probably still good, but the additives couldn't hurt.

Finally, I replaced the cap and hopped up in the cab to fire it up. The damned thing cranked over sluggishly a couple of times, so I juiced the portable battery booster with an additional touch of magic. The next try proved to be the winner, and the Cummins engine cranked over like a champ, belching black smoke into the sky like an angry dragon.

I let the engine run, not bothering to cast a silence spell on it yet since I needed to conserve magical energy. Then I did a quick check of all the fluids, topping off the ATF in the five-speed Allison transmission. Thankfully, this model had a central tire inflation system, so I was set and ready to haul ass in under five minutes.

I dropped the hood back down, securing it before I hopped in the cab to check all the gauges one last time. The thing had to make it to Austin with a load of kids in the back, so an abundance of caution was in order.

Gauges look good. Now, I just need to wait for Guerra.

That was my plan, anyway—until I looked through the sideview mirrors, past the busted chain link gates, in the direction Guerra had led the horde.

The 'thrope was almost a blur as he hauled ass up the highway, making a beeline toward the opening in the makeshift shipping container wall. About an eighth of a mile behind him lumbered a creature that almost defied description. It was easily fifteen feet tall and growing, picking up bodies to add to its mass as it moved toward us. I searched my memory, but I'd never seen anything like this grotesque amalgamation of dead bodies held together by some unknown magic in a general humanoid shape.

"Well, that's new," I said as my jaw hit my chest.

Guerra sped through the shattered gates, past my undead wards, to jump into the cab with me. "Drive, drive, drive!"

"What the hell is that thing?" I asked as I put the truck in reverse to create room to move.

"You want to stick around to find out?" he replied.

"Where did it come from?" I demanded, watching as the monstrosity grew ever larger in the mirrors.

"Hell if I know. I was a mile down the road, dealing with a few ghouls that had gotten ahead of the horde. Next thing I knew, that thing came running up the highway like the Stay-Puft Marshmallow Man. Soon as I saw it, I beat feet around the horde and headed back here to warn you."

I backed up slowly, using the truck's mass to push cars out of the way so I could have space to pick the best path through the cars that blocked our exit. Then, I slammed it in drive, goosing the pedal until the front bumper made contact with a police cruiser. Tires and rims screeched against the asphalt surface of the highway as I forced a path out of the checkpoint. It was slow going, because I didn't want to bend the bumper into the front tires and brick the truck, nor did I want to do something stupid like puncture the radiator.

Guerra craned his neck as he hung his head and shoulders out the window to look behind us. "*Vamos*, druid—that thing is almost on us."

"Dude, this isn't a *Furious* movie. I can't just bash these cars out of the way. This rig'll take a lot of abuse, but it's not indestructible." I gave a dismissive wave as I looked in the rearview mirror. "Besides, that thing is made of zombies. No way it'll make it through my wards."

"You better hope not," the 'thrope replied, muttering something about '*loco gringo magos*' or some-such.

I turned my full attention to getting us the fuck out of there, slowly pushing my way through the minefield of battered and burned-out vehicles. There were only a few more cars in the way, then we'd be home-free. I edged the front end against the driver's side rear bumper of a police SUV, just as Guerra yelped in surprise.

"You were saying, *culero*?" he exclaimed as he slapped me on the shoulder.

I looked in the sideview mirror again, just in time to see a huge hand-like appendage reach over the top of the container wall. The 'hand' was made of the legs of a couple of zombs, their bodies somehow glued or meshed together to make the palm. I was momentarily distracted by the weirdness of it all, which caused me to take my foot off the fuel pedal.

And that's when the truck sputtered and died.

"What're you doing?" Guerra yelled. "That thing is coming over the wall!"

"I know, I know," I said as I tried to start the truck. The engine cranked over with a sound reminiscent of a dying sea lion, then the noise faded away as the battery drained itself completely.

"Well, fuck—that's not good."

Guerra pulled himself back into the cab, settling into the front seat with his arms crossed over his chest. "You think?"

"Give me a second. Sheesh." I tried juicing the battery with druid magic, but it wasn't taking.

Obviously, the truck's battery had breathed its last, and I didn't have time to change it. A glance in the mirrors revealed that the undead golem thing was almost over the wall.

"'Nothing can get past my wards. I'm the greatest druid ever,'" Guerra chided in a high-pitched, child-like voice.

"That doesn't sound anything like me," I said. "And besides, your criticism isn't helping."

"Criticism is all I got in a situation this fucked up. Hell if I'm going to go out there and fight that thing. So, if you don't have anything else up your sleeve, I'm out of here."

He reached for the door handle, so I put a hand on his arm to stop him. "Wait," I said with a sigh. I reached into my Bag and pulled out a fresh car battery, a crescent wrench, and a tool bag. "Change the battery while I take care of this."

"What's next? You going to have me cut your lawn?"

"Come on," I groused as we both jumped out of the truck. "The ability to fix cars is *not* a racial stereotype. Now, if I had asked you to open a used tire shop, that would've been a thing."

"Oh, go drink a latte and watch a Wes Anderson movie, *gringo*," he deadpanned.

"Hey, you started it. And don't cross the cables up."

"*Chingao*, druid. I'm not fucking stupid."

"No, you're a grouchy old pain in the ass, is what you are," I replied as I peeled off my clothes. Once I'd stripped down to my spandex undies, I pulled my giant-sized great-sword, Orna, out of my Bag. "Be right back," I said, keeping my eyes on the monstrosity that now stood atop the wall.

"Yeah, yeah," Guerra replied. "You go kill the *cucuy*, and I'll just stay here and fix the truck like a good little Mexican."

"Geez, I'm sorry, alright? Can you let it go, already?" I groaned as I started to shift into my full Fomorian form.

"Fine. But I'm driving," he replied as he opened the hood.

12

The change went quickly, as it had gotten a lot easier for me to switch forms over the last year. By the time the zombie golem had jumped off the wall, I'd transformed into a nearly ten-foot tall, muscular, deformed humanoid that looked like a cross between Quasimodo and Paul Bunyan.

Since I'd discovered I was half-Fomorian, I'd often wondered why my Fomorian form was so hideous, while my mom looked like a normal, if very fit, human female. I hadn't thought to ask her before she disappeared, but if I had to guess, I'd bet it was the mix of human and Fomorian DNA. According to legend, some Fomorians were incredibly hideous, while others were as beautiful as any of the gods. My assumption was that, when the Fomorians conquered a race or culture and interbred with them, that was where the deformities began.

I could've been wrong, but I wasn't going to complain about the benefits this form afforded me. When I shifted, I was strong enough to bench-press a Buick, my skin was thick enough to repel small arms fire, and my bones were stronger than steel. In this form, I was functionally invulnerable against any mundane threat, and only the strongest supernatural beings posed a threat to me.

Speaking of, let's see what this thing is all about.

The weird amalgamation of dead bodies was lumbering toward me, so I tossed a concrete barrier, staggering it. That gave me a few seconds to scope it out in the magical spectrum. Shifting my eyesight to perceive that frequency on which magic resided, I looked at the thing again—and what I saw turned my stomach.

Necromancy.

The thing practically gave off necromantic energy in waves, so much so that I could only look at it in the magical spectrum for a moment before I had to turn away. Now that I knew what sort of magic powered it, the real question was whether it was self-directed or externally controlled. I shifted my gaze back to it again to search for some magical link that would indicate a necromancer's influence, actively probing it with my druid magic in an effort to find weaknesses that would make it easier to defeat.

Unfortunately, my efforts were interrupted when I got struck in the chest by a flying police cruiser. The impact knocked me flat on my back with the car on top of me. As I pushed the car off my chest, I considered that the creature wasn't as slow as it looked. The necro-golem, as I'd decided to call it, must've thrown the vehicle at me when I looked away for that split-second.

Tricky and quick. Huh.

The patrol car toppled as it fell off me with a crash of groaning metal and shattered glass, just in time for me to see a huge fist made from dead bodies coming down at my head. I rolled to one side, using the momentum to deliver a roundhouse kick to the inside of its knee.

My shin sank into the necro-golem's leg with a sickening squishing sound as the corpses that made up the appendage were crushed. The creature stumbled, then it caught and righted itself as more bodies shifted around from its upper thigh and back to repair the damage. I watched in horrid fascination as the dead flesh that comprised the creature crawled and shifted, each individual zombie and ghoul moving of its own accord within the whole.

It was then I realized the zombs were still moaning, albeit in muffled tones. At first, I had thought the low droning noise I heard was the remainder of the horde outside the check point. But no, it was coming from the necro-golem itself.

Okay, that's fucked up.

Despite the overt weirdness, I had little time to consider these oddities. After only a moment's hesitation to reorient itself, the necro-golem lunged at me for another attack. Rather than be crushed under its weight —or worse, be forced to grapple with it—I braced against the ground to plant both my feet in its chest, kicking the thing off me with all my might.

It flew through the air some twenty feet, landing with a crash against the container wall, which tottered and leaned precariously before settling back in place. The collision had obviously injured it, as its body had been deformed from the impact. Yet, as it pushed itself upright, more corpses shifted to replace and repair the damaged areas.

Okay, so blunt force isn't working. How about some tactical dissection?

After rolling to my feet, I leapt at the creature with Orna held high overhead. Landing in front of it, I cut it in half, straight down the middle of its grotesque, bulbous head, through its torso, all the way to its groin. As the blade cleared flesh, the thing fell apart, each half tumbling to the ground with a sickeningly mushy sound as dead flesh and skin burst apart on impact.

The smell was horrendous, although it didn't really bother me in this form. Fomorians reveled in battle and death, and when I went full Hyde-side, that part of my personality was dominant. Secure in my victory, I scoffed at the now dissected necro-golem and turned to walk away.

"Druid, look out!" Guerra yelled.

I half-turned, just in time to take a strike on my shoulder that had been aimed at my head. The force of the blow spun me around, causing me to stagger against a burned-out husk of a Humvee. As I recovered, I took in my new predicament. Now there were two necro-golems, instead of one—and each of them was busily Hoovering up the crawling dead around them, gaining in size and mass before my eyes.

"Oh, come on," I said as stood upright, yanking on my right arm with my left to set my dislocated shoulder back in place. "Why can't anything ever be easy?"

Behind me, the truck's engine sang to life, a welcome sound if ever there was one. Still, we couldn't just drive away, not with these things running loose. For all we knew, they were headed into College Station—or worse, they'd follow us to Austin.

Oh hell no. But if brute force and swordplay isn't working, then it's time for some druidry.

Necromancy was a weird, fucked up kind of magic, one that distorted the natural order, subverting death until it became a sort of second life of its own. Zombies could be created by necromancy, and those created that way were functionally identical to the infected variety. Some even believed that the undead vyrus was derived from the version that created 'thropes, having been mutated in a necromantic experiment eons ago.

It made sense. The therianthrope vyrus was basi-cally life on steroids, enhancing human DNA by magically grafting it to animal DNA. On the other hand, the vampire vyrus was full of death, killing the host and reanimating them in a permanent state of undeath.

Maybe 'thropes had come first, a part of the natural order, and then some necromancer had decided to experiment with their blood to see what they could create. Who could say? All I really knew was that druidic magic was the antithesis of necromancy. If anyone could fuck up a necromantic working, it was a master druid.

I shifted my vision back into the magical spectrum, forcing myself to examine one of the necro-golems in detail while they were busy adding more dead to their frames. The death magic coming off them in waves made me nauseous, but it was nothing that my Hyde-side couldn't control. Soon, I managed to spot details in the necromantic spells that powered them that I hadn't seen before.

Tiny lines and flows of magic held the corpses together, like stitches in the patchwork of a quilt. As the necro-golems neared one of the dead, the magic pulled the corpse toward it like iron filings to a magnet, drawing it in and securing it with tiny lines of dark energy. And deeper within the golems lay a magical core, a mass of necromantic energy that both fueled the spell and provided a rudimentary intelligence for the creature.

Now that I'd stopped fighting them, I observed that the creatures weren't interested in me at all. I wondered what had caused the first one to charge us, then I realized it might not have been coming after us. After all, it hadn't attacked until I tossed a concrete barrier at it.

Shit, I bet these things weren't even meant to attack us. They're probably the work of some crazy necromancer, who sent them out to gather bodies for his experiments or some shit.

My guess was that their primary function was Hoovering up the dead. They probably only attacked anything that appeared to be a threat, and if I hadn't confronted it, the golem might've ignored me completely. The question was, what did their maker want with hundreds of undead corpses? As I pondered that mystery, my mind immediately turned to a certain shadow wizard who might very well still be alive in the Hellpocalypse.

Crowley.

If anyone was behind this, it'd be him. For one, I didn't know of many wizards who were leery enough to evade a surprise assassination by a vampire hit squad. From what I'd gathered, the vamps sent teams after every wizard and sorceress they could find, likely with help from the fae, to thwart any latent magical defenses.

All at once, in a perfectly timed attack, magic-users all over the world had been taken out, just like that. Yet, Crowley had spent years of his adult life being hunted by assassination squads. No way a few vamps would get the jump on him.

I was tempted to leave the golems alone so I could

follow them back to their master's lair, then I could see if it really was Crowley who made them, but I didn't have time for that shit. Besides, once I killed these things, he'd come looking and recognize my ward work. I had a flash of an idea, but first I needed to end these corpse collectors before they did someone harm.

Fucking necromancers. Ugh.

Taking my time with the casting so I didn't wear myself out, I drew every bit of heat out of the air in an inverted cone several hundred feet high. I took that heat energy, combining it with combustible gases that I drew from that same cone of air, compressing the lot of it until I had two massive, ten-foot diameter fireballs floating in the air in front of me.

Then, I turned them loose on the necro-golems.

The fireballs flew with unerring accuracy, each finding its target and engulfing the golems in a conflagration that was hot enough to melt metal. The corpses that made up each of the golems lit up like wicks, the fat in each dead body fueling the flames. Hundreds of dead moaned and groaned with muffled cries as the flames consumed them, until finally, nothing was left of each golem but a smoldering pile of greasy ash.

"Damn, druid—when they say you don't fuck around, they mean it," Guerra remarked from somewhere behind me.

"No time to fuck around," I replied. "Give me a second. I need to leave a note for someone."

After I shifted back into my half-human form, I

walked over to the interior wall of a container, right next to one of the smoking piles of ash and soot. There I wrote the following in Ogham script, down the side of the container.

castle II coves austin find me

Few people would know what the lines and slashes meant, but if Crowley came here, he'd decipher it immediately. Guerra was already in the driver's seat of the truck when I got there, and I decided I wouldn't complain about it since he did get the truck running. I took a moment to get dressed before hopping in, wondering what the hell Crowley would be like after six months of this hell.

"What was that all about?" Guerra asked.

"Leaving a calling card, is all. Let's get out of here."

"Yes, Miss Daisy," Guerra said in a smart-alecky tone.

"You're not going to let it go, are you?"

"Nope."

After that, it was mostly smooth sailing. We had to dodge a bunch of dead to get back to town, and once we ditched them, we hid in a garage on the outskirts of town until dark. Then, Guerra and I headed on foot back to their camp.

Unbeknownst to me, the only reason Guerra went back was to tell Sledge that he was going with me to Austin. He said he wanted to see if he could find any

Pack members there who hadn't turned feral. Sledge and Trina okayed it since they both wanted to know where to find me when they were ready to turn the humans.

Once that was settled, Guerra and I drove in the dark back to my group, and we had few issues with the dead thanks to a silence spell on the truck. We arrived shortly after dawn on foot, after hiding the truck down the road. After all, Mickey and Anna were armed, and we didn't want to get shot coming into camp.

I signaled the sentry on duty, and when we got an answer, we headed down the road to the RV fort. As soon as Anna saw me, she let me have it.

"Damn it, Colin—where the hell have you been? We've been worried sick, thinking something happened to you. Half the kids have been crying their eyes out every night, Mickey's been jumping at every little sound, and here you come strolling into camp like you just went for a hike around the lake." She paused to take a look at Guerra, who was obviously enjoying seeing me get my ass chewed. "And who the hell is this?"

"Nice to see you too, Anna. This is Guerra. He's a friend from—well, from back when. He helped me secure transport for us to Austin, and he's going to ride along with us." I pointed my thumb at the 'thrope next to me. "He might be ugly, but trust me, he's good in a scrape."

"Screw you, druid," Guerra replied.

Anna narrowed her eyes at the both of us. "Um,

that's my biker nickname," I said, doing my best to recover.

"You, a biker," she replied.

"Yep."

"Liar. Anyway, there's soup and beans over the fire if you want it. We've spotted some zombs up the road, but they seem to be avoiding this area for some reason."

"Huh, that's weird," I said. "Right, Guerra?"

He looked at me, then at Anna. "Dude, I'm just here for a ride. Leave me out of it."

Guerra walked off, leaving me stranded with Anna. She looked around, checking to make sure all the kids were okay with Guerra's presence. A bunch of them were already crowding around him, asking him about his scars and tattoos. Anna leaned in close, whispering so only she and I could hear.

"I don't know how you're doing this, and frankly I don't care. Just don't freak out the kids, okay? They've already seen enough."

"Huh?" I said.

"Fine, be that way. Now, tell me about this ride you guys found."

"Oh-kay. I was going to try to bring a couple of APCs —armored personnel carriers—"

"I know what an APC is."

"Right. But then Guerra said he had a better solution, so we got this armored military truck instead. It doesn't have a roof on it, which means we'll have to cover it with tarps, but otherwise, I think it'll get us to Austin just fine."

Her brow furrowed as she considered what I'd said. "And when we get there? What then?"

"There's a place I remember, up in the hills in the southwest part of the city. You know, where the rich people lived. I think it'll be a good place to set up. There's a big fence around the whole thing, and it's secluded. You'll see—it'll work out fine once we get there."

"You sure we can do this? I mean, it's a long trip, and there are a lot of variables. Roadblocks, fuel, food and water—not to mention those other things."

I placed a hand on her shoulder as I met her gaze. "Anna, don't worry about it. I got this, okay?"

She sighed heavily, shaking her head. "You haven't let us down before—I know that. And you've never led us astray. But since we left the camp on the peninsula, something's different about you, and I can't put my finger on it. I mean, never mind how you somehow seem to defy death and pull miracles out of your ass all the time. I kind of got used to that. But you seem a little too damned cheery for someone who just spent six months in the same hell as the rest of us."

I squeezed her shoulder and let it go, allowing my arm to fall to my side. "Fair enough. Let's just say that escaping certain death gave me a new perspective. I want to get you guys someplace safe, and then—"

I stopped mid-sentence, because I hadn't told her

about the rest of my plan. Now that I thought about it, Guerra would likely stay and watch them until I got back. He wouldn't admit it, but that was probably the main reason why he'd tagged along. Still, Anna was going to freak out when I told her I was going to be gone for a while.

"And then what?" she asked.

"Then, I guess we just take things one day at a time," I said with a smile.

Anna hung her head, then she poked me in the chest. "Just don't abandon us, or I swear I'll *never* forgive you."

13

The trip to Austin was about what I'd expected, with the biggest challenge occurring before we left. Namely, convincing Anna and Mickey that I wasn't going to drive us into a radiation zone. After their initial freak out, I explained how I'd figured out that southwest Austin was safe, detailing weather patterns on the day of the strike, the size of the blast, and how far fallout could travel based on wind speed and direction.

After a lot of back and forth, Guerra jumped in to say he'd been in Austin just after the bombs fell, so he heard firsthand which areas the authorities said to avoid. That was total bullshit, because the EMP had knocked out communications all over the Austin metro. Regardless, Anna and Mickey seemed to buy his story. However, Anna made me swear that we'd alter course at the first sign of any dead birds or animals—in which case it'd be too late anyway, but I didn't tell her that.

I had to deal with a few other hitches before we left, namely how to keep revenants and nosferatu from jumping in the truck, and how to silence the engine and exhaust without freaking Anna and Mickey out. Well, the kids too—the little ankle-biters were a lot more observant than I'd given them credit for at first, that was for damned sure.

Since I had to tarp the top of the truck bed anyway, I decided to ward the shit out of the tarps before I put them on. A couple of the kids asked what I was doing, and I said I was decorating it for good luck. Before I knew it, I had a mess of boys doodling on my tarps. I waited until they got bored, then I finished the job and put it on the truck.

As for silencing the thing, that was another matter. I'd been casting my silence spells on the exhaust and engine, because it took less energy to cast it on smaller areas. None of my group was dumb enough to believe I'd found the quietest diesel truck in Texas, so I needed a different approach to keeping the zombs from hearing us. Finally, I settled on casting a spell that would contain all sounds within fifteen feet from the epicenter, which I set as the dead center of the bed. That would keep the undead from hearing us unless they were right on top of us, and it'd solve the issue of keeping the kids quiet in case one of them started freaking out.

We drove at night to avoid attracting attention, using a night-vision monocular to explain how Guerra and I could see in the dark. We stuck to the backroads, taking the little two-lane highways that crisscrossed the state like varicose veins, all across the map. First south to LaGrange, then parallel to I-10, heading west while skirting Lockhart by a wide margin, because I could sense the sickness there from miles away. It wasn't a ton of radiation, but plenty enough to make me want to steer clear.

Next came the really sketchy part, because the I-35 corridor was heavily populated, all the way from Austin to San Antonio. We scouted it for several miles at a distance, finally crossing the interstate near Hunter. I cleared the underpass by hand while Guerra waited with the group a mile distant. From there we headed north to pick up Ranch Road 12, cruising through Wimberley and Dripping Springs without incident. Then we took Hamilton Pool Road and Bee Cave Road toward the 360 Loop, which wasn't a loop at all, actually, but a major north-south artery that cut through west Austin.

That's when I saw it, about a mile east of the city of Bee Cave. I'd directed Guerra to stop along the side of the road, because the sun was about to come up and I needed to scout a place for us to hole up. I made the excuse that I needed to go potty, which of course meant we had to escort a dozen kids into the trees to do the same. Guerra stood watch, sneaking off now and again to silently take out stray zombs, while I hiked a few more yards into the woods for some privacy.

As soon as I was alone, I sat cross-legged on the

ground, slowing my breathing to drop into a druid trance. Then, I pushed my consciousness out in an ever-expanding bubble, until I was flitting in and out of the minds of small animals across a mile-wide radius from where I sat. Soon I spotted a suitable location to hide for the day, in the middle of an unfinished neighborhood development north of the road.

It was roughly two-hundred acres of woods with a few paved roads running through it, and not a whole lot else. I could park us in the middle, set up a ward cordon, and everyone could sleep while I scouted ahead. After I chose the spot, I was just about to exit my trance when I felt a familiar *presence* brush across my consciousness.

What the hell? Oak, is that you?

Then, it was gone, like a skittish deer spooked by a noise in the forest. I tried reestablishing contact for a few minutes, but the sky was already starting to brighten. It was time to get back to the group and guide them to our hiding spot for the day, so I relented and chalked it all up to my imagination and wishful thinking.

When I got back to the truck, the kids were loaded up and Mickey and Guerra were keeping watch. I nodded to the tall, thin older man, who stood by with a loaded crossbow held at a low ready position as he scanned the woods around us. After meeting my gaze as I passed, he placed a hand on my arm to stop me.

"Everything alright, Colin? You look like you've seen a ghost."

I patted his hand, because Mickey was touchy-feely like that. He'd been a volunteer at the Ren Fest, but before that he'd been a marriage and family counselor. He still wore a thick, worn gold wedding band on his ring finger, but I'd never asked him about it, and he'd never offered. He was a good man, one who adapted to unfamiliar and horrid conditions because he had people depending on him, and that's all that mattered to me.

"I'm okay. It's just—you know how it is. Sometimes you see stuff that can't be unseen. I'll be alright."

"Okay," Mickey replied, keeping his eyes locked on mine. "If you need to talk about it, though, let me know."

"Thanks, man, I appreciate it. Anyway, it's time to load up. I think I remember a place where we can safely rest until tonight."

"Sure thing. I'll do a head count, and then we can roll."

I kept watch as Mickey climbed into the truck bed and counted heads, but all the while I wondered if I wasn't alone here after all.

When the kids had gone down for the day, I checked my wards and then I headed into Austin. The only person I told was Guerra, as I didn't want to have to explain my actions to Anna. Things had always been a little tense between us, and since I got back from my own timeline, it was getting worse. Partially because she knew I was hiding something, but I also got the feeling she thought I wanted something from her, in a quid pro quo kind of way.

Could I blame her for being suspicious of my motives? No, I couldn't, but little did she know that I had a hot alpha werewolf waiting for me back home. That was, if I managed to make it back home, but that was a bridge I'd cross when I came to it. For now, the only thing on my mind was getting this group to our new home safely.

One thing at a time, Colin. One thing at a time.

Once I was away from camp, I stealth-shifted and cast my concealment spells, then I took off at a run, heading east on Bee Caves Road at full speed. All the while, I used my druid senses to check for radiation, making sure the area was safe for human travel. I couldn't really *see* nuclear radiation, but I could sense it as a sickness in the earth, plants, and animals when dangerous levels were present.

As for the dead, they were out and about, but not as many as I might've expected. This part of town was less dense than Austin proper, occupied as it had been by the area's wealthier residents. That meant a lot of big homes and bigger yards, including acreage plots that were more like ranches than homesteads.

The bottom line was that this area had been less densely populated before the bombs fell. That meant fewer dead, and if my radiation theory held up, fewer humans as well.

I kept my head on a swivel and my senses on high alert as I ran, not because of the zombs, but to look for hidden threats. It wasn't the zombies I was worried about, but the vamps. All we needed was to be attacked by a nasty nos' or a higher vamp while we were on the road. Either one would throw a wrench in the gears of my plan, not to mention scaring the ever-loving shit out of the kids.

Nope, not going to happen. Not if I can help it.

All I saw were a scattering of wandering dead and a single ghoul, which I dispatched by beheading it without slowing down. Everything was relatively quiet, and I fell into a steady rhythm that allowed me to eat up the miles at a decent pace. That was, until I reached the Orthodox church near the Capitol of Texas Highway.

I smelled it from the road, the telltale scent of clotted and spoiled blood, graveyard dirt, and decomposing flesh. That could only mean one thing, that a vampire had set up a lair nearby. I was standing smack between two large churches, the Presbyterian church to the south, and the Orthodox church to the north. The wind was blowing from the south, so I headed for the post-modern, jumbledy-gook structure to the southeast.

I'd attended the church across the street a couple of times back when I was struggling with Jesse's death. It was nice, but a little too flashy for my tastes, and I eventually settled on St. Elias downtown. My therapist had told me to join a faith community, but there was no way I was going to do the evangelical thing. All that singing and shaking hands? Nope.

But the Orthodox faith, that was an easy sell. Show up, chant the liturgy, stick around for a meal with the other parishioners every now and again, then go home. All without that fake niceness, Sunday-best behavior bullshit. My kind of church.

Which was all well and good, but now it seemed a vampire had decided to set up camp on the grounds next door. They liked desecrating holy places, and it didn't matter if it was a church, synagogue, temple, or mosque. Why the vamp had chosen this one instead of one across the way was anyone's guess, but man, did it stink of death.

Moreover, the vamp had hung dead bodies all over the building in a mockery of religious iconography. What compelled them to do such things, I had no idea. To me it was just a building, so I could care less how a vamp decorated it—the only thing I really objected to was the fact it was killing humans. It would likely attack us when we passed through its territory tonight, so I had to take care of it no matter what I thought of its design sensibilities.

Time to get to work.

Young vamps tended to sack out during the day, but older ones often stayed awake during daylight hours. Sure, you might get lucky and find a young vamp asleep in their lair, and you could stake them with little fuss if you were good and quiet.

But mature vamps were different. Give them a century or so of un-life, and you practically never caught them sleeping during the day. The only advantage humans had against older vamps during daylight hours was the sun. Direct sunlight would absolutely toast most vamps who were younger than a few centuries, unless they had some crazy strong blood in their veins. That old trope about busting out windows to fuck with vampires was about the only thing Hollywood had gotten right.

For those reasons, I wasn't expecting to catch this thing off guard. So, I entered a side door of the church with a spell at the ready and my sword in hand. As for whether I was sure this was the place, there was no mistaking it, because it looked like a fucking carnal house. Old, dried blood stained the tile floor in long streaks like paint, and blood spatter was evident everywhere, even on the ceiling tiles. It looked like a serial killer's playground, which in a way I guessed it was.

But then I noticed something odd—multiple sets of bloody, adult-sized human handprints on the walls, and footprints through the blood stains on the floor. These weren't the kind of prints you saw at a crime scene, the sort of frenzied smears you found in the aftermath of a bloody fight or murder. No, these had been left intentionally but at random, like a bunch of people had walked through here decorating the walls with human blood.

That's when I heard the chanting coming from another part of the building. Dozens of voices, combined in a creepy mockery of a Cistercian chant that was reminiscent of the Halo soundtrack. Not in Latin, but in English, and the words were definitely not your standard Catholic fare. They were chanting about blood, and death, and sacrifice, and describing really fucked up acts.

Wondering what the hell I'd stumbled into, I renewed my concealment spells before heading further into the church.

After a few minutes of wandering around, I ended up in the sound booth for the main worship hall, on a balcony above the nave below. The first few rows of pews were full of people, all adults, standing with hands raised to the sky as they sang their hellish chant. And up on the stage sat an altar, built from limestone blocks with a huge flat slab of white stone on top, stained with the blood of untold humans.

A kid was on the altar, gagged and tied hand and foot in spread eagle fashion. He was nearly naked except for a pair of soiled white underwear that had been stained yellow by the piss that puddled between his legs. The child was no more than ten, with dark, close-cropped hair, fair skin, an emaciated frame, and big brown eyes that were wide as saucers as they darted around the room. I'd seen that look before, here in the Hellpocalypse—the "I don't want to die" look.

Standing behind the altar was a naked woman—or rather, not a woman per se, but a female vampire. Like most vampires she was attractive, in a Lake Bell, "you're hot but you also intimidate the shit out of me" sort of way. She was also either very old or she'd been turned in her late forties. I could tell that by the way her breasts sagged slightly, the crow's feet around her eyes, and the salt and pepper in her long black hair.

Vamps did age, but very, very slowly. Luther looked to be in his early forties, and from what I gathered he'd been turned a few hundred centuries prior. They didn't normally turn people who weren't in their prime, so I was guessing she was at least as old as Luther, maybe more. Which meant she could be dangerous, never mind the peanut gallery worshipping her. No telling how many people in the audience were willing participants, and how many had been cowed into doing this shit by threat of violence.

What was clear was that this bitch had set herself up a little vampire worship cult, complete with a temple and followers who could lure in fresh victims. It was the perfect set up for an older vampire who was too lazy to hunt. And this turd looked like she enjoyed having things done for her, even before she'd been turned. I mean, talk about bitchy resting face, sheesh—she had it in spades.

I only spent a few moments to take it all in while I sized up the scene. Despite the complications due to the crowd and the unknown participant factor, I still wasn't going to let that kid die, and I sure wasn't going to let this shit go on. Besides, I came here to kill a vamp, and that's what I was going to do.

But how to get the kid free while dealing with the vamp? I needed to get her away from him and deal with her before she fed on the kid. If I just wounded her, she'd likely try to feed to heal herself, and in a room full of humans, she'd have her pick. That meant I'd have to disable her on the first go.

Ninja time. Better bring out the big guns.

I snuck out of the booth, circling around to find the pastor's entrance to the stage. They always liked to enter and exit the pulpit in a way that avoided their parishioners, like some sort of self-absorbed celebrity who wanted to avoid mixing with the common folk. That meant there was usually a back entrance to the stage in these churches, one that would provide a way to sneak up on Cruella down there.

As I picked my way through the back corridors, through the pastor's study to the backstage area, I shored up my concealment spells again. Then, I reached into my Bag with one hand and queued up my sunlight spell in the other. Once ready, I tiptoed to the side-stage entrance, waiting for the right moment to attack as I listened to the vamp's crazy bullshit.

"My children," she crooned in a voice that was one part velvet, two parts whiskey neat. "Again, you have brought me a worthy sacrifice and stayed my hand against my people."

"Blood brings mercy," the cult members responded.

"And blood is life," the vampire said. "This young boy's blood will not be spilled in vain, oh no. His life force will become one with the collective, a part of me, as each of you will eventually become as well. In this way, he will not pass into darkness, but instead he'll live on, immortalized with me, feeling no pain, no suffering, but only eternal bliss."

Holy shit, but this bitch is laying it on thick. Or unholy, I guess. Sheesh.

She appeared to be building her rhetoric to a crescendo, at which point I assumed she'd rip open the kid's neck and drink him dry. That, I could not let happen, so I readied my spell and prepared to fly. The plan was to run up behind her, cut off her head, and then cut the kid loose and run outside where other vamps would be hard-pressed to follow.

Then, I'd deal with the cult members.

Piece of cake.

14

Using every bit of Fomorian speed I could muster, I zipped behind the vampire, drawing Dyrnwyn in one smooth motion from my Bag. Against any non-evil opponent, the sword was nothing more than a mundane, if finely crafted, weapon. But against evil beings, it was effectively the original lightsaber—a flaming sword that burned so hot it could cut through weaker metals.

The blade lit up as soon as it cleared the Bag, and I sliced at the vamp's neck in a sweeping backhand motion that was sure to do the trick. As was typical in these situations, everything seemed to slow down. Just as the sword reached her neck, the vampire turned into a thick, smoky mist.

Now, where have I seen that trick before?

I only knew of one other vampire with that skill, and that was my friend Luther, who I intended to rescue just as soon as I got my group settled in. Luther could *bamf* around like a superhero, teleporting from place to place as he disappeared and reappeared in a cloud of black smoke. This leech seemed to have the same ability, because she immediately reappeared on the other side of the church.

Well, shit—Luther never told me he had a sister.

Obviously, she wasn't his real sister, but vampire talents ran through bloodlines like male pattern baldness, from maker to spawn. Not only were first-gen vamps—those made by primaries—stronger than your average bloodsucker, but they also were more likely to inherit their maker's gift. Second generation vamps might develop a gift as they grew older, while third-generation vamps rarely—if ever—had such skills.

Which meant that this vampire shared a lineage with Luther, who was one of the most dangerous bloodkin I'd ever met. I'd only met two vamps who were stronger—one was an ancient nosferatu who'd been around to see the pyramids built, and the other was supposedly a primary. I couldn't beat either of them, at least not before I became a druid master, and to be honest I'd be hard-pressed to beat their asses now.

Luther would certainly give me trouble, and that was a fact. Ergo, this bloodthirsty bitch was likely to be a handful. I met her gaze where she stood, near the doors to the chapel and well beyond my reach. She only had eyes for me at the moment, while her followers were muttering and looking about in confusion. They'd catch on momentarily, probably when she ate one of them.

"Dauphine—where'd she go?" I heard one mutter.

"Look, she's up there."

"Who's that?"

"Blasphemer!"

Ah, looks like we found the ass-licker in the group. That motherfucker will die next.

"Dauphine, is it?" I asked, cutting the kid loose with the sword while I kept my eyes on her. "How'd you know?"

She looked down her aquiline nose at me, her voice full of contempt as she spoke. "You reek of magic. I'd have left earlier, but I needed to see for myself who was wielding magic in my territory."

I helped the kid off the altar, whispering as I lowered him to the ground. "When the fighting starts, run and hide."

"Yes, do run and hide, Richard," she said, pronouncing his name with the faintest French accent. "It'll make things that much more interesting."

I ignored the confused mutterings of the crowd, choosing instead to focus on the master vampire. "So, how many of these people are willing participants?"

"Some? All? Who can say? Your kind are always willing to turn on their own when given the choice between savagery and self-preservation."

"Huh. So, are we doing this, or are you just going to let me disrupt your little cult with zero repercussions?"

She smiled and ran her tongue around the edges of her lips, ending the gesture by pricking it on a very long, sharp canine. "Oh, we're very much doing this. But first, a little snack."

She disappeared in a burst of smoke, reappearing behind a heavyset middle-aged man with a beard and a broken nose. The fact that he was overweight told me a lot about his willingness to participate in this farce. Nobody ate well enough to stay fat in the Hellpocalypse without fucking someone else over.

Regardless of his culpability, he was fucked. Dauphine bit his neck so deep, it looked like half of it was gone when she reared back to let the blood flow. Arterial spray squirted in her mouth, and as their vampire priestess or god or whatever she'd made herself out to be fed, the crowd stayed put. Every last one of them.

I fixed my gaze on a gray-haired woman in the front row. "Aren't you even going to resist, or try to get away?"

"Would it make a difference? At least this way, some of us live," she replied.

"They were all in on it," Richard whispered from behind me. "All of them."

"Well, that settles that," I said as I queued up a fireball.

I needed to get Dauphine in the open so I could blast her, and the crowd was in the way. Without hesitation or remorse, I cut loose with the fireball, aiming for the center of the cult members, right where Dauphine stood. It struck with the desired effect, consuming a half-dozen of those murderers and the middle of two pews instantly, and scattering the rest in an explosion of fire and heat.

When the smoke cleared, there were a bunch of dead and wounded—and no sign of the vampire. I scanned the room quickly, my eyes darting here and there for the telltale wisps of smoke that would mark her passing. Failing to find any trace of her, I decided to employ a bit of chronomancy to even the odds.

In less than a millisecond, I flipped through the most likely futures, looking just a few seconds ahead. In the vast majority of them, Dauphine materialized above me, landing atop me and ripping my throat out with her razor sharp, metal-hard nails. Whether that would kill me was a toss-up, as my Hyde-side usually took over when I suffered life-threatening injuries. Personally, I didn't care to find out, so I readied my sunlight spell and counted down the seconds to her likely attack.

Three...

Two...

One.

I dodged sideways with superhuman speed, opening my hand overhead at the same time as I released the spell. At the same moment, Dauphine appeared in the air above where I'd stood, just in time to catch the full intensity of the spell across the right side of her naked figure. Immediately, her skin bubbled and blackened, then it ignited, causing her to catch fire across an entire hemisphere of her body.

She shrieked like a banshee, and then she disappeared once more in a cloud of smoke and fire. But before she dematerialized, I saw the look of horror on her face, and fear—which must've been a shock for a vamp of her age to feel. I stood there at the ready for several more seconds, eager to finish the fight, but when Dyrnwyn extinguished itself, I knew she'd fled.

I took Richard to the pastor's office, instructing him to wait for me. Then I went back to the worship hall to kill the cult members who'd survived the fireball. Every last death was a mercy, as the blast had fairly decimated their number and seriously wounded those who remained. I was tempted to let them suffer slow, painful deaths from their burns and wounds—but I wasn't a monster.

Besides, some of them might have survived.

Once that chore was finished, we found Richard some clothes. The kid led me to a classroom inside the church that had been piled high with child-size clothing items, proof positive of the cult's previous sacrifices. Once he was dressed, we went outside into the sunlight so he'd feel a little safer.

"You think she's dead?" he asked between sips of water and bites of an energy bar.

I shook my head. "I doubt it. She's old and powerful, and vampires like her are hard to kill."

He took a bite of the energy bar, chewing thoughtfully as he stared at the horizon with his big, dark eyes. "She'll be back."

"I know. And we'll be ready for her." I waited for him to finish his meal, then I pointed to my back. "Hop on, because I need to get back to my group." Richard hesitated, his eyes darting around for an escape. "Whoa there, no one in my group will hurt you. I have a truck full of boys who are your age and younger, and we're on our way to set up a safe house here in the city."

He shook his head. "Lots of those vampires here. Werewolves, too. It ain't safe."

"It'll be safe once I'm done. Trust me on this." I looked around, taking in the corpses that still hung on the outside walls of the church. "And besides, where are you going to go?"

He frowned, hanging his head. "I guess you're right. My family's gone. I thought these turds would take me in, but you know how that went." The kid paused for a beat, then he squinted and looked up at me. "Your people know you're a wizard?"

His frankness made me chuckle, and I knelt down to get eye to eye with him. "Actually, they don't. And you can't tell them. It'll freak them out, maybe cause some of them to lose trust in me, and I can't have that. So, this needs to stay between you and me. Deal?"

Richard thought about it, then he held up a closed fist. "Deal."

I bumped his little fist, then I let him climb on my back and we were off. He jumped a bit when I triggered my concealment spells, but then he relaxed, and I felt the tension ease out of his limbs. By the time we made camp, I was carrying him, because the kid was sound asleep.

After giving the signal, I dropped my chameleon and silence spells and stepped out from behind some trees. Guerra was standing guard, and everyone else was sacked out in the truck or on the ground. He lifted his chin to acknowledge me, then he noticed the kid and gave me a quizzical look. I laid Richard in the front seat of the truck, then I went back to speak with Guerra.

"You smell like you just did a lot of killing. Who's the kid?"

"Found him at a church when I was scouting. It's a messed-up story. I'll tell you later once we have some privacy."

"Sure thing. We clear to the safe house?"

I shrugged. "Not sure—I still need to go back and check the rest of the route. Only made it to 360 before I got sidetracked."

"Anything I need to know?"

"Master vamp, an old one," I said, lowering my voice so only we could hear. "I wounded her badly, but I have a feeling she's not done with me."

He grunted. "Could be messy, with all these kids around."

"I'll clear the safe house before we get there, and ward it up good. So long as the kids stay within the perimeter, they'll be safe."

"I dunno, druid. It seems like they'd be better off with their own kind. Word is there's some settlements forming out in the sticks. Safety in numbers, and all that."

"No one's safe in this world, not anymore. They're better off with me."

He picked his teeth with his thumbnail. "And when you leave for Dallas?"

"Yeah, I know. But I figured since you're already here..."

"*Pinche cabrón*, I knew this was coming."

"I thought that's why you came along—to help."

He scowled. "First I'm a mechanic, now I'm an au pair. You going to want me to be your gardener, too?"

"Oh, quit your bitching. Once I get the place set up, we'll have all the food and game we want. And as for gardening, I'm a fucking druid, remember? You can leave that to me."

"If you say anything about beans and rice, I'm going to kick your ass."

I held up my hands in concession. "I didn't say a word, man."

He squinted as he looked into the distance, then he gave a half-shrug. "Plant some squash, find some yardbirds, and I'm in. No lie, Holmes—I could really go for some *calabaza con pollo* right about now."

I'd only napped for a few hours in the truck on the trip down, so I was dog-tired. But with the group exposed, there was no time to rest. Finnegas and Maureen had trained me to go days without sleep, a frequent occurrence when you were hunting supernatural creatures. As I slammed a packet of freeze-dried coffee with a swig of water, I heard the old man's voice echo in my mind.

You can sleep when you're dead.

With Guerra keeping watch I took off again on foot, taking time to pass through the church once more to see if Dauphine had returned. Wherever she went, it wasn't there, because a thorough check with my druid senses turned up jack squat. She had to be close by, but I didn't have the time to hunt her down, not with everyone out in the open and exposed.

Later, then. But I'll get to it soon.

My next stop was a hardware store and garden center down the road, on the other side of 360. The hardware store had been looted, but not badly, and I was able to grab some gardening gear along with some decent machetes and axes. As for the main items I'd come for, I found them almost untouched.

Seeds.

Most folks wouldn't think about shit like that in an

apocalypse, at least not the type you'd find on the bougie side of Austin. If I'd been out in a small town out in the Hill County or on the East Side, the whole display would've been gone. But here in the Hills? Hell, all the hippies left ages ago, forced out by rising rents and gentrification. And rich people didn't grow gardens—they had *people* for that.

I took only a couple of packages of each, leaving the rest for some other enterprising survivor to find. Then, thinking better of it, I found a plastic tub and put all the seeds in it, sealing it tight before I marked the outside so people would know what was in there. If I'd left them out, it wouldn't be long before the packaging broke down, then the mice would be all over them. At least this way, they'd be preserved until someone needed them.

After that, I headed for the place I'd chosen.

Years ago, one of the guys who pioneered the MMO genre of computer games built a mansion up in the hills that was designed like a castle. I'd seen pictures of it online, and the place was massive. The guy had it built out of stone and stucco, with thick wooden doors, a tower, the whole bit. The best part was the tall wrought iron fence around it, and the fact that it was situated on the top of a high ridge with nothing but trees and parks surrounding it.

Sure, there were other mansions up there, but I seriously doubted anyone was still there. My guess was they split when things went to shit—rich people always had a back-up plan, like flying to the Bahamas or some crap like that. Most of the people who lived in that neighborhood had probably been eaten on their way to the airport, the idiots.

And if anyone was there? Well, I'd deal with that problem when and if it appeared.

Thankfully, the neighborhood was dead. Quite literally, in fact. A few zombies wandered around, likely local residents or staff who died here and never wandered off. I dispatched them in an unceremonious fashion, promising myself I'd bury them later when I had time. Then, I hopped the fence to the castle mansion.

There, two more zombs patrolled the fence line like guard dogs, wearing a barren path through the tall weeds as they trudged around in a gross imitation of their former lives. Since the fence was still intact, likely as not they'd holed up here, and one of them had gotten bitten on a trip outside the compound. They likely got home before the vyrus took hold, only to wake up in the middle of the night with brains on the brain.

Fuck me, but that sucks.

I killed them both, then I cleared the house of the last zomb, dumping all three bodies over the fence. After that, I opened some windows to air it out, then it was time for some serious druidry.

My first order of business was securing the area, so I went over the fence to make permanent changes to the perimeter defenses. That involved using druid magic to etch runes and wards into the iron uprights all the way around the house and grounds. It was a time-consuming task, but much more durable than permanent ink, and the place was nigh impervious to undead and 'thropes alike when I was finished.

Next, I needed to make it difficult for anyone to get in and out of the neighborhood. There were two routes of ingress and egress, and for now we only needed one. So, I found a decent choke point and used magic to cave the road in, making it look like it had been washed out by a flood. Later, once I got the group settled, I'd do the other side—but for now, this would do.

After that, I used more druidry to seal off all the first-floor windows. One of my powers was the ability to shape earth and stone with magic, so I "borrowed" natural materials from the grounds, using them to brick up all the openings on the ground level, except for the glass double doors in front. I covered the windows that flanked the entry with stone, then I borrowed a large wooden door and thick iron hinges from inside the place, reshaping the door frame to make it all fit.

Then, I checked the mechanicals inside and outside the building. Solar panels had been installed at some point, and while the system needed work, it was serviceable. The rainwater catchment system would provide all our needs quite handily as well. I'd need to come up with a water filtration and purification system before I left, but the fact that I didn't need to dig a well was a definite bonus.

Finally, I planted a large garden—tilling the ground and making the plants grow with druid magic, of course. After I had finished, I was thoroughly exhausted but quite satisfied with my work. Now, all that remained was to bring the group here and get us settled in.

Then, I hunt.

15

A few weeks later, everyone in the group was finally comfortable with the new digs and used to the idea that we weren't going to be overrun by the dead. I'd washed out both roads in, and we were on a pretty steep hill, so it was doubtful any roaming herds would wander this way. And even if they did, the fence would keep them out—and anything else that decided to get stupid.

Speaking of which, we'd seen no sign of Dauphine, but that didn't mean she wasn't out there. The upside of running into her was that the area was clear of other supernatural predators for miles around. No nosferatu, revenant, or lesser vampire would even think of crossing a master vampire, so they steered clear of this part of town.

I kept looking for her, of course, but she was either too injured to be a threat or staying away out of fear I'd burn her with sunlight again. Guerra and I remained vigilant, and I scanned the surrounding area with my druid senses nightly. It was all we could do—that and keeping everyone inside the perimeter after dusk.

As for getting everyone situated, my chores were done. I solved the water purification issue with magic because it was easier to just put some glyphs on the water catchment system and call it a day. We'd assigned the younger boys to tend the garden, and the older ones began receiving training in hand-to-hand combat from me and Guerra.

I'd also built a small forge, and I began making spears for them to wield, teaching them how to kill the odd shambler by stabbing them in the head through the fence. As kids will do, they made a game of it, and soon they were counting kills to see who could turn the lights out on the most zombs.

Not once did I stop and ask myself what I was doing, teaching kids to kill. I'd made peace with that decision not long after I rescued them. This was a harsh world, and it was no different than I would've trained my own children—except someday I would push my own kids much, much harder.

The walls inside the house were decorated with a plethora of medieval weapons as well, and some of them were battle ready. I picked out a few for Anna and Mickey to use, giving the kids those weapons that weren't suitable for combat. Guerra and I started giving the two of them lessons as well, and I discovered that the 'thrope was well-versed in the *Destreza* school of fencing. Yet, his movements were much more refined than any modern master I'd seen, more proof of his age and experience.

Finally, I could wait no longer, and I decided it was time to leave. Guerra knew it before I told him because he could sense the restlessness in me. Mickey merely took it in stride, but Anna? That was another matter.

"How can you leave us at a time like this?" she asked as she paced back and forth in the wine cellar.

It had been left well-stocked, and there were some expensive bottles down here. The room was also nearly soundproof, which was why we decided to have the conversation there. Currently, I was letting her wear herself out, at which point I expected a concession and an apology. Or maybe just guarded resignation because she was pretty freaking pissed.

"I'm leaving because it's the best thing for the group, in the long run," I said. I sat atop an empty wine barrel that was there for show, leaning against the wall while I engaged in practical stoicism. "For one, we don't know what's out there. There might be safe zones set up by the government, or settlements where the boys could live somewhat normal lives. Or there might be a million-strong horde headed this way. We won't know unless I go on a long-range scouting run."

"Send Guerra, then, if it's so important. He's more than capable."

"Yes, but I have people I need to check on, Anna. I had a life before all this, you know."

"We all did," she exclaimed, throwing her hands in the air. "You think I don't want to know if our parents are alive? Brian asks about them, every single night."

I sighed and ran my fingers through my hair because this was a pointless discussion. Anna didn't check on her parents because she knew she wouldn't make it, and she also knew that I was a different story. She just didn't want me to go because I'd become their security blanket, the group's magic feather.

"Look, I know you feel safer with me here, and believe me when I say I'd rather hang around the compound than head out there. But this is something I have to do, and not just for you guys."

"What is it with you, Colin? Why do you act like you're the only person who can save a soul in the apocalypse? What makes you so special?" Rather than give her a lame answer, I sat stone-faced, returning her icy stare. "You know what? Be that way. If you want to abandon us, you go right ahead. But just remember, I'm the one who has to deal with the kids when they cry every night, asking for their parents, their families, their freaking woobies—me. Not you."

"I have to do this, Anna. But I will be back. And the bottom line is—"

"Yeah?" she said, leaning in until she was up in my face. "Say it."

"I don't owe you or anyone else a thing."

She slapped me, and I allowed it, because it would do her some good. Plus, she'd regret it after she cooled down. This was a bandage that had to be ripped off, better sooner than later, because Anna needed to consider what she'd do if I wasn't around. For all I knew, I might *not* come back, if not from Dallas, then from my own timeline. She needed to accept that possibility, and steel herself to survive anyway.

We stared at each other as the echo of her palm striking my face faded away, my expression calm, hers murderous. After several seconds, she shook her head and turned toward the door.

"I knew you'd abandon us. I knew it all along."

After Anna slammed the door behind her, I took several moments to calm myself, because that had been a hard thing to do. Then, I grabbed a bottle from the shelves, Montrachet Grand Cru something or other, and I popped the cork with magic. I took a long draw off the bottle, wincing at the fact that I'd accidentally picked a white instead of a red.

I'd give my left nut for some bourbon about now.

That said, the wine tasted like citrus and spice, and in truth it wasn't half-bad—although I couldn't tell if it was a good vintage or not. Resigned to my limited choice of drink, I raised the bottle in a general northerly direction, toasting the sky before I took another swig.

"Well old man, you prepped me for a lot of shit, but you never prepared me for a divorce with kids involved." For some reason, I found that to be really funny, and before I knew it, I was laughing hysterically. When my tittering subsided, I wiped my eyes and raised the bottle again. "Here's to you, Finnegas. I miss you, you crotchety old fart."

I left early the next morning, before anyone else was up. Well, almost anyone. While Richard had taken well to life in the compound, he had trouble sleeping after the experience he'd gone through at the church. When I snuck up to the rooftop deck to let Guerra know I was leaving, Richard was sitting on the stairs by himself, staring out into the darkness.

"Good morning, Richard."

"You leaving?" he asked as I passed by.

I stopped to address him, leaning on the wrought iron rail. "Yes, for a time."

"You coming back?"

"Sure, but I don't know how long I'll be away."

The kid gave a pensive nod of his head, then he turned back to staring at nothing. Hopefully, he wasn't thinking of leaving. I'd left the adults with instructions to allow no one outside the perimeter until I got back. We'd gathered plenty of food from the surrounding mansions—one of the previous owners must've been LDS, because they had canned and dried food out the wazoo—so there was no need for anyone to go wandering about.

"Kids are getting restless," Guerra remarked as I joined him on the rooftop deck.

"They have plenty of room to play here, and if they get bored, just ask Anna or Mickey to assign them some chores."

He chortled. "'Ask' Anna. More like suggest it, and then wait for her to decide it's her idea."

"Hey, man, I just work here. She's the one who's in charge."

"Heard you arguing last night. Then I heard someone singing Irish ballads at the top of their lungs, way off-key."

"Was it loud enough for anyone else to hear?" I asked, trying to hide my embarrassment.

"Nah." He scanned the darkness all around the perimeter. "You good?"

"I'm good. Or I will be, once I deal with a few personal issues."

"When you get back, I'll need to take care of my own stuff. Pack stuff."

"You got it," I said, clapping him on the shoulder. "Thanks for having my back."

"Pack for life. Just don't ask me to iron your shirts."

"Never going to let that shit go, eh?"

"Not on your life, *guero*. Now get the fuck out of here, before the kids wake up."

After I hopped the fence, I headed south. It was stupid and risky, because the radiation was likely to be worse in that area of town, but I had to see for myself what had happened.

The junkyard was pretty much how I'd left it in my

own timeline, except it was as dead and quiet as a cemetery. The place had been buttoned up tight, but by who I
couldn't say. I found a few graves, one with a marker that
was nothing more than a rusted longsword and a with-
ered mistletoe wreath.

I didn't bother finding out who occupied those
graves. Fact was, I didn't want to know.

Wait a minute... is the old man still alive in this timeline?
And if so, where'd he go?

Where would the old man go if I died, his last
apprentice? What would he do if the future hope of
druidry went up in a mushroom cloud of death and
destruction? I pondered that question as I continued
searching and inspecting my former home.

My wards were intact, so I took some time to shore
them up, just in case I needed to come back here. Mirac-
ulously, the junkyard was outside the fallout zone,
which was good because all that metal would be deadly
once irradiated. Speeding up the half-life decay of
radioactive material meant releasing all that energy at
once. No bueno, at least not up close. Anyway, right now
the radiation was providing us some cover and keeping
humans out of the city, so I'd leave it be.

While I was there, I checked my weapons stashes,
taking time to oil and re-wrap the swords and firearms
I'd hidden beneath the floorboards in the warehouse.
Then I grabbed a couple of incendiary grenades before
making sure the ammo containers were sealed up tight.

I had no need of them now, but I might later. It never hurt to be prepared, after all.

What I'd come here for was to find some sign that the Oak was still around here. According to my own timeline, the Oak had been in existence when the bombs fell, but this version of me hadn't bonded fully with the Oak and Grove yet. That would mean they'd been orphaned completely when the other me died. I wasn't completely sure of the implications of that particular series of events, but what I did know was that I could really use the Oak and Grove right about now. If I could find the Oak in this timeline and bond with it...

Just as that thought passed through my mind, I felt it again, a familiar presence that could only be one entity. It brushed against my consciousness with a feather-light touch, just for a moment, and then it was gone again.

It's the Oak—has to be. But why isn't it communicating if it knows I'm here?

That was a question for the ages, and one I'd toss around after I freed Luther. Right now, my chief concern was gathering willing allies and doing recon on the vamps in Dallas. Once I knew exactly what I was dealing with, then I'd enact a plan to free this timeline from vampire rule.

I skirted downtown Austin on my way north, if only to satisfy my curiosity. From what I could tell, ground zero was somewhere between the capital building and Camp Mabry, and everything was toast from the epicenter out to the river and parts beyond. A few buildings across the river south and west still stood, but if there was an intact window anywhere, I didn't see it.

As for Luther's cafe, it and all my old haunts were just... gone.

It was a sobering sight, especially considering that some other version of me got vaporized in the blast. I steered well around the radiation zone, jogging in a generally northern direction until I found what I was looking for—a motorcycle dealership.

The front of the store had been trashed, and the dead wandered all over the parking lot and in and out of the showroom. I avoided all that by jumping the back fence, where I killed a zomb wearing a mechanic's shirt with a name tag that said "Dave." Then, I broke into the shop through the dock entrance.

Bingo.

No one had touched anything back here because no one had time to do so. There were a dozen or more bikes in crates, all waiting to be assembled and placed on the showroom floor. I had my pick, and I went for a KLR 650, the classic dual-sport with enough speed to outrun a revenant, enough maneuverability to get through tight spaces, and enough off-road capability to go off the highway whenever necessary.

I spent a few hours assembling my find, foregoing the saddlebags and disconnecting all the lights, the horn, and instrumentation audibles. After filling the engine fluids, I siphoned some gas from another bike and dropped some fuel stabilizer in the tank, just in case.

The coup de grace involved etching glyphs and runes for a silence spell onto the crankcase and exhaust. Once that was done, it was quieter than an electric bike, and a hell of a lot easier to refuel.

One of these days, I need to figure out how to charge the batteries on an electric vehicle. But for now, this will do nicely.

Stuffing a couple bottles of fuel stabilizer and some extra bike batteries in my Bag, I cut open the chains on the back gate and took off up IH-35, heading north to Dallas.

It was normally a three-hour drive at highway speeds, and a straight shot from North Austin to the downtown area. Vamps loved fancy shit, and I knew where I'd stay if I had my choice of digs as a post-apoca-lyptic dictator. The area between historic downtown Dallas and Uptown was full of all that bougie crap, including some pretty decent museums, expensive restaurants, and hotels like the Ritz-Carlton. I'd bet my left nut that's where I'd find the primary, and whatever else waited for me in vampire central.

As for my trip, it was surprisingly uneventful, at least until I hit the outskirts of Dallas. The vamps had cleared the interstate from Waco north all the way into Dallas. I steered clear of major cities, which were certain to be

crawling with zombs, so it was mostly smooth sailing—
right until I heard the low rumble of a semi a few miles
south of Red Oak.

Only running vehicle I've seen or heard since starting this
trip. Weird enough to check it out.

I pulled off the road into the trees, relying on my
chameleon spell to keep me hidden. Keeping the bike's
engine running, I waited until the big rig came into
view, then I enhanced my eyesight with a cantrip to get a
good look. And, boy, was it an eyeful.

The thing looked like something out of a Mad Max
film, all armored up with spikes and blades coming off
the center hubs of the wheels and welded iron grates over
the windows. It had all been professionally done, as the
work was anything but haphazard. The armor looked like
it had been cannibalized from a military vehicle, because
much of it was composite and not metal. As for the grates,
the cuts were symmetrical and the welds were neat.

When I saw what it was hauling, though, that's when
things really got interesting. At first, I thought they were
delivering livestock or going to pick up a load, because
the metal, cage-like trailer behind the rig was the same
kind I'd seen used to haul hogs and cattle. Yet it didn't
smell like a pig farm, nor did it smell like cow shit. It
wasn't until the vehicle passed that I recognized what
was in the back.

Humans. They're hauling humans like cattle.

After waiting until the rig was a quarter mile down

the road, I pulled onto the highway, crossing the median to head south after them. Unfortunately, I hadn't gotten a good look at the driver and whoever else was in the cab. However, the way that the dead had dispersed as soon as the truck came within hearing range told me they had a powerful vamp on board, one who could control the dead.

Or a necromancer.

I ruled the second option out from the get-go, because if there was one thing vampires feared, it was a necromancer. A powerful necromancer could make second and third-generation vamps into virtual thralls, all with just a few rituals. Heck, even a run-of-the-mill practitioner could control a few dozen lesser undead. A while back in my own timeline, we'd had an undead outbreak that was clearly the work of a necromancer, and even Luther went into hiding until I ferreted out the culprit.

No, it was definitely a higher vampire, likely a master. Many of them could exert some mental control over the lesser undead, and a few had talents that allowed them to control greater numbers. It was my bet that they kept a master in the cab to scare away the dead with the vamp version of repulsion field, one that was keyed specifically for zombs and ghouls.

I definitely wanted to know more about this whole slaver thing the leeches had going on, and I could damned sure use some intel on Dallas before I snuck into the city. Plus, there was no way I was going to let what I'd seen pass. Uh-uh, not in a million years.

So, I trailed the tractor-trailer until it pulled into a highway rest area, just before dusk. After hiding my bike alongside the road in some undergrowth, I slipped through the trees that ran parallel to the highway, moving unseen until I was within hearing distance of the truck.

Let's see what the hell these fuckers are up to.

16

After stealth-shifting and casting a hearing enhancing cantrip, I was able to pick up some chatter from inside the cab. There were three male occupants, and they were discussing whether they should feed on one of the slaves in the trailer or roam out into the surrounding countryside for a meal. Since all three were engaged in the discussion, I figured they were all vamps.

The sun had not quite set, so I decided now was the best time to act. The question was whether or not the anti-dead zone would remain after I killed the lead vamp, and for how long. There were at least a dozen humans in the trailer, and if I freed them, they'd need a way to get to someplace safe. On the other hand, there were three vamps in the cab, and one of them was likely a master.

For all I knew, the leader was another Dauphine,

and hell if I wanted to take on a vamp like that at night
with limited magic. So, I rummaged around in my Bag
until I found what I was looking for, then I snuck up to
the passenger side of the truck. The side windows had
been removed to allow for replacement with armored
panels, but the view slot in the window armor was just
big enough for me to slip my payload through.

"You smell that?" one of the vampires said.

"Smell what?" another replied.

"Smells like magic."

"Ain't no more wizards," the third vamp chided.
"Y'all are just imagining shit."

While they argued, I pulled the pin on a white phosphorous grenade and slipped it through the slot.

"What the fuck?"

Then, *pop-hiss*! The "Willy Pete" grenade detonated,
filling the cab of the vehicle with burning phosphorous
and tons of white smoke. It was a horrifying weapon to
use against humans, but incredibly effective against
vamps, who were quite susceptible to fire.

The cacophony of screams and howls from inside
told me that I'd caught all three of them in the blast. As I
backed away, the passenger door opened and a burning
figure zipped away into the twilight, almost faster than
the eye could see and screaming his bloody head off.
That would be the leader, and it remained to be seen if
he'd survive those wounds or not.

The other two vamps were still screaming in the cab,
although their screams had faded away to faint squeals

and moans, which told me they were on their last legs. I let them suffer, pulling a Halligan bar from my Bag as I walked to the back of the trailer. I busted the lock off the door with the pry tool, then I swung it wide, smiling at the huddled, confused people within.

"You're free, and you'll want to be coming out of there in a hurry. It's hard to get a diesel fuel tank to explode, but it can happen. I'd say we have about, oh, three minutes before that burning phosphorous reaches one of the tanks."

"You just killed us all, mister," a thin, thirty-ish woman with dirty blonde hair and a pallid complexion said.

"Not if you get out of there in a hurry. Let's go, before that other vamp decides to come back and feed on one of you so it can heal."

She shook her head, cowering inside the cattle cage with the rest of the captives. "He's the least of your concerns. When the coven in Waco figures out that we didn't make it, they'll send a group to come find us. And if they think we helped you, they'll kill every last one of us."

The other captives nodded and muttered in agreement, while I stood there dumbfounded. "Yeah, but you're free. You can escape, go somewhere else, and live without worrying if you're going to be the next meal for a vamp."

"Go where?" a forty-something man with a slight paunch said. "Whole state's full of zombies, and anywhere outside the Vampyri outposts is a no man's land. Those ugly ones are out there, too, and they're worse than the ones that look like us. At least they'll let you live, if you don't fight and show you're useful."

The flames were getting hotter, but still the people weren't budging. "And just what was supposed to happen to you, once you got to Waco?"

"We were going to be cattle and servants for the master and his coven," the first woman said. "It might sound bad, but it beats being alone out there. Hell, I know—I lived in the badlands for two months before I gave up and surrendered to the vamps in Dallas."

"Whoa, whoa, whoa," I said, waving my hands back and forth. "You went there *willingly*?"

"Sure. What's a person supposed to do, get eaten by zombies?" Potbelly replied. "Like I said, it's better in the Vampyri strongholds. You get fed, you get a warm place to sleep, and they have electricity and running water. Out here, you got nothing but sleepless nights and staying one step ahead of the undead. No thanks."

Un-fucking real.

"Well, I have some bad news for you. You can't stay in there, because you're going to die, and let me tell you, death by immolation sucks." I knew, because I had tried it once. "So, you're either going to file out in an orderly fashion, or I'm going to start tossing you out."

"Once that master is gone, the dead'll come," the dirty blonde said. "We're better off dying in here."

The others agreed with her, nodding and mumbling

in support of her assessment. "Fine, then. We'll do this the hard way."

After I had tossed every last one of them out of the trailer, I herded them away from the flames, toward an RV that sat on flat tires a good distance away from the burning semi. These people might've been cowards, but they were right about one thing—the dead would be drawn to the light and noise. If I was going to keep them alive, I needed to do something, and fast.

"Alright, people, get inside the camper and get some sleep. I'll stay out here and take care of any zombies that wander near."

"You one of those other things?" the dirty blonde asked while the others filed into the RV.

"Meaning?"

"You know, those werewolf things. We seen some, and they was eating people. Then some vamps came, and they fought." She paused with a resigned expression on her face. "Are you going to eat us?"

"What? No, I'm not going to eat you. I was just trying to do a good deed, is all."

"Fat lot of good that'll do us," she said. "Been better off if you'd minded your own business. And you still didn't say you were human."

I resisted the urge to show a bit of my Hyde-side, just to get her to move her ass. Instead, I counted to ten and held the door for her. "You'll be safe in here. Get some sleep."

"Yeah, until a mob of zombies or one of those ugly vamps comes by," she remarked as she entered the camper.

I shut the door behind her, taking a moment to holler at the idiots within before I set about securing the area. "And lock the damned door. It'll keep zombs from opening it by accident."

"We ain't stupid, mister," someone replied.

"Could've fooled me," I muttered as I began to ward cars and light posts in a roughly ten-yard perimeter around the camper.

Once the ward barrier was done, I set about finding food and water. The vending machines had already been ransacked, and the only other RV had nothing but a pack of spearmint gum and a half-eaten Clif bar that had petrified months ago. I hiked a mile down the highway before I found a van with a case of bottled water and a cardboard box full of canned food in the back.

When I returned with the supplies, I had to knock on the door to get the former captives to let me in. "For gosh sakes, I just rescued you. You can see it's me out here."

"No, we can't. It's dark."

Son of a—

"Well, it's me, so open up. I have food and water."

"Alright." *Click.*

The RV smelled like the inside of a longshoreman's boot after a double-shift at the docks, and the people inside looked worse than they smelled. I set the food on the counter, then I started handing out water bottles. Nobody said a word. They just took the bottles and passed them down.

Potbelly looked in the box and frowned. "Canned food. I bet the propane tanks on this thing are empty. How are we going to heat it up? And did you bring a can opener?"

"For cripes' sakes, look around. There's bound to be one in here somewhere," I snapped. The guy had the gall to give me a wounded look, so I rummaged through a few drawers 'til I found a can opener and some silverware. "Alright, why don't you start telling me your stories?"

"Whadya mean?" the dirty blonde asked.

"Like, how did you end up in Dallas? What's it like up there? How many vampires live in the city? What are the boundaries? Do they have defenses set up—walls, fences, gates, checkpoints, and the like? Who's in charge? That sort of thing."

Potbelly shook his head as he opened a can of beans and passed it along. "That's an awful lot of questions. You plan on attacking them or something? If you are, you may as well put a bullet in your head now."

This is getting old.

"Vampires don't scare me."

A younger guy spoke up from where he sat on bunk

near the back of the RV. I had marked him earlier because he walked with a pronounced limp, and he was missing a few digits on each hand. "You're a hunter, right?"

"Depends on what kind of hunter you're talking about."

He scoffed. "Yeah, you know what kind I mean. I was too, before all this shit happened. Worked out of Fort Worth, mostly hunting rogue vamps and fae. Killed a lot of zombies at first, saved some lives. Then I thought I'd be a hero when the vamps started taking over." He held up his hands, and I realized he was missing the index fingers on both his hands. "They did this to me and sliced my Achilles. Said I was lucky I was healthy, because it was the only reason they let me live. Yeah, right."

"I'm sorry." It was the only thing I could think to say.

The look he gave me could've frozen lava. "I don't need your sympathy, mister. All I'm saying is what everyone else has already told you. You got no chance against them, none. The vamps they got up there make the ones we used to hunt look like pussy cats. And their leaders?" He shook his head. "They're like gods."

"Gods don't scare me, either."

"Maybe you oughta start being scared," he said. "Cause if you go against them, you're signing your own death warrant."

The guy clammed up then, laying back on the bed with his maimed hands interlocked behind his head. He stared up at the bunk above him, and I was pretty sure tears were running down his face.

"Okay, then. I guess Q&A time is over." I scanned every face for a smile, the will to live, something. What I saw was a lot of despair and people who'd already given up. "If anyone wants to leave, tell me now."

Silence, then the dirty blonde spoke. "We're going to wait for the coven in Waco to come get us. If we're lucky, they'll let some of us live. You go on now, mister, and the next time you see a slave truck pass, you leave it be. Folks don't need your kind of help in these times."

No amount of argument could convince the slaves they were better off being free of the vampires' control. I spent forty-five minutes trying to persuade them to come with me, or failing that, to get the RV running so they could drive away during the relative safety of the daylight hours. Eventually, I gave up and left them in the middle of the night.

On one hand I was disgusted by their cowardice, but on the other hand I couldn't really blame them. The strongest of the group was the former hunter, and he stood as a testament to what happened when humans defied their vampire overlords. It sucked, but that's the way it was in the Hellpocalypse, and it would stay that way until I did something to change it.

The one positive that came of my chance encounter

with the slaves was the acquisition of intelligence on the vamps in Dallas. Although none of the others were willing to talk, I eventually got the hunter, Dane, away from the group. Once we were alone, I plied him for information on what I could expect when I got there.

Dane said that the city looked and operated much as it had before the bombs fell, except for a few key differences. For one, he said I could expect heavy security, both in the form of human patrols during the day and vamps at night.

The daytime patrols were made up of Renfields, human sympathizers, and ass-lickers who had either been in league with the leeches before things went to shit or who got in line quickly once they realized the vamps were in control. Those with previous experience in the military and law enforcement were recruited for the vamp's human security force. Dane said they dressed and operated much as local police agencies had before the apocalypse, wearing similar uniforms and patrolling in police vehicles that had been appropriated for that express purpose.

Every human in the city had assigned roles, and everyone had to have their vamp-issued ID on them at all times. The security forces were familiar with the neighborhoods they patrolled, and would stop anyone they didn't recognize, questioning them to determine if they belonged.

At night, vampire enforcers patrolled the city, looking for humans who were out past curfew, and for resistance fighters who occasionally caused trouble for the Vampyri governor, Alan Garr. If they caught a human out after dark, they took them to one of the local security stations for "questioning." Rarely did anyone return after being taken by the Vampyri enforcers.

Based on what Dane told me, Garr and all the high-ranking vamps occupied the former Ritz-Carlton downtown. The former hunter said Garr's coven preferred to cluster together, both for the company and because of safety in numbers. I saw that as a tactical error, but I didn't mention it during our discussion.

Interestingly, Dane also said the Ritz was rumored to be where they kept vampire defectors and human political prisoners. Whenever they caught a leader in the resistance, they were taken there for questioning. Once these prisoners were determined to be of no use, they were sent to a converted football stadium to fight for the amusement of the vampires and their Renfields. Sometimes they would have to fight lesser undead, other times they'd be forced to fight each other. As for the defectors among their own kind, they were slowly starved to death.

It was all exceptionally weird and incredibly brutal, and exactly what I would expect of the Vampyri. Although I'd mostly only interfaced with Luther's coven, who were much more civilized than other covens, I had plenty of experience dealing with rogue vampires. I'd also dealt with the New Orleans coven, who were as bloodthirsty as any group of vamps you'd find before they took over. Vampires were generally cruel, callous creatures who saw humans as nothing more than livestock and prey. And while they often hid among us, they shunned human company except when it came time to feed.

Luther was the exception to the rule, and that was one of the reasons why I was determined to free him. He'd also be a valuable source of information on the Vampyri, and possibly an ally in my fight against them. Besides, he was my friend. No way was I leaving him to starve to death in that tower.

The only question was how I was going to sneak all the way into the heart of Dallas, avoiding human patrols and Vampyri enforcers, and then break into a high-rise that was full of powerful vampires and at least one primary.

Very carefully. Very, very carefully.

17

Getting into Dallas wasn't a problem, as there were no walls, roadblocks, or even check points to stop me. I'd cast the strongest obfuscation spell I knew on myself and the bike, the one Mom had taught me when I was running from Badb and Fuamnach. That spell had been enough to fool a goddess, but it took a lot out of me to cast it, and I'd need time to recover before I went after Luther. That would mean finding a place to hide out near my destination to rest, but I'd worry about that later. Right now, the absolute weirdness of what I was seeing had my full attention.

I had left IH-35 east as soon as I started seeing patrol cars cruising around the city, just north of Interstate 20. From there, I headed west and took Polk, then Tyler all the way north to the Trinity River, cutting through a slew of residential districts along the way. Everywhere I looked, I was absolutely dumbfounded by how *normal* things appeared. There were vehicles driving on the streets, albeit not as many as before, but people were using them to get from place to place. Restaurants and corner stores were open, with customers coming in and out, chatting with each other and going about their business as if the apocalypse didn't exist right outside their city limits.

Yet, it was all just a bit *off* somehow. The people I saw looked skittish and haggard, even though they were much cleaner and better dressed than anyone I'd seen since the bombs fell. And folks didn't walk where they were going, they scurried, heads lowered and eyes downcast all the while.

But the most blatant difference between pre-apocalypse Dallas and the version I was witnessing were the blood "donation" centers that sat on almost every street corner. At each one, people were lined up around the block, waiting to give for the cause. Most of them were pale and anemic, an obvious effect of all the "volunteer" blood donations they were being subjected to—likely on a much more frequent basis than the Red Cross recommended.

I bet they have a ration ticket system set up. Every family has to donate so many pints a week to get their rations for the following week. And if you don't show up to donate, you get a knock on your door from the Stasi, stopping by with a friendly reminder to "do your part." Geez.

Another sight that surprised me were the working traffic lights, verifying rumors that the entire city had electricity—or at least the parts the vamps occupied. I could only assume they were running the city on nuclear, because I couldn't imagine they could keep the natural gas plants going out in North and East Texas, even with the influence the Vampyri wielded over the dead. They were probably just barely keeping enough wells and refineries open to provide gas for those who merited those rations.

As I'd been warned, the "police" were a constant presence, wearing neat blue uniforms and driving black and white patrol vehicles. Every so often, I'd see them stopping someone at random, just to ask them for their papers and to find out where they were going. Everywhere I looked, catchy slogans on billboards and signs encouraged "citizens" to do their part:

SEE SOMETHING, SAY SOMETHING. REPORT DISSENT.

WORK. GIVE. SERVE. THE COUNCIL REWARDS OBEDIENCE.

And my personal favorite:

GIVE BLOOD. THE LIFE YOU SAVE MIGHT BE YOUR OWN.

Obviously, the vamps had taken a lesson from history, because this whole damned set up had "fascist playbook" written all over it. It all had a Cold War-era East Berlin feel about it, giving the impression that the "State" was constantly watching everyone to make sure they stayed in their lane and did as they were told. As I silently observed the many ways that the vamps were using fear to control the populace, I wondered how many of the ruling Vampyri in the city had been involved in the rise of fascist regimes in the past.

Weird. Nothing is keeping these people here but their own fear. Ben Franklin was right when he said people who would give up liberty for temporary safety deserved neither.

Once I got over the revulsion I felt at all the sickly, fearful faces I saw, I thought of Dane, the hunter I'd "rescued" from the slave truck. How many dissenters had the vamps tortured, mutilated, or killed to drive home the point that resistance was futile? These people had no reason to think they could fight back, and the majority of them lacked the skills to survive in the Hellpocalypse. I understood why they'd chosen to live in invisible chains, but I didn't have to agree with their decision.

The question is, what the hell are these people going to do once I free them from the vamps? Most of them are probably like the slaves I rescued last night—they don't even want to be saved. Should I even free people who don't actually want to be free?

I wasn't sure of the answer to that question. All I knew was that my friend was dying in a cell in the basement of the Ritz-Carlton, and I was going to get him out. Continuing north until I hit the river, I took the riverside trail all the way to the Design District, which took me within walking distance of the International Center and State Thomas districts. The Ritz sat smack in the middle of those two neighborhoods, right on the edge of Uptown, and that's where I was headed.

It didn't take long to find a place to hide out, considering how most of the businesses in the Design District were out of business. After hiding the bike in an alley between two warehouses, I broke into the most neglected looking of the two using magic to avoid leaving evidence. Once inside, I cleared the building to ensure there were no zombies inside—or worse, down-on-their-luck vamps—then I found a place to sleep until nighttime fell over the city.

It might have seemed counterintuitive to attempt a breakout at night when the vampires would be most active, but the fewer vamps who were in that tower when I went in, the better. If there were two things vampires loved to do, it was drinking blood and partying. And if I was right, most of them would be out and about, meeting up with other vamps and high-ranking Renfields at the restaurants and night clubs that were scattered all over the Uptown and Downtown districts.

The primary challenge I faced in getting around Dallas at night was avoiding the attention of all the vamps. Younger ones weren't an issue, because they lacked the sensory advantages of their older kin. No, the older ones were the real problem, because they had noses like bloodhounds, and many of them possessed a rudimentary ability to sense heat. Never mind that they could hear a human heartbeat from a block away.

To go completely incognito, I'd either have to pose as a Renfield—one who actually had business being out at night—or I'd need to conceal myself perfectly using magic. The truth was, magic was more reliable and predictable. But if I spent my innate magical reserves on casting concealment spells, I'd be shit out of luck if I had to fight my way out of the Ritz.

Besides that, some vamps could "smell" magic. I doubted they actually picked up a scent per se, but the older ones could sense the presence of magic when in close proximity to an active spell. For that reason, I chose to do things the hard way, and the best possible disguise I could think of was posing as a member of their "police" force.

Finding a mark wasn't hard. All I had to do was drop my concealment spells and wait in a conspicuous place where a patrol unit would find me. After all, I stood out like a sore thumb because I looked like I'd just been through hell, which I had.

But before I triggered my trap, I had to deal with a few problems. The first was taking out the cops without killing them. For all I knew, the vamps were forcing these cops to work for them, and I figured they likely had families as well. As much as I despised them for turning traitor, I didn't want to deal with the guilt that would follow killing a couple of cops, no matter who they worked for or why.

And my second problem was hiding them where no one would find them, at least not until after I'd retrieved Luther and GTFO'd. Once they failed to check in, their fellow officers would come looking for them, and a Vampyri enforcer would be sure to follow once night fell. If they were found, there'd be an all-points bulletin issued for anyone matching my description, and it would make it that much harder for Luther and me to escape.

Which led me to my third problem, that of being identified. As soon as the cops started chasing me, they'd call it in to dispatch. So, I needed to make sure that they couldn't reach their HQ on their radios.

It would only take a small amount of magic to jam the signal. Just to be safe, I put on a ball cap and sunglasses, and I tied a bandanna over my face. Hopefully that would keep them from providing a matching description, should my spell fail.

Now, it was time to get my disguise. I chose a spot in the Design District, where the alleys were too narrow for a patrol car to enter, which would force them to chase me on foot. A few minutes after I dropped my concealment spells, a passing patrol car flashed its lights and pulled into the warehouse parking lot. As for me, I ran into a nearby alley and waited to spring the trap, listening in as they reported their status to their dispatch center.

"Dispatch, this is unit twenty-three. We are on foot in pursuit of a suspect wearing an Astros baseball cap and a black trench coat. Suspect is roughly six feet tall, and concealing his face with a bandanna, over." After a few seconds of static, the officer tried again. "Dispatch, this is unit twenty-three. Do you copy?"

"Maybe they're on break or tied up with another call," his partner suggested.

"Nah, we'd have heard it. Probably another power surge at HQ. Fucking vamps can't get anything right when it comes to technology."

"Shit, Dominguez—keep it down, will you? I have a family to feed, and the last thing I need is to get shit-canned and sent to run security at one of the blood processing centers."

"Don't get your panties in a wad. There aren't any of them around—too early."

"That's what you think. Those old ones stay up all day sometimes. Mostly indoors, but still..."

I got tired of listening to their chatter, so I tossed a rock at a nearby wall.

"You hear that?"

"How could I not, shit for brains?"

"Fuck you, Riley. I don't like this." I heard the sound of blued metal clearing leather. "If that fucker pops out at us, I'm capping his ass."

"You keep wasting blood bags, you'll never get that promotion."

"Yeah, but—"

Dominguez never got the chance to finish his sentence. When the two turncoats stepped between the runes I'd drawn on either wall of the alley, the wards lit up like Christmas, hitting each of them with 50,000 volts. For their sakes, I'd designed the spell to act just like a stun gun, dialing the amperage way down to ensure I didn't kill them. It'd still hurt like hell, though. *Good.*

As soon as I heard them fall to the deck, I leapt into action. The ward was set to release another shock every minute or so until I turned it off, so Dominguez and Riley wouldn't get up any time soon. First, I drove their patrol car through a bay door on the side of the building, pulling it in as far as I could and dropping a look away, go away spell on it. It cost me less magic to cast than a chameleon spell, although it wasn't nearly as effective, so I threw a tarp over it, just in case.

Next, I carried the patrolmen into the warehouse, hauling them up to the offices on the second floor. There I stripped them of their uniforms, using Riley's t-shirt to make gags for each officer and tying them hand and foot with the flex cuffs they carried on their duty belts. I drained them of a pint of blood each, using blood donation kits that I'd placed in my Bag back in my own timeline. Then, I tossed Dominguez and Riley in a supply closet, hoping they wouldn't be found before I freed Luther.

The officers both carried Glock pistols, so I switched Riley's sidearm and spare mags out for my own, which were loaded with silver. Hopefully, no vamps would get close enough to smell it on me, as that would make for an awkward conversation. I also took Dominguez's hold out, a snub-nosed .38 that he wore in an ankle holster, stuffing the hollow point with silver beads that I had in my Bag. It wasn't as good as a silver-core JHP, but it'd do in a pinch.

Dominguez's uniform and all my gear and clothes went inside my Craneskin Bag, then I put on Riley's uniform since he was close to my size. After I'd donned my disguise, I emptied a small lunch cooler I'd found inside the warehouse, stuffing my Craneskin Bag in the bottom. Using druid magic, I created a block of dry ice, laying it atop the Bag, covered with a towel. Then, I threw the blood bags on top. Now I had an excuse to be in the Ritz, in case anyone stopped me.

So long as hotel security doesn't know Officer Riley, I'm golden. Time to get Luther.

The Ritz had been the only Forbes five-star hotel in Texas before the apocalypse, and it was still about as opulent as a hotel could get. Marble floors, coffered ceilings, crystal chandeliers, and gold leaf everywhere. However, I didn't go in through the front door. Instead, I drove the patrol car around to the loading dock, dropping the look away spell just before I turned the corner into the rear drive.

According to Dane, all the highest-ranking vamps lived in the very upscale townhomes next door to the hotel or in sub-penthouse suites. Their subordinates lived in the condo tower or in the middle floors of the hotel itself, with lesser vampires occupying the lowest floors. As for the governor, he lived in the penthouse of the hotel, taking the entire floor for himself and the bevy of thralls who sated his every urge and hunger.

In other words, it was a building full of mature and master vampires, with at least one primary in attendance. I showed up just before dusk, so if I was lucky, at least half of the bastards would be busy waking up and getting ready for a night on the town, drinking bloody Bloody Marys and fucking with their human thralls. Also, it was the right time for a shift change, when the human security would switch out with their vampire counterparts. Hopefully, I could sneak in during all the confusion.

As for where the prisoners were kept, they were supposed to be on the lowest subfloor of the hotel, a storage level that had been converted into a jail of sorts. Dane said it was rumored to be a real charnel house, a vampire's BDSM dream. There they could torture human political prisoners to their cold dead hearts' content, without worrying about spooking the human "citizens" too much with the screams of their victims.

My plan was to go in through the back, heading downstairs using the maintenance elevator. Once I was on the prison level, I'd bluff my way to Luther's cell, then cut loose on whatever vamps were guarding him. After I fed Luther, I'd have him *bamf* us the fuck out of there. Or, if he was too weak, I'd have him don the other police uniform and we'd walk out the back.

Easy peasy.

I got into the hotel without a hitch. When the door security saw a uniform carrying a cooler, all I had to do was show them the blood inside and they waved me on. Interestingly, these cats were much more heavily armed than the cops I'd seen on patrol. They wore body armor, earpieces, and they carried AR-15s and Tavor X95s. Full auto capable too—kind of gave me a woody seeing them, and I made a note to snag one if given the opportunity.

There was a freight elevator just off the dock, but the buttons inside told me it didn't go all the way down to hell. I navigated the labyrinthine halls beyond on instinct and, after getting lost a few times, I finally made my way to my immediate destination. Two human guards stood post at the elevator, both similarly armed as the door guards and a hell of a lot more intimidating.

Just my luck. These guys look like pros.

"Hang on," one of them said. He was a tall, Viking-looking guy with a beard and tats covering both arms. "What's a uni doing heading downstairs?"

"Hell if I know," I said, opening the cooler and showing them the contents. "The duty sergeant told me to deliver two pints to the jail at the tower, and that's what I'm doing."

He kept his eyes on me, while his partner glanced

inside the cooler before scanning the hallway behind me. "Nobody told us jack about this. Graves, call it in."

Shit.

I leapt into action before the guy could activate his earpiece, attacking with Fomorian speed and strength. In the same motion I bounced Graves' head off the wall with a vicious jab and struck the Viking guy in the throat with a nasty web-hand strike. Both guards went down without so much as a whimper. Now, I had to deal with the bodies.

"Fuck it," I said, forcing the elevator doors open.

The cab was a couple of floors above, so I shoved both bodies over the side and slid the doors closed once more. I slung one of their Tavors over my shoulder, stashing the other one behind a trashcan, then I hit the call button. When the doors opened again the elevator was empty, so I stepped inside and hit the button that said "SB3."

Hang on, Luther—I'm on my way.

The ride down to Sub-level 3 seemed to take forever, and by the time I heard the floor bell ding, I was wound up tighter than a two-dollar pocket watch. As the doors slid open with a mechanical whoosh, I stood on the balls of my feet, ready to pounce on whoever or whatever might be waiting on the other side. When I saw the hall was empty, I breathed a quiet sigh of relief before exiting.

The floor was industrial and sparse, with no decorations to speak of besides the smeared bloodstains that ran up and down the hall. The floors were clear-coated concrete, but they hadn't been mopped since ever, and the place stank of spoiled blood and human waste. Thick black arrows had been painted on the white cinderblock walls, pointing left and right to "Storage" and "Mechanical." Someone with a twisted sense of humor had crossed out both words, finger-painting "HELL" and "PERDITION" below each in bloody, smeared strokes.

Heartwarming.

I heard human screams to my left and nothing to my right, so I took a chance and headed toward the silent end of the hall. I followed the hallway around a corner, after which it was sheer darkness. It seemed that since this side of the hall contained nothing but vampires, only other vampires attended to their needs, if at all. Thus, no light was needed.

I doubted they got many visitors, considering how long-lived vamps were and how long it took to starve one to death. The isolation was likely part of the torture process because vampires were surprisingly social creatures. They craved the company of their own kind—that is, so long as those interactions happened in the proper social order. "Families" were made of bloodlines first, coven second, and everyone knew the pecking order.

It wasn't much different than pack life, actually, except that vampires held their positions by force. In the packs, dominance prevented most challenges to the hierarchy. In the covens, it was fear.

I didn't need much light to see by, but I did need some, so I pulled a small LED flashlight from Riley's duty belt, covering most of the lens with my fingers. If I had to drop the flashlight to fight, it might be to my benefit to maintain my own sight while blinding an attacker.

Soon, I came to the cells, marked by the smell of death and decay that comes from the physical deterioration of a blood-starved vamp. First, they became weak and even more pale, then they grew lethargic as their muscles and connective tissues began to harden and dry and their brain activity became ever more basic and feral. Finally, their skin and flesh became desiccated, eventually dry-rotting and falling off the bone until only their crumbling internal organs remained.

I'd been told that very old vampires wouldn't rot away, but instead they became petrified in a sort of hibernating state. I had no firsthand experience with such a creature, but I had no reason to doubt what Finnegas and Maureen had taught me about vampire physiology, either. Their lessons had saved my tail countless times over the years, and now, the one fact that stood out most about starved vampires was that they'd do anything to feed.

Chances are good that Luther won't recognize me. Gotta keep that in mind.

I was more worried about being found out than

being attacked by my friend, but time was ticking away. Each cell door had a window and a meal slot, and I checked every one as I passed. Most were empty, while a few contained barely moving corpses that seemed to be on the brink of death. Those who still had some life in them whispered as I passed.

"Blooood…"

"Feeed meee, please."

"Just… one… sip…"

I ignored their pleas. Sure, I might recruit some allies to my cause down here, but I'd be first on the menu once I opened those doors. And I didn't have near enough blood for Luther, much less the lot of them.

As the minutes ticked by and the chance of someone investigating the missing guards grew, I began to think Luther wasn't down here. I'd checked nearly every door, and I was almost at the end of the hall.

One door left.

I peered through the cell window, hoping against hope that my friend was inside. At first it looked empty, then I saw a dark, emaciated form hunched up against the far wall. It was pitch black inside the cell, so I risked shining the light through the window to see inside. As the light reflected off the back wall, it illuminated an ashen figure laying in a layer of filth on the floor beneath.

The sudden change inside the cell must've activated some feral stimulus deep inside the occupant's brain, because its head popped up with uncanny speed. The thing's eyes fixated on the window, and it bared its teeth with an evil hiss. Then it leapt at the door, ramming the plexiglass face first, as if to bite me through the pane.

I leapt back involuntarily, both due to the sudden ferocity of the attack, and because I recognized the face on the other side of the window—if only barely. His features had morphed into something that was a combination of bestial and human, and his skin was so thin and drawn as to look painted on his skull.

But it was him. I'd found Luther.

18

As Luther clawed and bit at the plexiglass, anti-magic runes flared up on the outside surface. He was probably too weak to teleport right now, but mere contact with the wards triggered their magic, making it that much more difficult for him to escape. Apparently, the Vampyri Nation knew how to prevent their kind from escaping captivity, no matter their specific talents. It made sense, after all.

Suddenly, a man's voice startled me from my reverie. "It's amazing how a few weeks or months of hunger can reduce one of our kind to this, isn't it?"

The soothing, mildly accented voice came from the darkness at the very end of the hall. I dropped the light and drew my Glock, aiming it at the short, lean figure emerging from a cloud of gloom the reflected light could not seem to penetrate. As he stepped fully into view, darkness ran off him in rivulets like water droplets, falling to the floor in puddles that gathered around his feet.

He was not a tall man, maybe five-foot-six or so, with a lean build, swarthy skin, and short, neatly trimmed black hair, with just a hint of grey around his temples. His nose was prominent and hawk-like, but strangely complementary to his high cheek bones and square, masculine jawline. The vampire moved with an effortless, predatory grace, like a lion stalking a gazelle through tall grass on the savannah. Every nerve ending in my body told me he was an apex predator, and despite his easy smile and casual demeanor, my first instinct was to blast him with sunlight and get the hell out of Dodge as fast as my feet could take me.

But I couldn't do that, not without harming Luther. He was still slavering and biting at the plexiglass, gouging long scratches in it with his teeth in an attempt to get at the meal standing on the other side. In his current, weakened state, I doubted he could survive a direct blast from my sunlight spell. So, I'd have to bide my time until I figured out a way to deal with this new threat.

"I take it you're the big cheese around here," I said, keeping the muzzle of my pistol pointed at his center mass. "Strange, I can't seem to place your accent. Is it Egyptian?"

"Older, actually. Governor Alan Garr, at your

service," he said, taking a perfunctory bow. "We've met before, you know. More than once, in fact. Indeed, I've been keeping an eye on you for some time now."

"Ah, you're Clarence's maker. Sadly, he didn't make it."

The vampire gave the slightest hitch of his shoulder. "He was expendable." He turned his eyes to the cell door window. "But Luther here is another matter."

"You made Luther?"

"Indeed, many lifetimes ago by your mortal conception of time, although it seems like it was just yesterday. Of all my children, he remains among my favorites."

"Which is why you're starving him to death in your dungeon," I said, rolling my eyes. "Ought to at least get you an honorable mention for father of the year."

"He was always headstrong, and a bit too softhearted when it came to his thralls. I am merely reintroducing him to his more bestial nature. The hunger brings out the Vampyri while suppressing whatever mortal tendencies remain. A few more months of this, and he'll come around."

"See, that's where you're wrong," I said. "He's coming with me."

"Oh?" Alan replied as an amused smile played at the corner of his lips. "And what makes you think you're leaving, druid?"

This.

I snapped off three rounds, two at Garr and one at

the corner of the plexiglass window. Without bothering to see if I hit the vampire, I dropped the pistol and punched the window with every bit of Fomorian strength at my disposal, popping it out of the frame with enough force to snap Luther's head back.

Sorry, bro, I thought as I opened the cooler, slamming the open end against the window so that the bags of blood flew through to the other side. Holding the cooler over the opening, I raised my hand and triggered my sunlight spell.

"*Solas!*"

The narrow hallway lit up like high noon as I released all the solar energy I'd stored. Squinting so I could protect my eyes from being completely blinded by the light, I scanned the hall where the ancient vampire had stood seconds before. Everything before me was illuminated by the spell, except for a mass of darkness in the center of the corridor that seemed to repel the light completely.

Shit.

As the spell petered off, the cloud of darkness dissipated, revealing a very unharmed Alan Garr standing with his hands clasped in front of his waist. Not a single hair on his head was singed, not a thread of clothing out of place. In fact, he looked as fresh as he had just moments before.

"Impressive," he said, sparing a glance at the open window in the cell door. "Now, that is unfortunate. It'll take weeks to get him back to a state of emaciation again."

"Well, shit. I guess we're doing this the hard way, then."

Alan Garr smiled, and as he did, his canines extended an extra inch from his gum line. "If you insist."

Going into this fight, I had three problems. First, my magical weapons were in my Bag, at the bottom of the cooler. Second, I couldn't shift into my full Fomorian form, because there simply wasn't enough room in this hallway for a ten-foot giant to move. And third, I had no idea what I was dealing with when it came to Garr's powers. Sure, I knew he'd be fast and strong, but other than that, his abilities were a toss-up.

Rather than wait to see what he could do, I went on the offensive, exploding forward with Fomorian speed with a strong right cross aimed at his jaw. Before the strike even connected, he disappeared in a cloud of black smoke, causing me to stumble as the blow hit empty space. I recovered and spun around to find him standing several feet behind me, hands clasped behind his back.

"You're quite fast for a human—which tells me you're not entirely human, of course—but you'll have to do better than that if you're going to be more than a nuisance."

It was obvious that I wasn't going to hit him with the direct approach, so I switched tactics. I bellowed like an angry ape and charged him at full speed, leading with an obvious punch that was meant to be a feint. As I stepped into the punch, I pushed off the floor with my front foot to move in the opposite direction as I launched a side kick at the space behind me.

My foot seemed to connect with something, but it felt like kicking water, because whatever I connected with gave and then dissipated away. I managed to turn my head in time to see whether I'd hit him, but all I saw was a puff of black mist that evaporated completely, even as I recovered from the attack.

"That was much better," Garr said behind me. "But not good enough. Let's hope that the third time is a charm, for your sake."

Now you're really pissing me off.

With a roar of frustration, I snapped off a lightning spell from each hand, filling the hallway with 100,000 volts of arcing, popping electricity. Again, the vampire's form dissolved in a puff of inky blackness that my spell passed through harmlessly, only to detonate as it struck the end of the hall some fifty feet away.

This is getting me nowhere. Time to pull out the stops.

I slowed my breathing, calming and centering myself as I opened my mind to the Twisted Paths. All I needed to do was anticipate where Garr would appear after my next few attacks. If I could catch him as he materialized, I could hit him with a spell or a strike, and hopefully stun him enough to finish him or get Luther and me the hell out of here.

Time slowed down around me as I mentally flipped through the various branches of time that represented all the possible permutations of action that could occur over the next few seconds. As I reviewed the many possibilities, I focused on those that followed a similar, reoccurring pattern, identifying that short sequence of events as the most likely response that Garr would make to my next attack.

Then, I fired another lightning spell at him with one hand, immediately following it up with another spell directed where he was most likely to appear next. As the first spell reached him, he faded away into smoke, reappearing in the hall to my left, just as the second spell arced through that spot. When the vampire materialized, the lightning bolt struck him in the chest, detonating with a resounding thunderclap that blasted the vampire off his feet and down the hall a good twenty feet.

Rather than give him time to recover, I blasted him again and again, each time tossing him further down the corridor like a rag doll. I must've hit him a half-dozen times before my internal magic reserves began to peter out, leaving me gasping for breath while Garr lay in a smoldering heap near the terminus of the hallway.

Standing with my hands on my knees as I caught my breath, I watched the vampire's lifeless corpse for several seconds, just to make sure he wasn't moving. Then, I turned around and headed back up the hall to get Dyrnwyn from my Bag so I could finish him off before he recovered. I'd almost reached the cooler where it sat on the floor in front of Luther's cell when the vamp grabbed me from behind and slammed me against the cinderblock wall of the corridor.

Garr held me off the floor, his claw-like nails digging deep furrows in my chest as I struggled against his vice-like grip. His clothes and skin were a smoking, charred mess, with the left side of his face having been burned down to the bone. But as I watched, the flesh grew in and reformed, filling the void space that had been obliterated by my magic. Soon, his cheek and orbit were whole and complete once more.

"Color me surprised—you actually managed to injure me, something I've not experienced in over a millennium," he said as his eyes narrowed dangerously. "But now, it's my turn."

Garr's fingers were starting to hit bone, so I kicked him off me with both feet, sending him flying across the hall. Before he hit the opposite wall, he vanished in a puff of mist, reappearing on my left even as my feet hit the ground. I barely had time to raise my hands in a guard before he hit me with a jackhammer right across the jaw, so fast I barely registered it coming, even with my enhanced Fomorian senses.

The blow sent me reeling, and as I staggered, he appeared again to my right, striking me on the other side of my face with another right cross, and then again with a vicious left hook to the liver. I attempted to return the favor with every bit of speed I could muster, but he dissolved into mist before my strike reached him, only to materialize behind me.

From that advantageous position, he rained jackhammer blows on my head, ribs, and kidneys, striking me dozens of times in the span of perhaps a second. I felt and heard my ribs break, despite my much denser and more durable Fomorian skeleton. Even worse, based on the explosion of pain in my right lower back, I was pretty sure he'd burst one of my kidneys as well.

Knowing I needed to prevent him from flanking me again, I backed up to the wall, bringing my hands up to guard my head and keeping my elbows close to protect my ribs and organs. Meanwhile Garr kept up his onslaught, disappearing and reappearing at will to my right, left, and in front of me at seemingly random intervals, each time landing savagely powerful strikes and punches anywhere and everywhere that wasn't covered with my hands and arms.

At first, I tried to return the attacks, but it only made things worse as I got hit every time I left myself open. Finally, I just shelled up the best I could, covering my head to hopefully diminish the damage as I tried to think of some way to counter Garr's relentless onslaught.

All the while, Garr beat me like a drum, shattering my ribs until the broken ends grated together in multiple places. My insides felt like they'd been turned to mush, and the accompanying pain and nausea became nearly overwhelming. Even worse, I was pretty sure he'd punctured a lung, because I was finding it difficult to breathe.

My thoughts became sluggish and jumbled, both from shock and from the multiple concussions I sustained as the ancient vampire spread his strikes around, going upstairs and then downstairs to ensure I didn't recover. I tried my best to formulate a plan, come up with a spell, trigger my full Fomorian form—anything to defend myself against this seemingly unstoppable creature. But every time an idea formed, those fists of stone bounced my head around, muddling my thoughts and putting me in survival mode once more.

The beat down probably lasted no more than a minute, but when you're being beaten by a creature that can move faster than the human eye, a minute is a very long time. Eventually, I lost consciousness, and when I regained some semblance of awareness, I was lying in a bloody, semiconscious heap on the cold concrete subbasement floor.

My right eye was swollen shut, or possibly Garr had pulverized it completely, but I managed to crack my left eye open to look up at him. He stood upright and proud, covered in my blood and of course not the slightest bit winded, because vampires didn't need to breathe. The ancient vampire licked a fleck of blood from his knuckles, shivering with delight as he savored the taste.

"Mmm, delicious. I've not tasted titan blood in several millennia." He glanced down at me, watching as I struggled to push myself to a seated position on broken arms that refused to obey my commands. "You are full of surprises, druid. Obviously, I can't let you live, because where would I keep you that you couldn't break free? I suppose I'd better drain you, before all that delicious lifeblood flows out of your body on its own accord."

The vampire leaned over me, his jaw opening impossibly wide as his canines extended even further than they had previously. As his mouth loomed closer, I tried to summon magic to release a spell, but neither my fingers nor my mouth would obey, as they'd been shattered and broken along with the rest of me.

Sure, my Fomorian healing factor was trying to repair the damage, but I simply couldn't heal fast enough in this form to fix the massive injuries I'd sustained at Garr's hands. Even now, I could feel my internal organs shutting down as proteins flooded my bloodstream from the damaged tissues, while internal bleeding caused my blood pressure to drop precariously low.

For a moment I wondered if my Hyde-side would

take over and save me from the brink of death, now that I'd fully integrated it with my human side. I doubted it would because my human side was too dominant to allow it. And in my current state, there was no way I could muster the energy to transform on my own.

Whelp, I guess this is it. What a punk-ass way to die.

19

Garr was just about to sink his teeth into my neck when a shimmering black oval appeared in the hallway behind him. He paused and glanced back, just in time to see a flood of zombies, ghouls, and revenants come pouring through. The vampire hissed at them as if to warn them away from his prey, but strangely they barely slowed, rushing him while completely ignoring me.

The ancient vampire struck a ghoul in the face, ripping the thing's head clean off its shoulders. Meanwhile, a revenant jumped on his back, scratching and tearing at his shoulders, head, and neck with abandon. A trio of zombies grabbed at his arms and legs, but the vampire flung them away as if they were made of paper mâché. Meanwhile, dozens more undead flooded out of the portal toward the vampire.

"Necromancer," he hissed, sparing me a final

glance. "Next time, druid," he promised before dissolving into a black mist that dissipated into the darkness.

The dead looked about for several seconds after the powerful vampire disappeared, searching for some sign of where their target had gone. Then their eyes turned to me where I lay helpless on the floor. I was certain I was a goner, when a tall, dark-robed figure strode out of the portal. The newcomer raised his arm, pointing a long, slender finger down the hallway.

"Secure the corridor. Ensure that no reinforcements make it through."

Instantly, the undead heeded his commands, the faster of them loping down the hall with the much slower zombies trailing behind them. As they passed, they completely avoided and ignored me, much to my relief. I was a mess of open wounds, and all it would take was a single drop of putrefied flesh or saliva to infect me with the deader vyrus. That was the last thing I needed.

The stranger strolled toward me with certain, unhurried steps. His face was concealed beneath his hood, but I'd recognize that voice anywhere. Crowley knelt beside me, pausing to survey the massive damage I'd sustained during my brief, one-sided fight with Alan Garr.

"We must get you out of here. Their next step will be to send human reinforcements, and the dead I managed to gather can only hold them off for so long."

"Wait," I managed to croak. "Luther's in that cell. And I need my Bag."

He stood, crossing the hall with two quick strides. As he peered through the window, he shook his head. "Empty. The walls are covered in runes, but apparently something you did broke the continuity of the anti-magic field. It appears he escaped."

"Good," I whispered, wincing at the effort.

Crowley snatched my Bag from the floor, tossing it to me with a tsk. "You need to shift, or this effort will have been for naught." He knelt beside me, pulling a flask from his robes and unscrewing the cap. "Drink this."

"What is it?"

"It will help you focus your will, so you can heal yourself."

He held it to my lips, and I gulped a few swallows, nearly choking in the process. It was bitter, yet it burned like fire on the way down. When it hit my gut, that heat went through me like a jolt of electricity, clearing the fuzzy headedness caused by the head trauma I'd sustained.

"Can't shift here. Not enough room."

"Fine," he replied in a tone that sounded more than a little peeved.

The shadow wizard sprouted several black, oily, semi-transparent tentacles from his torso. He lifted me off the ground with two of them, while the others stabilized against the ground and walls to offset my weight.

Gunfire and screams erupted from down the hall, signaling that it was time to leave.

Crowley calmly walked through the portal, his shadow limbs trailing behind him. The tentacles turned to orient me so I entered the portal feet-first, then they pulled me through behind their master. It felt like diving into a pool of motor oil. As soon as my head passed the threshold the lights went out, and shadow magic tried to force its way into my mouth and nose.

Instinctively, I fought it with druidry, pushing the stuff back with a brief effort of will and a flash of silver light. As the druid magic illuminated the darkness, it appeared as though I was traveling down a long, ribbed black tube, filled with the black, inky magic Crowley used. Outside whatever membrane made up the boundaries of his weird portal spell, things moved in the darkness, brushing up against the tunnel and then skittering away from the light.

Seconds later, I emerged from the portal, gagging and spitting out black gook and snorting it from my nose. I could barely see, because my eyes were gunked up with the same clingy, oily substance. And the taste—ugh. Worse than the time I barfed up beer and Jäger boilermakers and German food at Octoberfest.

"Gah, what the hell was that? And where exactly did it take me during transit?"

"The shadow realm. Now, you had best shift, and quickly, before your organs give up on you completely."

"Fine," I groaned. "Just don't take me through that thing again."

By the time I shifted into my full Fomorian form, enough of the shadow gunk had dissipated so that I could finally see where we were. According to my geospatial druid sense, the spell had transported us fifty miles southwest of the city. As for our surroundings, we were inside an old barn that was full of rusted farm equipment, mildewed hay, and cobwebs. And thankfully, no undead.

Crowley stood by the doors, peering outside every few seconds. While he kept watch, I spent several long minutes in silence, focusing on the extremely painful process of shifting bones back into place as my healing factor knit my skeleton and soft tissues back together. Once I'd healed fully, I shifted back into my human form, collapsing against a hay bale in a cloud of dust and straw as I stared at the full moon shining through an open loft door above us.

"Thanks for the save. If you hadn't showed up when you did..." I left the sentence unfinished, as the shadow wizard seemed uninterested in my gratitude. "Anyway, how'd you find me?"

Crowley pushed back his hood, and I released an involuntarily gasp at what the moonlight revealed. His eye sockets were two swirling pools of blackness, like two spinning chunks of coal in a snowbank. His skin was streaked with black lines, and a dark mist swirled in random patterns over his exposed flesh.

"Holy shit—what happened to you?"

"Normally I'd have followed the trail of death and destruction," he said, ignoring my second question. "But in this case, I relied on simple deduction. It took me some time to decipher that cryptic message you left. But then it was only a matter of asking the lycanthrope where you'd gone."

So, we're not going to talk about the fact that you look like walking death. Right.

"Okay, but how'd you know I'd be at the Ritz?" I asked as I rummaged around in my Bag for a bottle of water. I was parched because the healing process had left me thirsty and weak.

"Mere ratiocination. Once I knew where you were headed, I decided it was only a matter of time before you confronted the most powerful vampire in Dallas. Since you had been traveling via conventional means, it stood to reason that you were under-magicked and at a severe disadvantage. If you were still alive, the tower was the most likely place to find you."

"You knew I was going after Luther." I took a slow, conservative swig of water. Drinking too much when you were dehydrated was a good way to make yourself puke. "How'd you know I'd get my ass whipped by their governor?"

"I take it you mean Alalngar?"

"You say that like it's one word. I thought his name was 'Alan Garr'?"

"That is merely the name he has adopted since his return from across the Veil. As for how I knew you would fail, Alalngar is a 5,000-year-old vampire, possessing power and strength to match any of the Tuath Dé." He gave a dismissive wave. "It was a foregone conclusion."

I sat down on a discarded tractor tire because I was too tired to stand. "Yeah, I guess I am a little underpowered. Bit off more than I could chew."

"Obviously. The real question is, why are you in this timeline?"

His inquiry caught me off guard. "Huh?"

Crowley scowled. "Don't play coy. You died, druid. I saw it, perhaps not firsthand, but you were at Luther's cafe when a cruise missile struck downtown Austin carrying a one-hundred-fifty-ton nuclear payload. Everyone within a half-kilometer radius was instantly vaporized. Thus, I can only deduce that you are another Colin, from another timeline."

"And how do you know I'm not a doppelgänger?"

He shook his head. "I know how to spot the fae. Besides, no one but you would be foolhardy enough to leave a note giving away their location."

"It was written in Ogham."

"Colin, this world is now populated by creatures with extremely long lifespans. The possibility that a vampire could read an ancient language is quite high, and not just because they might have lived contemporaneously with its usage. Species that live very long lives get bored, and they must find ways to alleviate their boredom. Learning languages, even dead ones, is a common distraction."

"Something you learned when you lived in Underhill, I take it."

"Indeed."

"In that case, I can neither confirm nor deny your allegations, for obvious reasons." He gave a single nod, as if to say, 'I knew it.' Meanwhile, I took another sip from the bottle, savoring the cool wetness while I scrambled for a reason to change the subject. "Why risk helping me? Hell, why risk helping Luther?"

"It was not that much of a risk for me to enter the city. I have more to fear from the fae than from most bloodkin, although primaries such as Alalngar are another matter."

"Necromancy. That's why they fled."

"Yes. I may be the last necromancer on Earth. That makes me someone to be feared, even by master vampires. The only members of their race that can resist my spell craft are very old masters, and primaries." His brow furrowed. "It has also made me the most hunted man alive. The vampires want to see me dead, very badly."

"Shit, Crowley. Then why don't you just go hole up somewhere—I don't know, like Underhill? Surely there's a place there you can hide out from everyone, fae and vampires included."

"I stayed for good reason." He exhaled heavily, as if what he was about to say would cost him a great deal. "Belladonna is dead, and I now exist only to exact retribution on those responsible."

The revelation struck me like a hammer blow. Suddenly I felt dizzy, and it was hard to breathe. I had to prop myself up by placing a hand on the tire next to me, so I didn't lose my balance. It took me a minute or two before I could collect my thoughts enough to speak.

"How—I mean, how'd she die?"

"Meeting you, actually."

"At Luther's, I take it."

"Yes. She was returning some things you'd left at her apartment, and—well, she died when you did."

"Damn it. I am so sorry."

Those two swirling pools of blackness that served as his eyes churned for a moment, like clouds above a stormy sea. Then, the moment passed, and he shrugged. "What's done is done. What remains is revenge."

"You still haven't told me what happened to you," I said, pointing with two fingers at my own eyes. "You've changed."

"After Belladonna died, the vampires came after me in force. Obviously, the city was in chaos, but my only concern was verifying Belladonna's passing. They caught me unaware while I was tracing her last known whereabouts using a tracking spell I'd placed on her motorcycle."

"Don't tell me—they attacked shortly after you realized she was really gone."

"Yes. I lost control, and for a time I gave myself over to my darker proclivities. After I regained my senses a few days later, I'd changed. I was stronger than before, but I paid a heavy price."

"Again, I'm sorry."

"Unfortunately, your sympathy does nothing to further my cause. Yet, it appears our goals align. If you wish to provide succor, help me destroy the Vampyri."

"Gladly. What's the plan?"

"It certainly does not involve committing suicide by staging a full-frontal assault on a Vampyri stronghold. But before I share my intentions, there are things you should know. Sit, and listen to what I have to tell you."

Half an hour later, I had a pretty good idea of what the vamps had done after the bombs fell. "That's what the fae wanted in return for their assistance? I can't believe they'd give up their demesnes on Earth so easily."

"You gave the lesser fae little choice, Colin. After you closed the gates to Underhill, they lost access to the primary source of their magic. It would be like taking electricity and fossil fuels away from humanity. In their eyes, you sent them back to the figurative Dark Ages overnight."

"That's why they rebelled. Shit, you mean I caused this?"

Crowley grunted. "Your actions certainly contributed to the chain of events. The Vampyri had been planning their takeover for centuries, but two things stood in their way. First, the human magic users had to be eliminated, not just because of the power they wielded, but also due to the possibility of closet necromancers among their ranks."

"And the second obstacle were the fae. So, they had to offer them something in return for forsaking their place here on Earth."

"The Fae Courts wouldn't have even entertained such a proposal, at least not the more influential of their number. Those fae kings and queens who had the most influence were also the ones who still wielded considerable power, as they had ways to access the magic of Underhill. But the rest were left magically destitute, as it were. Unwittingly, you caused a sort of class warfare among the fae."

"So, they went behind Maeve's back, cutting a deal with the vamps. What happened to Maeve?"

"Her courtiers and subjects turned on her, and she was forced to flee to Underhill. As I understand it, she resides at her father's house, on *Emain Ablach*. She stands in league with the Tuath Dé who are at war with the fae of Earth."

"Wait a minute—you mean to tell me that the Earth-bound fae actually invaded Underhill?"

"With the help of the Vampyri, yes. The bloodkin have no fear of the sun in Underhill, and they enjoy the taste of fae blood. For those reasons, they gladly volunteer to help the rebel aes sídhe fight their civil war in *Ildathach*."

I covered my face with my hands, groaning with remorse over the chain of events that I'd put in motion. Of course, I'd stopped the Vampyri plot in Texas in my own timeline. However, they were likely still working behind the scenes back home, cooking up other ways to execute their batshit crazy plan.

After several moments, I rubbed my face with my hands and stood. "I'm going to need to get to Underhill."

Crowley shook his head. "The battle with the Vampyri is here. Besides, you would not wish to visit The Multi-Colored Lands if you saw the atrocities being committed there. Powerful fae fight against the gods, and the lands are in total chaos."

"Maybe so, but my little excursion to Dallas has shown me that I need to level up if I'm going to take on Alan Garr and his merry gang. To do that, I need to speak with the Dagda."

The shadow wizard's brow furrowed. "You wish to grow a Grove."

"Got it in one."

"Hmm. There is something you should know. Among the Vampyri and Fae alike, stories abound of a great oak tree that appears out of nowhere. Wherever it goes it leaves destruction in its wake. They call it the *Ubivanje Drvo*, the Killing Tree. Several smaller Vampyri outposts have been utterly wiped out by it."

"Could be a *jubokko*, a Japanese vampire tree. Or a Green Man who has it in for vampires."

"A jubokko feeds on the living, not the undead. And all the woodwose fae retreated to Underhill with the rest of their kind. Besides, they would not violate the pact they made with the Vampyri. No, I believe this is your Druid Oak—or rather, your counterpart's. And I think it went mad after your counterpart's death."

Fatigue was taking its toll on me, and all this bad news wasn't helping. I hung my head and knuckled the corner of my eyes before I answered. "You might be right. I think I felt its presence once or twice when I was performing druid magic."

"Did you attempt contact?"

"Yeah, but it slipped away before I could establish a connection. Listen, the connection a druid has to his oak is incredibly strong, and it deepens over time. If this timeline's version of me bonded with his Oak before he died, then his death may very well have driven the poor thing crazy. And if that's the case, I doubt I'll be able to bond with it."

"The creature might very well think you're some sort of fae doppelgänger. It may even turn on you."

"Or it might think I'm an undead version of myself. Who knows? But if I could connect with it, it would solve my magic deficiency, for sure. Still, it's a long shot, and I'd feel a lot more comfortable creating a fresh bond with a new oak."

"Which means finding the Dagda."

I nodded. "Yep. Will you help me?"

He stared at me with his creepy missing eyes. "If we are to work together to obliterate the Vampyri, then I need you at your full strength. Therefore, I suppose I have no choice. But I must warn you, this will be an arduous, perilous journey. You should return to your keep in Austin to rest and prepare. I will find you there two weeks hence."

"Sounds like a plan." I extended my hand. Crowley stared at it for a moment before clasping forearms with me, old-school style.

"I will see you in two weeks," he said. Then, he stepped back and vanished in an oval of smoky darkness.

That's going to take some getting used to. Now, to find some wheels.

20

After Crowley did his shadow wizard disappearing act, I scrounged around the barn for something that could get me from wherever we were to a more reliable form of transportation. Eventually I found an old Yamaha 125 dirt bike under a tarp, someone's restoration project before the shit hit the fan. The outside was rough, but the mechanicals were in good working order, and with a little elbow grease and a lot of druid magic, I got it running, and silently to boot.

The farm was relatively free of the dead, which likely meant Crowley had landed us in the middle of BFE. Once I got my bearings, I headed in a general southeasterly direction and eventually ran into Highway 281, a north-south artery that ran more or less parallel to IH-35 all the way to the Hill Country west of Austin. I took the highway for a few miles until I saw signs telling me I was near Stephenville, home of Tarleton State U and not much else.

I vacillated back and forth on navigating the former college town, which was certain to be crawling with undead co-eds, finally deciding I needed better transportation. The town wasn't nearly as busy with the dead as I'd anticipated, having been nearly leveled by a passing horde sometime in the recent past. I found a CBR 1000 in a parking garage near the university, got it running, and after casting silence spells on it I hauled ass back to Austin.

Six hours later, I crossed the Pennybacker Bridge, then I took Courtyard Drive as far as the point where I'd washed out the road. The dead were almost a non-presence, which I assumed was the result of Guerra hunting them when he wasn't guarding the Castle House. I hiked the rest of the way to the compound, taking time along my route to check my wards to make sure they hadn't been disturbed.

When I got to the house, nobody was outside, and I heard no sounds of children playing quietly in the backyard. I jumped the fence, drawing my sidearm in one hand and my greatsword in the other as I crept around the perimeter to scope out the house and grounds.

Garden's been left untended for days. Not good.

The first thing I did on approaching the house was creep up the outside steps to the roof. No one was on duty, and our makeshift guard station looked like it hadn't been used for days. I crept back downstairs, attempting to enter through the front door, which was, of course, locked.

At least that means someone is inside.

After unlocking the door with a cantrip, I tried it and found that it was barred from the other side. Just as I was about to knock, gunshots echoed from inside the house, and the thick wooden door sprouted several brand-new peepholes across its width. I hit the deck, rolling to the side as I hollered to announce myself to whoever was trying to kill me.

"Stop shooting, it's just me!"

Anna's voice answered from the other side of the door. "Colin?"

"Yes, damn it. Shit, you almost shot me."

I heard the bar being tossed aside, then the door opened. After I stood, I brushed myself off and then entered the house. Anna stood in the entry foyer holding an AR-15 at low ready, and several older boys were spread out behind her with their PVC bows and crossbows nocked at full draw.

I took the scene in, then I asked the obvious question. "What the hell happened, and where's Guerra?"

Anna pushed past me, shutting the door after nervously looking outside, then barring it again. "He's off looking for Brian."

"What do you mean, looking for Brian? And where's Mickey?"

Matthew lowered his bow and motioned for the others to do the same. "Mr. Mickey got hurt. He was on guard duty, and we found him on the deck with a sharpened tree limb stuck through him. Mr. Guerra and Ms. Anna got it out, but he's been real sick ever since."

I rubbed my temples, then I turned to address Anna, just in time to catch her glaring at my back. "When did Brian disappear?"

"Yesterday," she spat, "which you'd know if you had been here. The day after Mickey was attacked. Guerra put us on lockdown, and then he went looking for him. We haven't heard from either of them since."

A million thoughts went through my head, none of them healthy. After a moment's deliberation, I decided to prioritize and do the most good I could in the shortest time possible.

"Take me to Mickey."

One of the boys led me to an upstairs bedroom, where the quiet, reserved man tossed and turned in the throes of a fever dream. He was sweating and his skin was burning up, and from the looks of it, the attack had gone through the fatty tissue and muscle of his upper abdomen without hitting any internal organs. *Lucky.*

I checked under his dressings, examining both the entry and exit wounds. They had done a decent job of stitching him up, but both wounds were infected and leaking pus with hot, red streaks leading away from the epicenter.

"Thomas, go get me some hot water and towels."

"Yes sir," he said, hopping away to his assigned task.

In truth, I didn't need either. I just wanted some

privacy so I could heal Mickey. Before I chanted the *teinm laida*, I'd always been shitty at healing magic. But after I gained the knowledge of druid mastery, I at least had the principles down, enough to cast simple healing spells. While Thomas was gone, I laid my hands on Mickey's wounds, slowing my breathing as I dropped into a meditative state.

When I was ready, I released the magic from my hands, and bright, silver light poured out from the spaces where my hands had not made a perfect seal with his skin. Probing his tissues with my druid sense, I traced the infection wherever it went, drawing it out until thick, yellow pus ran in rivulets all over the bed beneath my patient. Finally, I infused his blood with more magic, strengthening his immune system so it could deal with the sepsis that had been trying to shut down his organs and end his life.

After I finished, I staggered into a nearby chair, just as Thomas returned with the items I'd asked him to bring. I used them to wash Mickey's wounds, turning him over so I could change the bed linen and then replace his bandages. Already the wounds were closing and healing, but I didn't want anyone to see it happening so quickly. I instructed Thomas to make sure no one changed his dressings until I said so, then I washed my hands and headed back downstairs.

All Anna seemed capable of was pacing and scowling, so I recruited Matthew instead. "Show me the stick they pulled out of Mickey."

He shrugged as if to say, "why not?" and led me to the kitchen table, which was still a bloody mess. Apparently, this was where Guerra and Anna had saved Mickey's life. Lying on the ground next to the table was a five-foot-long length of Osage Orange, smoothed and carved into a point at one end. I picked it up, sniffing the tip first, then the shaft. The sharp end had been dipped in animal excrement, while the handle carried a most familiar smell.

Vampires.

I tossed the makeshift javelin down, brooding over the implications. Leaning with my hands on the table, I looked up to see Matthew staring at the ground. Something about his demeanor told me there was more to this tale.

"Tell me everything that happened leading up to the attack and Brian's disappearance."

It didn't take long to get a clear picture of what had occurred in my absence, and by the time Matthew was done, I was kicking myself for not seeing it. After I left, Richard started acting strangely. He became more and more aggressive with the other children, and ever more rebellious when Mickey and Anna would ask him to do his part of the chores around the compound. The other children began to avoid him, while the adults left him alone, figuring that he was simply having a hard time dealing with what had happened to him back at the church.

The night Mickey was attacked, Brian disappeared while Anna and Guerra were busy trying to save Mickey's life. When they discovered Brian was gone, they found the rear gate unlocked and open, the chains and lock sitting on the ground nearby. I had locked that gate myself and given only Guerra and Anna the key, so someone had to know where it was kept, taken a key, and then unlocked the gate.

When the boys were questioned about it, Richard made an offhand comment about seeing Brian wander off. He was the only one who'd been outside when it happened. While the adults didn't want to accuse him outright, Guerra said that Richard smelled of vampire. That Anna didn't question the accuracy of Guerra's sense of smell said a lot about her state of mind, or perhaps that she suspected a lot more than she let on.

Shortly after that, the boys reported seeing Richard sneaking out of the house. Anna caught him trying to unlock the front gate, and when she confronted him, Richard slipped through the gap and took off. That was the last they'd seen of Richard as well.

A brief search of Guerra's room turned up some hairs and clothing that I would use for a druid tracking spell. Finding unadulterated DNA and clothing items belonging to Brian was another matter, as the boys routinely shared clothing and personal grooming items. I decided to seek Guerra's trail instead, hoping that he'd found Brian and that would be how I found them both.

Before I left, I checked in with Anna. "I'm going after them. Keep the kids inside until I get back."

She failed to make eye contact with me, busying herself with loading magazines as she guarded the front entrance. "If you don't find my brother, don't come back at all."

Hmph.

I was almost certain I was going to find Brian, but I seriously doubted that I'd find him alive. As for Richard, he was obviously a Renfield, and he'd likely been turned already. That had been Dauphine's plan from the start. She wasn't going to sacrifice him, but turn him—something I should have considered based on what she'd said. Mentally kicking myself for not hunting her down and ending her wasn't doing me any good, so I focused instead on picking up Guerra's trail.

After I double-checked the gates and my wards, I vaulted the fence then headed a short way into the trees. Once I found a relatively safe spot, I knelt in *seiza* and dropped into a druid trance, searching the surrounding hills until I found what I was looking for, a grizzled old coyote on the hunt for a meal.

Once I entered his mind, I gained his trust and convinced him to approach. Then, I produced Guerra's hair and an item of his clothing, allowing the coyote to get a good whiff. The scent made the 'yote skittish, but after a little encouragement, I got him back on course.

The grizzled old canine spent a few minutes sniffing around the compound, then he caught the trail and took off at a trot down a deer path, with me jogging along behind him.

The coyote led me down the ridge and through the woods to Emma Long Park. There we continued southwest, past Turkey Creek Trail, until the spoor ended on the banks of the Colorado River, only a mile or so from the compound. When we reached the water, the 'yote sniffed around the shore, then he sat on his haunches and let out a low whine.

I entered the coyote's mind again, seeing through his eyes. He wanted to continue the hunt, but the scent led across the river and he didn't feel like getting wet. I knew that his species were excellent swimmers, so I gave him a gentle nudge. Soon we'd both crossed the river to the other shore, where my companion picked up the trail again.

This time, however, he only traveled a hundred yards or so before stopping in his tracks, ears erect and tail held high. The coyote snarled softly, keeping his eyes trained on a smallish, two-story house up the hill. I cast a cantrip to enhance my senses, and with one good whiff, I knew exactly what had the old 'yote riled up.

Decaying flesh, dried blood, and graveyard dirt. Bingo.

I sent the 'yote on his way with a scratch behind the ears and a stick of jerky in his mouth. He loped off quickly once I released him from my mental influence, making a beeline away from the suspected vampire lair. After the 'yote was gone, I checked the skies and surveyed my surroundings, noting that the sun would be going down soon. If I was going to act, I'd need to do it fast.

After my disastrous run-in with Alan Garr, there was no way I was fucking around when it came to confronting Dauphine. She'd already proven herself to be a powerful master vampire, and based on the talent she displayed, she was likely one of Garr's get. That told me she might be stronger than I'd originally anticipated, and that eventually more of her kind would come, regardless of how I handled her now.

Time to get ugly.

I stripped down to my lycra skivvies, stuffing my clothes in my Bag before I started my transformation. On the way here, I'd remained in my stealth-shifted form, knowing that it would make the full shift that much easier when I needed it to happen. Within the span of no more than thirty seconds, I made the painful transition to my fully Fomorian form.

After the transformation, I took a few moments to stretch and reacquaint myself with this form. Ten-foot-nothing of twisted steel and no sex appeal, when I went full-Fomorian I was the ugliest motherfucker on the block. Toughest, too, which is what I'd need to defeat Dauphine.

I had recharged my magic after my battle with Garr, but not enough to make a significant difference in the coming fight. Lacking a good night's rest, at best I'd be able to muster one or two strong spells before my magical reservoir was depleted. I didn't bother queuing up any spells, because there was no sense wasting magic on the first engagement. Instead, I'd save it until the moment was right, when I was sure she wouldn't slip away.

If they're dead, I still have to kill her. Not just for revenge, but to keep the group safe.

Once I'd resolved to end Dauphine, I pulled Orna from my Bag and silently stalked up the hill, taking care to avoid alerting the home's occupants of my presence. When I reached the top, I came to a yard bordered by a short, wrought-iron fence, beyond which sat a badly neglected pool and a concrete patio that led to the back door of the house. There were signs of conflict here, not of a struggle, but a full-on battle.

Lawn furniture had been smashed and scattered, and sections of the fence were twisted and even crushed in places. Something had cracked the concrete in a sort of star-shaped pattern, as if the ground had been struck with tremendous force. I knelt to sniff a pool of dried blood, shaking my head at what I discovered.

'Thrope blood—Guerra's. This is not looking good.

I was just about to enter the house when the last rays of sun winked out behind the hills to the west. No sooner had the sun disappeared over the ridge, than I heard a rustling, both from the wooded areas around the house, and from the residences to either side. The wind shifted, and the smell I'd caught earlier intensified dramatically, carrying the scent of dozens of undead. Not just vampires, but revenants and ghouls as well.

Dauphine has been busy in my absence.

Only a master vampire or better could reliably make other vampires. As far as I knew, there were no other vampires living in the area when I left for Dallas. That meant Dauphine had been capturing humans and turning them, or she called in the cavalry. Either way, her brood was likely only meant to be a distraction, something to keep me occupied while she waited for the perfect moment to strike.

I stood on the patio next to the pool in a fighter's crouch, sword held at the ready as dozens upon dozens of undead flooded out of the surrounding woods toward me. Some climbed the fence, others vaulted it, and still others leapt through the air, all of them clearly coming for yours truly. I tightened my grip on the giant-sized great sword, confident that its supernaturally sharp edge would be sufficient for the coming task.

21

"**O**h, master, are we fighting the undead this evening?" the sword asked. Orna was a sentient artifact, and I was fairly certain it was senile, as it chose the strangest times to speak. "This reminds me of the time when my former master, Tethra, battled the Tuath Dé at the second battle of Mag Tuired. They swarmed upon him like locusts, coming in wave after wave, yet he cut them down like stalks of wheat, never tiring until the witch Morrígan sang and turned the tide of battle. Why, I recall—"

"Shut up, Orna," I growled, as I swung the blade in a broad arc that swept through the first line of undead like a scythe. I spun around with a short pivot step, swinging the sword in a tight arc overhead so I could carry the momentum into the next cut. "There'll be plenty of time for you to recount my deeds when I'm dead."

"Balor forbid, master!" the sword replied. "And

besides, I was recounting the deeds of my former master, who you helped slay—at the hands of a master vampire, no less. Let us hope that's not a foreshadowing of current events."

"If it wasn't for your sunny attitude, I don't know how I'd go on," I replied as I punted a linebacker-sized ghoul through the wrought iron fence with a front snap kick. "Now, hush and let me work."

"I exist to serve, master," the sword said before going silent.

Thank heavens. Not as if Dauphine doesn't know I'm here, though.

As I recovered from that kick, two young vamps came at me from each side in an attempt to flank me. The dumb fuckers didn't realize all they had to do was wait for the next wave to attack, and instead they saw the gap I'd created by cutting down the first wave as their opportunity to attack. *Idiots.*

Young vamps were faster than any human, but generally slow when compared to mature bloodkin and 'thropes. Mature leeches were faster than 'thropes, and mature 'thropes were stronger than vampires of a similar vintage. And me? I was almost as fast as a mature vamp in this form, and stronger than any lycan-thrope, but my real superpower was my Fomorian battle instincts.

Back in the day, the Fomorians were the most feared race of the old world. They were the original sea-faring raiders, sailing around the known world in vast armadas and descending like a bloodthirsty plague wherever they went. They were born and bred for battle, trained from the time they were young to wage war. Every Fomorian possessed an instinctual cunning for warfare, a brutal analytical mind that did battlefield calculus, showing the warrior the most efficient and devastating ways to deal with their opponents.

Before the vamps reached me, my Fomorian mind had already worked out their most likely angles of attack. The pool was too large an obstacle for them to traverse, so one would approach around it, and the other would leap off the house in an attempt to attack me from above. The first was a distraction, the second was intended to succeed in a sneak attack.

Subtle.

Rather than let the vamps know I saw them, I turned to face the half-dozen ghouls coming from the west, turning my back to the vampire on the roof. Then, I waited for the one on the ground to rush me, extending my hand at the last moment to catch him in a vice-like grip around his neck.

Meanwhile the female vamp on the roof was already mid-leap, diving through the air at me with her jaws open and hands extended. Her plan had been to land on my back and sink her teeth into my neck, ripping out my jugular. I foiled that plan by pivoting and punching the other vamp's head at her, using his neck like a fist load, accelerating his body so quickly that his spine snapped with a loud *crack,* just before his skull smashed into the female vamp's mouth with a sickening crunch.

Following through with that motion, I pinned them both to the pavement with my free hand. Then, I drove the sword's tip through both their hearts, pulling the blade out sideways with a forehand slash that nearly cut their torsos in half. With a snap of my wrist, I slung black blood from Orna as I faced the second wave.

After that, the battle was a blur. *Spin, cut, kick, punch, slice, turn, repeat.* When I was done, dismembered bodies were strewn everywhere across the patio, inside the pool, and even out in the woods beyond. The fight lasted less than a minute, and I was hungry for more.

Yet Dauphine still hadn't shown. I was certain she'd attack while I was distracted by her underlings. Slinging the blood, guts, and putrefied flesh off my blade, I headed for the house.

I found Guerra inside, bound with silver chains and pinned to the concrete floor with hooked rebar spikes, just like the ones I'd used time and again on vamps I tortured for information. His left leg had been hacked off below the knee, and his right arm was a stump that ended just above where his elbow would've been. Both limbs ended in open wounds that wouldn't heal while he was bound by silver. It was doubtful they'd grow back, but he was old, so there was always a chance.

Already practically on my hands and knees as I navigated the low ceilings in the house, it didn't take much more effort to kneel beside the 'thrope as I snapped the locks and removed the chains. Where Dauphine had gotten this much silver was a mystery to me, and how she had forged it into chain links was anyone's guess. Maybe the Vampyri Nations manufactured equipment like this en masse for their enforcers—I'd be sure to ask her, just before I shoved all that silver down her throat.

Guerra was breathing, but he wasn't moving, even after I got all that silver away from his skin. "Hey, man, you with me?"

He cracked an eyelid, and I noted that he'd been beaten badly. "Setup," he gasped.

"I can see that—"

He rolled over, grabbing my wrist with his remaining hand. "Distraction, *pendejo*. Kids are in danger." Then, he collapsed and fell silent.

"Fuck!" I growled, slamming a fist on the floor.

I checked to make sure Guerra was still breathing— he was, barely—so I tossed him over my shoulder, exiting the house in a crouch. Once I cleared the back door I took off at a sprint, running at top speed, about fifty-five miles an hour. A minute later, I crested the ridge behind the Castle House. As I neared the fence, I scanned it in the magical spectrum.

Ward wall is broken.

There were only two ways that could happen. One involved unraveling my wards with magic, and I doubted anyone was left alive who could do it in the fifteen minutes since I'd left. And the second was to unlock the gate and break the continuity of the ward circle.

I leapt the warded fence with Guerra still slung over my shoulder, then I ran to the front gate, laying him down on the ground inside the perimeter. He was unconscious, so I lightly slapped his cheek to bring him around.

"Guerra, wake up. I need you to watch this entrance, and when I give the word, you have to shut the gates."

"Might need a... hand with that," he croaked, wriggling his stump as he opened his eyes.

"She should've cut out your tongue, to save us all from the dad jokes," I quipped, pasting a smile on my face despite the fact that none of this was funny, at all. "I'm going to go find that bitch. When I tell you, shut these fucking gates."

"Just go," he said, pushing himself up so he sat against the gate post. "I'll take care of it."

I reached into my Bag and pulled out my Glock, which was loaded with silver-tipped rounds. After placing it in his hand, I took off for the front entrance of the house. Before I got near it, I heard Dauphine's Bacall-like voice ring out above me. When I looked up, I found her standing atop the observatory tower, dangling Brian upside down by one ankle over the side of the house.

She wore a strange outfit—black motorcycle leathers

and gloves, with the collar zipped up tight around her neck. She even wore the boots to match, big heavy things with buckles to secure them around her ankles and calves. Her hair had been pulled back into a severe ponytail, exposing her alabaster skin, perfectly plucked eyebrows, aquiline features, and blood-red, pouty lips that required no make-up whatsoever. Kevlar armor or no, I intended to beat her to a pulp, just as soon as she came within reach.

"My, what big muscles you have," she remarked, her voice going from silky sweet to barbed wire as she continued. "Despite the strength and speed you have in that form, don't even think of jumping up here. I'll snap his neck and vanish before you even get off the ground."

"Where are the others?" I asked, glancing back and forth between Brian and the house below.

"Hiding in the cellar. I was about to break down the door and introduce myself when I heard you approach." She turned her gaze to Guerra. "Ah, I see you brought my houseguest. Poor manners, that one. He left the kitchen a bloody mess."

"C'mon, Dauphine—you know you want a piece of me. Why don't you set the kid down, and let's step outside to settle this, just between us. Winner take all."

"A piece of you? Why, my dear druid, I want all of you. Dallas is a-buzz about your recent trip into the heart of Alalngar's domain, and how you freed my dear deluded brother, Luther. Rumor has it you're in league with the necromancer as well." Brian began to squirm in her grip. Dauphine paused to turn him around, holding him higher so he could see her bare her fangs. "You're hardly worth the blood in your veins. I will drop you, young man, make no mistake."

"Drop him, and you'll regret it," I growled.

"Oh please, you're in no position to make threats. Now, where was I? Oh yes, your visit to Dallas created quite a stir, and Alalngar wants you, dead or alive. Do you know how valuable that makes you to me? I've been stuck in this backwater, gathering slaves for the Dallas market, all because of a recent *indiscretion* with one of my master's newest progeny."

"Let me guess—you killed a potential rival."

"Of course. What was I supposed to do? There aren't many of us who've inherited Alalngar's unique talents, and with Luther locked up, I was first in line to rule beside my master. Then, he turned some rock star, and the impertinent twat had the audacity to teleport when he was only a few months old. It took me decades for that skill to emerge—decades. I'll be damned if I'm to see some upstart usurp my position in the bloodline. So, I spied on him while he was practicing his newfound talent, and when the time was right, I made sure he had an accident."

"But you didn't cover your tracks, and Garr found out," I said, biding my time while my Fomorian brain formulated a plan.

Her upper lip curled distastefully. "I was found out, yes, and banished here. But if I delivered your head, well—that would certainly put me back in his good graces."

"Yeah, well—you wouldn't be the first to try. Again, set the kid down so we can settle this beef, once and for all."

"Set him down, you say?" she arched an eyebrow. "Certainly."

Dauphine flipped Brian in the air, catching him by the neck. Then she spun once before tossing him in a high arc, over the front gate and toward the street beyond.

I heard the kid's neck crack, even before she let him go. The sound was unmistakable—I recognized it because I'd broken enough necks in my time to know it when I heard it. Despite that, I still sprinted at top speed to catch him, nearly a blur as I passed Guerra at the front gate, skidding to a halt in the middle of the street.

He might still be alive. Please let him be alive.

I pivoted like a wide receiver going out for a hail Mary pass, just ahead of the body that tumbled in rag doll manner through the air directly at me. Catching the kid in my huge, overdeveloped arms as gently as I could manage, I noted the way his head hung at a grotesque angle as I cradled him to my chest. It didn't take a medical degree to know he was gone, and tears of frustration and rage pooled at the corners of my eyes at the meaninglessness of it all.

As I lowered his lifeless body to the ground with tender-loving care, I thought about how the kid had a whole life ahead of him, even if it was a shitty one in this shitty world—the world I'd helped create. That life had been snuffed out, and for what? So Dauphine could distract me and create an opportunity to take my head back to her master?

Fucking vampires. *Fucking fae.* Fucking supernatural bullshit species who thought they were the apex predators, and we were just cattle. No, less than cattle—that we were nothing more than grass upon which they could graze. To them, we were lower than animals, so far beneath their consideration as to be trampled upon at will.

I was sick of it, sick and tired of seeing innocent people die because of their twisted games and inflated opinion of their place in the natural order. And that was just it—they were anything *but* natural. They didn't belong here, not really. Vampires and fae were only here because thousands of years ago their god-like forebears found a way to cross over the Veil into our world, taking on physical forms so they could prey upon the human race.

Fuck that. Fuck them all. It's time to disabuse them of that notion—starting with this disease-addled cunt.

I knew exactly what Dauphine intended, because my Fomorian battle instincts had already worked her plan out. She'd heard an account of how Garr had defeated me in the sub-basement of the Ritz in Dallas, and she intended to do a repeat of that battle. However, there were three things working against her.

One—I wasn't in my full Fomorian form then.

Two—I had nowhere to go when I was fighting her master.

And three—I wasn't nearly as pissed off then as I am now.

When Dauphine teleported behind me, I was ready for her. When she appeared, I turned and dropped to my back as I unloaded the full force of my sunlight spell right into her face. Light flared with day-glow brilliance from the palms of my massive, gnarled hands, blazing so bright as to illuminate the entire street and the homes beyond.

When the spell subsided, I blinked the spots from my eyes and searched the area for Dauphine's charred, smoking corpse. But what I saw instead was the bitch standing unharmed fifteen feet away, gloved hands on her hips wearing a full welding mask over her face and head. She yanked the shield off, letting it dangle from her fingers as she placed her other hand on her chest.

"My, but that was exhilarating. I can't remember the last time I saw sunlight." She paused, tapping a finger on her lips as her gaze momentarily darted up and to the right. "Oh yes, of course—it was the last time you tried that little trick on me. Well, fool me once, and all that."

I leapt to my feet, silently cursing myself for essentially blowing my wad when I unleashed that spell. I could only absorb and store so much sunlight every day, and I'd just released everything I had in an effort to fry that bitch to a crisp. My Fomorian mind hadn't accounted for this simple, cunning countermeasure to the one spell I knew that was faster than her teleportation talent.

Alright, then. Time to do this old school, I thought as I heard the gates clang shut behind me.

In this form, I was fast but not very nimble, more like a freight train coming down the tracks full tilt than a Mercedes-AMG GT carving up the Nürburgring. If I was going to defeat Dauphine without the benefit of my sunlight spell, I'd need speed and agility to match hers at least, which meant shifting back into my half-Fomorian form. As for her teleportation abilities, well—I'd work out a plan as I went along.

What was supposed to happen next, at least in that bitch's mind, was for me to stand my ground and go toe to toe with her. Like I said, fuck that. As Dauphine vanished in a dark cloud of smoke, I crouched and did a leaping backflip that took me over the gates and safely back inside my wards, barely escaping the vampire's initial attack. I landed in the three-point crouch on the front walk of the mansion, just as my enemy evanesced and then reappeared, just on the other side of the wrought iron fence.

Thin wisps of black smoke curled into nothingness as they peeled off Dauphine's lithe, dangerous form. The master vampire faced me three-quarters front, arms crossed over her chest, feet together, and shoulders held high and proud. She sneered, staring down her nose as she fixed me with a look that was contempt, personified.

"Fool. I can stalk you and those you protect during the day as easily as I can at night. And I am old, even for my kind, requiring neither sleep nor sustenance for days at a time. I will pick you off, one by one, just like I did the old man. Eventually, you will slip up, and then I'll be among you again, the proverbial fox in the henhouse. It is only a matter of time."

I triggered my transformation, shifting back into my semi-human form, mortal skin on the outside, wrapped around a skeleton and musculature fortified by Fomorian DNA. Calmly, I reached into my Bag, donning my clothing and strapping my weapons to my body—silver-plated knife, a spare pistol, magazines loaded with silver-tipped rounds, and Dyrnwyn slung over my shoulder. Dauphine looked on as I laced my boots up. I took time to cinch them tight, ensuring I'd have sure footing for what came next.

Guerra looked on from where he remained seated and propped up against the fence. His wounds had closed over, but there was no sign that his limbs would regenerate. A damned shame. I could find him a prosthetic, but he'd never be the same.

The old wolf chuckled as he looked back and forth between me and the vampire. "I think you got it wrong, *culera*. He's not hiding. He's getting ready to lay a smackdown on your skinny *gringa* ass."

I chuckled, because I had no intentions of fighting Dauphine face-to-face in a fair fight. I had learned my lesson about fighting vampires who could teleport during my confrontation with her master back in Dallas. In fact, during the entire trip from Dallas to Austin, I had mulled over how I might defeat Alan Garr should we ever meet again.

Like Garr, Dauphine was supernaturally fast, and combined with her teleportation talent, it was almost as if she could be in two or three places at once. That was the primary issue with fighting vampires of this kind, that there was only one of me and essentially multiples of them.

But I had seen Luther fight several times in the past. One time, he fought a challenge match against another very powerful master vampire. In that particular instance, Luther was almost defeated, not because the other vampire was a better fighter, but because he was cheating. That vampire had made an arrangement with the avatar of a lesser god, borrowing that lesser god's powers and magic to allow him to fight without tiring, no matter how long the fight lasted.

By watching that fight, I learned that even master vampires like Luther had limitations to their power. Luther could teleport at will to any place that he had a clear line of sight, but he couldn't do that forever. He almost lost because he began to tire toward the end of the match, slowing his reaction speed as well as the speed at which he was able to teleport.

That was the weakness I intended to exploit in this fight with Dauphine. I intended to wear her out and slow her down. Only then could I spring the trap I had planned out in my mind.

Dauphine looked at me condescendingly, sizing me up as I finished my preparations on my side of the warded fence. "We may as well get this over with, druid. You'll die sooner or later—why not make it sooner?"

"Well, one of us is bound to die," I said. "But it's not going to be me, bitch."

I waved Dauphine back with a shooing motion, which she answered with a roll of her eyes and an exasperated, affected sigh. Then, she teleported, disappearing and reappearing some fifty feet off. After she had cleared the way, I vaulted the fence, landing lightly on the balls of my feet on the other side as I drew Dyrnwyn.

It was really a dumb idea to carry a sword in a shoulder sling, but I had done it so often that I had little difficulty drawing the blade from its sheath. As soon as the blade cleared its scabbard, it flared into life, the flames that rolled up and down its length giving off a blinding brilliance in the presence of such an evil creature as Dauphine. No sooner had I drawn the blade than the fight was on.

Dauphine wasted no time teleporting behind me, landing a blow between my shoulder blades that staggered me forward, even though I was prepared for it. I rolled with the blow, rolling over my shoulder and sweeping the blade upwards in a circular motion, hoping to catch her as she appeared on the other side of where I'd landed. Instead, she teleported above me, appearing in the air where she could fall directly on top of me.

I swept the sword crosswise in front of me to prevent her from completing her attack. Her eyes widened as she realized she was about to fall into a sword blade that was essentially hotter than one of my lightning bolts. The vampire teleported away just before the blade touched her chest.

The momentary pause in the rhythm of the fight was all I needed to jump to my feet. Then, rather than wait for Dauphine to attack again, I jumped into action, sprinting in a random, zigzag fashion all around the street as I swung Dyrnwyn around me in looping, dizzying patterns.

This accomplished two things. First, it made it harder for Dauphine to get a bead on me, forcing her to teleport again and again in her attempts to attack. Also, it allowed me a bit of breathing room, even when she managed to teleport in front of me, correctly anticipating my moves.

With Dyrnwyn swinging around me, it was difficult if not impossible for her to land a killing blow. Not that she didn't land a blow on me, because she did manage to slash my flesh with her razor-sharp fingernails many a time over the course of the next minute or so. Yet, for every blow and slash she landed, she had to teleport half a dozen times in order to find a position that allowed her to successfully attack. Within two minutes, I was a bloody mess, while Dauphine's speed in teleporting from place to place was beginning to lag.

Time to finish this.

After my fight with Alalngar, I realized that my best bet for defeating him would be to use a stasis field. Yet, I couldn't do that here without revealing my knowledge of chronomancy and chronourgy to Guerra. Not that I didn't trust him, but I was afraid Click would find out, then travel here to kill him—a risk I wasn't willing to take.

What I needed to do was cast a stasis field in a way that no one could tell what I was doing. In other words, the effects had to look like it was all me, and not eldritch magic at work. And to do that, the timing had to be just right.

I continued zigzagging around the street, paying careful attention to Dauphine's reactions. Like most creatures of her ilk, she relied way too much on her talents and not enough on her intellect to win battles. Meaning, she had tells. Whenever she was going to teleport ahead of me, her eyes widened slightly in anticipation of her impending attack.

While I watched and waited for that tell-tale sign, I queued up a spell I'd recently invented—a stasis shield. This spell created a dome-like area around me only a few inches thick in which time was functionally halted. Any person or projectile that ran into it got stuck, like a gnat on flypaper, until I released the spell.

C'mon, show me what you got, Dauphine.

Finally, I saw it—that momentary widening of her eyes that happened each time she teleported in front of me. When she disappeared from sight, three things happened at once.

First, I thrust my hand out, as if to catch something in midair.

Second, I lashed out with Dyrnwyn in a horizontal, waist-high backhand cut.

And third, I cast the stasis shield not in a globe, but in a flat, inch-thick plane that bisected the space where Dauphine rematerialized, just above the cut I'd made with my blade. This meant that, while the rest of her could coalesce into solid form, the part of her that was caught in the stasis shield was out of phase.

In other words, the stasis shield cut her in two.

Dauphine met my gaze for a moment as she partially solidified, her eyes filled with horror when she realized what I'd done. I stepped back, releasing the spell, watching with satisfaction as her two halves tumbled to the ground, while an inch-thick section of her torso evaporated into smoke. However, she wasn't dead yet, so I leapt forward and thrust Dyrnwyn through her heart before she could teleport her upper half away.

With a final swing of the flaming blade, I chopped her head off. As her skull tumbled away, her entire body collapsed as it transformed into a pile of thick, black ash. Thinking she might have teleported after all, I kicked the pile, breathing a sigh of relief as a cloud of black dust scattered to the four winds.

22

When all was said and done, Dauphine lay dead —truly dead—on the pavement, and I stood over her remains, illuminated in the fading glow of Dyrnwyn's blade. Having spent the last dregs of magic I had left in me at the moment, I sheathed Dyrnwyn, then I fell to my knees in sheer exhaustion.

Guerra whistled, low and soft behind me, muttering curses in Spanish under his breath. To anyone watching the fight, it would've appeared that I cut Dauphine in two with my blade. My secret was safe, and so was the compound—for now.

Brian's body lay to my right, still and perfect, save for the odd angle at which his head hung. I couldn't stand the way he looked there, all cold and alone, so I stood and staggered toward him, intending to carry him to the relative safety of the compound.

I dropped to one knee next to him, but just as I was

about to pick him up, I heard rapid footsteps behind me. Before I knew it, a slight, feminine figure shouldered past me, knocking me sideways in frantic urgency.

"Don't you touch him!" Anna cried, tears running down her cheeks.

Anna took a good long look at his still, pale form, then she collapsed atop her little brother's chest, wailing and calling his name over and over again. Dutifully, I stood watch, knowing that the dead would soon be drawn to her cries now that Dauphine was gone. Still, I waited, giving her the space she needed to grieve.

After a time, Guerra cleared his throat. "Druid, I see movement off in the trees. Time to get inside."

I nodded, keeping my eyes on Anna and Brian, then I stepped forward and laid a hand on her shoulder. "Anna—"

"Get away from us!" she hissed, slapping my hand away. "It's your fault he's dead—yours. If you hadn't brought us here and left us helpless against that, that thing, Brian would still be alive."

I waited a moment, hoping that her anger would subside once she'd voiced her feelings. "The dead are coming, Anna. We have to go."

"The dead are already here," she said softly. "And we never had a chance."

With some difficulty, Anna scooped her younger brother into her arms and headed toward the gate. She took care to support his lolling head with her elbow, despite the effort it took. Suddenly, she missed her footing, and when I reached out to steady her, she hissed and pulled away from me, like a mama cat protecting her young. Then, she stormed off toward the side yard of the mansion.

I made to follow her, but Guerra's voice called after me. "Let her go, Colin. She needs to be alone. If you want to help someone, help me close and lock this gate and take me inside. Fucking ground is damned uncomfortable."

I mentally chided myself for my disregard, remembering that he'd been near death not more than thirty minutes ago. We locked the gate up, threading the chain through the bars and clicking the hasp shut on the padlock. Finally, I checked the wards to ensure their integrity, before helping the 'thrope limp back inside the house.

Outside, the dead trudged forth from the forest in twos and threes, gathering at the gates and wandering around the perimeter like funeral mummers. All the while they sang their song of death, a chorus of moans and groans that gained in volume as their numbers grew. Yet, whenever one of them tested the wards on the fence, deadly silver magic arced forth to discourage them, and I had no fear they would breach the gates.

Not this night, at least. Not this night.

After everyone had settled down and the kids were asleep—all of them choosing to remain locked in the wine cellar, sadly—I leapt over the fence with Dyrnwyn in hand. Then I set about the task of clearing out the dead who'd gathered after my battle with Dauphine. Once that grisly task was complete, I found Anna in the yard, cradling Brian's body in her arms.

There was a very real danger that he'd come back as a zombie, or worse. He'd been in direct contact with a master vampire, and for all we knew she'd purposely nicked him to infect him with the vyrus. Yet I gave Anna space, and instead of disturbing the sad, moonlit tableau, I grabbed a spade from the garden and spent the hours before dawn digging a grave for Brian.

When dawn broke, I dropped a loaded pistol on the grass next to Anna. "In case he comes back."

When she failed to answer, I loped off toward the fence, vaulting it and heading toward the medical park at Bee Caves Road and 360. There I found antibiotics, antiseptic, and bandages that I ostensibly gathered for Mickey, but really, I grabbed them for the next time someone was badly injured in my absence. Then I broke into a prosthetics design and repair facility, grabbing an assortment of limbs that I thought might fit Guerra.

Once back at the compound, I found the old 'thrope in his room. "Got a present for you," I said, dumping a pile of prosthetic limbs on his bed.

"Aw, you shouldn't have," he replied as he rummaged through the lot.

I watched as he tried several on. "Gonna take some modification. From what I understand, every limb is a custom fit."

Guerra gave me a nod and a grunt, then he grabbed a knife from his bedside table. He measured a replacement limb for length next to his remaining leg, then he eyed the fiberglass and plastic fitment sleeve. Setting the limb down next to his stump, he motioned me over.

"Gonna have to do this quick. As soon as I give you the signal, slap that thing on, hard, and hold it there."

"What—?"

Before I'd figured out what he intended to do, he'd started shaving flesh from his stump. Strips of skin and muscle fell on the bed, along with a good deal of blood.

"Do it," he said in a flat, tight voice.

I shook my head, but I did as I was asked, forcing the prosthetic over the bloody stump. Eyeing the alignment, I turned it a few degrees counterclockwise, making sure the "foot" section was in line with his knee. A minute or so later, Guerra grunted again.

"That should do it. It'll be enough to get around, make me a little less useless around here." He fiddled with the limb, wiping blood off it with his bedsheets. "Speaking of, what are you going to do now that Dauphine's dead?"

"I have to wait around to meet up with a friend, then we're going to find a way to bring the whole damned Vampyri Nation down."

"Tall order. Guess that means I'm stuck here on babysitting duty."

"Mickey'll be up and about in a day or two. Once Anna gets over her grief, she'll be able to help."

"That's if she don't lose her shit," he replied.

"She won't. I've been with her day in and day out for the last six months. That woman is iron wrapped in silk. She'll bounce back—maybe not soon, but she will."

Guerra cleaned his knife on his bedspread before sheathing it and setting it aside. "She's going to blame you for a long time, you know."

"She has to blame someone, may as well be me." I didn't tell him about the revelatory conversation I'd had with Crowley after the near-disaster in Dallas, although it weighed heavily on my mind. "I'll keep my distance for a while, until she can stand the sight of me again."

"He was a good kid. I did my best to save him, you know?"

"I know. Not your fault." Then I realized we'd only recovered one of two missing children. "Speaking of, did you ever see any sign of Richard?"

"Nope. The *pendejito* is still out there, somewhere. That is, unless Dauphine drank him dry."

"Hmph. Not that I'd wish that on anyone, but considering the alternative? Now that I think about it, I wonder if he wasn't a sacrifice, but a willing volunteer."

Guerra frowned in disgust. "I didn't think leeches turned kids."

"We're living in a vampire apocalypse. Pretty sure the rules have changed."

"Fuck."

"Couldn't have said it better myself."

Two weeks later, Crowley showed up at the front gate while I was on guard duty. I walked up and unlocked the chains, opening one side just enough to let him past.

"You could've just climbed over," I said, giving him the side-eye as he strolled into the yard.

"I didn't want to cause any unnecessary alarm amongst the younger members of your group—or the adults, for that matter. Besides, your wards might not have let me in."

It was dark, and he had his hood pulled up, but I could still make out those swirling pools of darkness against his ashen skin. "Yeah, probably best we don't let the kids see you come and go. Could give them nightmares for weeks."

He acknowledged the ribbing remark with the barest of shrugs. "Do they know you're going away?"

"Guerra does. He got a little banged up tussling with a master vampire, but he's well enough to cover for me while I'm gone."

"Gather your things, then. The sooner we leave for the gateway, the better. There are entities guarding it, and it may take us some time to circumvent their presence."

I patted my Craneskin Bag. "Got everything I need right here." I turned toward the house, speaking in a conversational tone that wasn't loud enough to wake the kids. "Guerra, I'm off."

A few minutes later the grizzled 'thrope strolled out the front entrance of the mansion, sipping a cup of instant coffee.

"Sure you don't want me to heat that up for you? Bad enough we have to drink instant."

He scowled. "Not a pussy like you, McCool. I like it cold and black."

"Like your heart," I replied.

"Shiiit. With a comeback like that, it's no wonder your people lost at the Alamo."

"Guacamole is just Mexican fruit salad," I deadpanned.

Guerra's eyes narrowed. "Hotdogs are just German tacos."

"I'm not German."

"Oh yeah?" he replied with a smirk. "I couldn't tell—all you *gringos* look alike to me."

"Oof—walked right into that one." Having gotten the worse of the exchange, I flashed a crooked smile. "Be seeing you."

He waved me off with the gaff hook that he'd made to replace his missing arm. "Don't worry, I'll look after them."

Nothing more needed to be said. Crowley and I walked out the gate, and I secured it behind me, leaving the key in the lock for Guerra.

"Where to?"

Crowley gestured northeast, toward the radiated devastation of downtown Austin. "To the former queen's manse, of course."

"Ah, hell."

"I said this would not be easy."

"Yeah, yeah. If we're going to be eaten by a real-life monster house, we may as well get it over with." He began making arcane gestures in the air, causing me to shake my head vigorously. "Uh-uh, don't even think about it. No way am I getting in one of those nasty shadow portals again. We're going on foot."

He gave a put-upon sigh. "If you insist."

Two hours later, we stood in front of a hole in the ground that, moments before, had nearly been covered by charred debris. I wondered if the blast had leveled Maeve's mansion, or if the rebel fae had done it during the coup. Standing at the edge of the hole, I looked down where crumbling stone stairs spiraled away into the darkness.

"Is that safe?"

Silence hung in the air for several beats. "Are you serious?"

"Never mind. I'm casting a light spell, by the way, whether you like it or not."

"I do not advise—" he said, stopping mid-sentence

as he raised a hand up in warning. "Hold. Something or someone comes."

Crowley sprouted a half-dozen shadow tentacles, while I summoned a fireball over each hand. The shadow wizard glanced at my spell work, rolling his eyes before scanning the darkness around us. We both homed in on it at the same time, just before the portal appeared in the air next to the stairwell.

The tension was thicker than the bottom of a peanut butter jar as we waited for whatever was coming out of that portal. After several long seconds, a familiar figure stumbled out, deftly avoiding the bottomless pit in front of him as he brushed bits of gray dust off the shoulders of his black leather jacket.

"Your timing is as impeccable as ever, Click," I said as I banished the fireballs so I could offer a hand to steady him. "What are you doing here?"

"What am I doin' here? I'm savin' ya', aren't I?" he replied with no small amount of indignation in his voice. "When ya' didn't come back, I assumed ya' got stuck here. Told ya' ta' anchor the time stream. Took me forever an' a day ta' track ya' down, but here I am."

I glanced at Crowley, getting the smallest tilt of his head in reply. "What do you mean, I didn't come back?"

"Well, lad, that's plain as day, innit? Ya' shoulda' come back ta' the instant ya' left our timeline, after ya' wrapped up yer' business here. But six months later, nothin'! Which I took ta' mean ya' got stranded here." He crossed his arms over his chest, squinting as he tapped a finger on his lips. "Hmm... or maybe tis' somethin' worse."

"What do you mean, worse?"

Crowley's gaze swiveled back and forth from me to the trickster. "Think about it, druid. If you never returned from this foray into an alternate timeline, and if you truly are not stuck here, that leaves only one other alternative."

"What, that I chose to stay?"

"No, that you died before you could return."

It felt like someone let the air out of me all at once. I slumped to a seated position on the ground, legs splayed out in front of me.

"Well, hell."

This ends Book One of The Trickster Cycle. But never fear, Colin's adventures will continue in Book Two, *Druid's Curse*!

Be sure to subscribe to my newsletter at MDMassey.com to get two free books and to find out more about the rest of my Druidverse novels!

Printed in Great Britain
by Amazon